C0-BWY-211

Praise for *Hostile Witness*

"Los Angeles lawyer Douglas Anne Munson has written a first novel that is . . . raw, poetic, . . . powerful and very moving. . . . It is the memorable work of one who has delved into a job that sometimes verges on nightmare, and brought it into the daylight."

—*California Lawyer*

"Douglas Anne Munson is a wonderful writer. Her novel is tough, sensitive, completely modern in its voice and views. A remarkable debut."

—*John Rechy*

"[HOSTILE WITNESS] is a book that will help lighten and light another dark corner of all our minds."

—*Hubert Selby*

"Munson asks primal questions and coolly answers a few of them . . . She takes us on a journey to the side where the line between victim and perpetrator is lost somewhere in a contagion of betrayal, in a ragged sequence of nuances out of order, in a cluster of squalid boulevards . . ."

—*Los Angeles Times*

PINNACLE BOOKS HAS
SOMETHING FOR EVERYONE —

MAGICIANS, EXPLORERS, WITCHES AND CATS

THE HANDYMAN (377-3, $3.95/$4.95)
He is a magician who likes hands. He likes their comfortable
shape and weight and size. He likes the portability of the hands
once they are severed from the rest of the ponderous body. Detective Lanark must discover who The Handyman is before more
handless bodies appear.

PASSAGE TO EDEN (538-5, $4.95/$5.95)
Set in a world of prehistoric beauty, here is the epic story of a
courageous seafarer whose wanderings lead him to the ends of
the old world — and to the discovery of a new world in the rugged,
untamed wilderness of northwestern America.

BLACK BODY (505-9, $5.95/$6.95)
An extraordinary chronicle, this is the diary of a witch, a journal
of the secrets of her race kept in return for not being burned for
her "sin." It is the story of Alba, that rarest of creatures, a white
witch: beautiful and able to walk in the human world undetected.

THE WHITE PUMA (532-6, $4.95/NCR)
The white puma has recognized the men who deprived him of his
family. Now, like other predators before him, he has become a
man-hater. This story is a fitting tribute to this magnificent animal that stands for all living creatures that have become, through
man's carelessness, close to disappearing forever from the face of
the earth.

HOSTILE WITNESS

DOUGLAS ANNE MUNSON

PINNACLE BOOKS
WINDSOR PUBLISHING CORP.

PINNACLE BOOKS

are published by

Windsor Publishing Corp.
475 Park Avenue South
New York, NY 10016

First Pinnacle Books printing: September, 1992

Printed in the United States of America

"One should be particularly on one's guard
against changes in the weather and
should avoid in such times all
bloodletting or the use of
the scalpel."

—HIPPOCRATES

1

The rains finally stopped in the first week of July. An unusual weather pattern known as El Niño had reversed the natural order of things. The temperature of the ocean rose. Trade winds changed directions and died. There were torrential rains in California, a drought in Mexico. The air was heavy. She stopped, lingering by the immense picture window that ran the width of the building. The climb up the stairs from the underground parking structure to the second floor of the criminal courts had left her sweaty and breathless. The palm trees in front of City Hall drooped. It was quarter after nine but it was already hot. The news on the radio promised smog for downtown Los Angeles. It looked like the weather was returning to normal.

Clouds of cigarette smoke hung in the gray hall. A long, tense line of people coiled around a wooden information desk. Children sprawled on the floor. Voices rose and fell. Sandy Walker was slightly hung over and the confusion made her head ache. Surveying the growing crowd outside the juvenile court, she quickly divided them into groups. The guy with the green plaid pants and striped shirt: child molester. The black woman, hair wrapped in an orange and white 'do rag and her feet in a puddle of coffee: PCP. The teenage girl with the skintight counter-

feit designer jeans: neglect and a possible concurrent misdemeanor charge for welfare fraud. Sandy Walker returned her attention to the limp palm trees. Undoubtedly
there would be someone, a man, either black or white, in
his midtwenties, who had submerged a baby in scalding
water. This happened at least once a month.

"Walker!" A voice interrupted her lethargic inspection
of the trees.

Despite the fact her head was beginning to pound and
she had just noticed a tiny rip in the sleeve of her new
jacket, Sandy smiled when she heard Michael Fillipini's
voice. The tough Italian neighborhood where he had
grown up in Pittsburgh had left him with an accent like a
bad character actor. He was peering around the door of
Department 28, the arraignment court. His face was fat
and boyish although he was in his late forties, and the hair
above his ears was turning gray.

"You working or are you going to stand there all day?"
he yelled across the hall at her.

Silhouetted against the window, Sandy Walker was
outlined by the sun, which seemed to be drawn to her
long wavy blond hair. She was only a couple of inches
over five feet, with broad shoulders and narrow hips. If
she ran into someone she hadn't seen for a few weeks,
they would invariably ask if she'd lost weight, because she
gave the impression of being bigger than she was. This
annoyed her. She always wore the highest heels she could
find to appear taller and more in proportion. People said
she was handsome, a term she had never understood as
applied to women. She supposed it meant she had regular
features conventionally placed. All that kept her face from
being ordinary were her eyes, which were a brilliant blue,
and a tiny jagged scar just under her lower lip.

Sandy Walker turned away from the window and the
sprawling city. She must have been daydreaming again.
Last night she had been reading about Kohunlich, a for-

mer ceremonial center of temples and observatories where the Mayans had measured the change of seasons. In the tropics the changes are so subtle they can only be seen in retrospect. The weather in Los Angeles was lousy and there was something bad in the air.

Michael Fillipini held the door to the anteroom open for her.

"You look like you were up late last night," she teased, brushing past him toward the courtroom. "Who was it this time? That secretary in your office, or did you go on another date with your ex-wife?"

"How can you accuse me of such things? Me, your mentor, a respected member of the state bar, an officer of the court," he mugged with mock indignation. "I was out with someone new."

"Of course you were." She straightened his tie. "That's the only kind you like." They had met two years ago on a molest case in Department 28.

"Walker, get in here," a woman's voice summoned. It was Wanda, the big-busted black social worker who assigned cases in the arraignment court.

Sandy opened the courtroom door as she looked back at Michael. "I can hardly wait till noon for the latest thrilling episode."

"Jealous? That means you must still be sleeping with that . . ."

She let the door swing shut behind her. The other lawyers were already there, reading files, taking notes, making phone calls. Sandy sauntered over to the social worker's desk and started to leaf through the stacks of paper on it.

"What's all the excitement, Wanda? Something new in the world of perversion?" For two years Sandy Walker had worked in the juvenile dependency court with child abusers and molesters.

Glancing up from the files piled on the right-hand

9

corner of her desk, Wanda smacked Sandy lightly on the wrist. "Those aren't for you. We got a special one for you today, don't we, Greg?" she said as she looked toward Greg Herbert, the county counsel who was sitting nearby with his feet propped up on the long oak counsel table. Sandy wondered if there was any real malice in this or if it was just the usual bantering.

Greg Herbert might have been a nice guy if he thought it would help him to get a transfer to another division of the county counsel's office. As it was, he was the number four man in an office that was ranked somewhere between probate and garbage collecting by its unhappy staff. The kindest thing Sandy had ever heard said about him was that he had a three handicap. He scanned the two women, first Wanda conspiratorially, then Sandy. "This is great. Check out what Walker is wearing today."

Discreetly, Sandy inspected the suit she had recently bought on sale and wondered if it looked cheap. It was red silk, narrow skirt, long boxy-cut jacket. Maybe she should have gotten the ten instead of the twelve. She always bought her clothes big because she didn't want people staring at her breasts. The saleswoman had shown her how to roll the sleeves of the jacket and push them up. It looked fine, she decided. The only thing wrong was that she felt guilty for shopping the garment district knowing the clothes were made in sweatshops by women paid less than minimum wage.

"We got a special momma for you; we know how much you love the real weirdos. Plus, she's Spanish speaking so she's all yours." Wanda handed her a file, then three more.

It was a mystery to Sandy Walker how she ended up in downtown Los Angeles in the middle of an incredibly hot summer holding a stack of petitions filed against parents alleged to have abused their children. She would not have predicted this when she was an anthropology student nor that the Spanish she learned would one day be used to talk to strangers about their children's private parts.

She had gone to Mexico City on a scholarship from her university. It was winter. The plazas were nearly deserted in the late afternoon, except for a few couples who lingered on benches catching the last of the sun. In the library of the National University someone had laid a rose on the table where she read. Later, in the spring, as her year of study was about to end and the azaleas and coral bougainvillea were blossoming in painted terra-cotta pots at an outdoor cafe where she was drinking beer, she concocted the idea of law school so she could avoid the real world for another three years. She would, she imagined, end up someday with several more degrees teaching about pottery and Toltec civilization.

Instead, she had become a defense lawyer specializing in child sexual abuse cases. When she started to work for herself, she was broke and had applied to the juvenile courts because it was said to be a source of easy money. The first time she was given a file with a police report detailing chronic and violent sodomy, she got a migraine. She read the report until the words lost their meaning.

"We save these cases just for you, even if you do get here late." It seemed Wanda gloated as she handed over four more files.

Sandy was late. She knew she was supposed to get there early; she was the only Spanish-speaking attorney assigned to pick up cases in the arraignment court on even-numbered Wednesdays of each month. And the only place there were more Mexicans than Los Angeles was Mexico City. Plus there were the Central and South Americans.

Greg Herbert thumbed his newspaper, pretending to ignore her. "Really, Walker, we were afraid we'd have to give the case to someone who wouldn't do it justice. We were afraid you wouldn't get here." He glanced over at

11

Wanda again, who muffled a laugh and ducked her head toward the work stacked in front of her.

Sandy wondered what they were getting at. She covered her mouth and coughed. No telltale breath. No obvious alcohol leaking from her pores. Everything was all right. She put her large scuffed beige leather purse behind the bailiff's desk, then felt in her pocket for her fountain pen and cigarettes. Starting for the hall, she remembered to go back to her purse for a supply of business cards, which she stuffed in the other pocket. Yes, she thought, patting both pockets, the suit is fine. The styrofoam cup of coffee she'd been carrying was lukewarm. She wished she had some aspirin. Maybe the court reporter would have some when she arrived.

"Butler," Sandy called, standing stiffly in the middle of the hall, which was getting warmer despite the sluggish air conditioning. "Butler." A group moved toward her.

A young white woman about twenty-four or five with long auburn hair locked in a tight perm, a frilly overblouse, and cranberry-colored pants of some synthetic fabric designed to resist all wrinkles stepped forward. She was followed by an older woman, probably the maternal grandmother, whose face was set and angry. Two more young women in short shorts and sleeveless blouses followed them. A flabby man in his late twenties wearing camel slacks that were too tight and a double-breasted navy polyester jacket trailed behind. All he needs, Sandy thought, is a pair of those thin green socks to look like an insurance agent.

"I'm an attorney." She flipped through the papers for a minute. "The court has asked me to speak with the mother, Joyce Butler. Is that you?"

The woman with the kinky hair nodded, so Sandy handed her a card.

"Great." Sandy's voice hinted at the boredom she felt. She had interviewed hundreds of these people. With her hand she gestured to the other side of the wide corridor, where there were a couple of tables with chairs. "Do you want to speak to me alone or do you want these people to come with you?"

"I want them to come," Ms. Butler said in surprise, apparently failing to grasp what was about to happen.

Silently they walked en masse to the tables. Sandy stopped at the first one, where a black woman was changing a baby's diaper. Tense with anticipation about their own case, the Butlers barely managed to feign apologetic smiles at the woman.

"I'm sorry, miss," Sandy said as she put her files and coffee on the table. "We need to work." The baby began to howl as the woman carried it away.

The Butlers looked at Sandy expectantly.

"I'm Ms. Walker," she repeated, her eyes traveling past them to the window at the end of the hall. "I'm an attorney in private practice. This court appoints me to represent people who are unable to afford attorneys." Her voice dropped apologetically in the event they were embarrassed.

"You know Ted Strumble?" demanded the man in the navy jacket. "I'm calling him and getting him here as fast as possible. I'm not going to let this go on. We've had enough of these accusations."

"No, I don't know him, but I'm sure he's a terrific guy." She pulled her attention back from the window to the Butlers and smiled a bit too broadly at them. Christ, this could get to be a long day.

"Now," she announced brightly as she launched into her formalized speech, "let me explain the way I want to do this. Our time's limited.

"First of all, I'll give you general info about this court system and the legal procedures. Then I'll read the petition that's been filed regarding your child and I'll read the police report that's attached. After that I'll specifically

13

discuss your case with you, Ms. Butler." Sandy added a gracious smile to encourage the woman's compliance. "You sure you want these other people to stay here while we're talking?"

The woman's head bobbed as she looked around the table.

Sandy shrugged and took out a cigarette, which the man hastened to light. She smoked gracelessly.

"This is not a criminal court, although it happens to be located in the same building as the criminal courts. It's a civil court with broad powers for the protection of children."

"We're not criminals," the man protested heatedly. "Somebody's gonna get sued for libel."

Sandy ignored him. The grandmother gave him a harsh look.

"A petition has been filed in the superior court by the Department of Social Services of Los Angeles County after the receipt of a complaint by some person or agency, such as a school or a doctor."

"Is my son's doctor going to be here?" the woman asked excitedly. "I've been taking my son to him since he was born. He'll tell you there's nothing wrong, that it's all been an accident."

"We can talk about that in a few minutes," Sandy said in an impatient effort to soothe the woman. She looked past the woman's head out the window again. It must be ninety already and the heat was rising. It was jungle heat. Febrile and green. It reminded her of the stands of dense bamboo, palm, and banana trees around Hichihuayan. She had been through there on the way to see the dances of the Huaxtec Indians. A group of men from the village had cut down a poplar while offering prayers of dedication to PuliMinla, the god of trees. They stripped the limbs and branches from the tree and dug a hole in the ground. Then they dropped a live hen into the hole and

14

impaled it with the immense tree pole. Costumed in feathers, they had attached ropes to the pole and suspended themselves from the top so they seemed to fly through the vibrating green air.

"Right now I'd like to finish giving you my talk, then you can tell me anything you want," Sandy offered half-heartedly. The grandmother nodded on behalf of her daughter, who appeared petrified.

"Good." Sandy flipped the petition over and drew a Roman numeral one. "Today is the arraignment-detention hearing. This court isn't a trial court, so it's not going to hear any evidence. The judge is going to assume the petition he reads is true and he'll make a very conservative order about where the child should stay between now and the second time you come to court."

"You mean I'm not getting my son back today?" the woman cried. The rest of the group leaned forward as though it would help them gain perspective on the problem.

"That's it," the man in the navy jacket shouted in a squeaky voice. "I'm calling Ted right now. He'll come down here and get things straightened out." He stood up, feeling for coins in his pocket. "No offense, miss, but I see we need a man for this job."

Sandy picked up the black book of matches she had dropped on the table—"Casa Alegria, fine food and drink from south of the border"—and played with them as she addressed the Butler woman. "Almost no one gets their child released at the detention hearing. The court feels it has to make an order to protect the child until the second time the parents come to court, when there's a full hearing and the judge can decide if the petition is true or not."

"It's not true. It was an accident. I told you," the woman pleaded. "Aren't you going to get my son for me?"

The drone of insistent voices was becoming practically

hypnotic in the heat. "Look, Ms. Butler," Sandy snapped, "it's not my job to justify this system to you. My job is to explain the machinery." She gave them all a second of significant eye contact. "I got a lot of work to do, so let's try to get on with this."

The family grew quiet again, as though willing a belief in her.

Sandy muffled a yawn. It was tedious to go through this with everyone but safer than assuming they had learned anything about legal procedure from watching television. "When you come back the next time you're going to do one of two things. You're either going to have a trial and the county'll have to try to prove what's alleged about you or you're going to enter a plea of no contest to some kind of amended petition and admit the allegations are true. . . ."

"Don't plead to anything," he hissed.

". . . or if you go to trial and lose, the result will be the same. The county of Los Angeles by the Superior Court will assume the right to decide where your child lives and under what conditions."

"Ohhh, I'm never getting my son back." Joyce Butler put her face in her hands.

Without looking up, Sandy drew a dot after the Roman numeral two. "They'll assign a social worker to interview you and the father."

The woman gripped the table. "No. I don't want him to know about this."

"I'm sure that's true, but as a parent he has a legal right to know about these proceedings and participate in them if he wants." Sandy dropped her cigarette on the floor, crushing it with the toe of her shoe while thinking, I should get a pair of navy heels to go with this suit.

"He doesn't even pay any child support," Joyce Butler whined.

Don't they ever contemplate the consequences of their

actions? Sandy marveled. If they knew it was going to cost so much for a piece of tail, would they even bother? The girlfriends crossed and recrossed their legs restlessly.

Sandy straightened herself on the hard chair. Had the court reporter arrived with aspirin? "The social worker will interview children, relatives, doctors, therapists, whatever's necessary to get an idea of the way the family functions. Based on these interviews the social worker forms an opinion about the best place for the child and then makes a written recommendation."

"Then do I get my son back?" Joyce Butler was suffering.

Why couldn't they follow the logical order she was giving them? she sighed. "Maybe, maybe not. There's a number of things the worker can recommend. The child could live with you under certain conditions, for example you take a parenting class or go to therapy. They could recommend the child live in the home of a relative, even a foster home."

They always get near the edge when I get to this part. Maybe I should work out another rap. Maybe I should just stop trying to give them any explanations. Impatiently, Sandy tapped her pen on the gold wedding band she wore on the middle finger of her right hand. It had been her father's. A mortician had given it to her when her father was cremated.

"You'll be given copies of this report," she said finally, taking the pen in hand as though she had some further use for it. "If it says something you don't agree with, like the boy should stay in a foster home, then you come back for a contested disposition hearing." She wrote this down by the Roman numeral three to have something to do.

She flipped the paper over. "Now let's talk about your case. This says there's a minor named Frances Lee Butler."

"Frankie," the woman interjected hopefully.

17

"Okay, Frankie. And that he usually lives with his mother and her male companion, Bud Simpson." It figures this jerk would call himself Bud, she thought. "At an address on Vallejo Street in Altadena. That on July twenty-seventh, 1982, and numerous prior occasions, the male companion inflicted injuries, including burns, to the minor's body. Furthermore, the mother was aware of this abuse and failed to protect the minor."

"It was an accident." The man frowned warily at Joyce Butler as she spoke. "It's not true," she added in confusion.

"Let me have a look at the police report." Sandy skimmed it quickly. The boy had gone to his father's house for a visit and had shown him a cigarette burn on his arm. When the father asked what happened, the six-year-old said Bud did it while spanking him for going into the kitchen after they'd told him not to. Sandy imagined the kitchen with its speckled linoleum floor, green refrigerator and stove, a plastic pitcher of tea cooling on the counter, the boy opening a cupboard looking for cookies. Then she read them the full police report so they could hear the child's statement. He said he didn't want to go home if Bud was still there.

The young Butler woman was looking at the police report like a passenger in a lost car stares at a map without knowing where to begin.

"You'll have to decide this morning how you want to proceed. Trial or plea."

The girlfriends looked uncomfortably away toward the plate glass window. Joyce Butler squeezed her eyes shut to keep from crying. "So where's Frankie going to stay?" asked the grandmother.

Joyce Butler slowly opened her eyes; she shook her head gratefully.

"The court won't allow Frankie back in the same house where this injury occurred, even if it was accidental.

18

You're going to have to get rid of Mr. Simpson here for starters."

The man glowered, jiggling change for the pay phone in his hand. A blue stone set in his high school ring caught the sun.

"Your best plan's to think of a relative who lives in LA County who could take care of him. Maybe for a few weeks."

"That's what I'm here for," the grandmother said.

Sandy lit another cigarette and stood, smoothing her skirt over her hips. "I'll be back later in the morning to find out what you want to do the next time you're here. Anybody got any questions before I go do some other work?"

Ms. Butler and Bud didn't hear her. They were already involved in a quiet but intense conversation. Sandy had noticed in the police report that Butler was the secretary at Bud's insurance agency in Glendale. The woman would tell him to get his clothes out of the closet. He would tell her to find another job. Sandy exhaled, letting the smoke trickle from her mouth and nose. It's not even ten A.M. It can all happen so quickly.

"Swanson. Swanson," she called as she moved away from them.

Before she had time to speak with the black woman who came forward, calendar call was announced over the loudspeaker and everyone trooped into Department 28 like contestants at a game show.

While the skinny red-haired bailiff was reciting the do's and don'ts (no hats, no sunglasses unless they're prescription, no gum, and don't stick it on the bottom of your seat, don't cry when you see your child), Sandy glanced through the rest of her cases.

"You got anything good today?" she asked, taking a seat next to Lacey Potter, an older black woman who was seated at the counsel table recording her work on finan-

19

cial forms. Lacey Potter was wearing some light and expensive perfume that reminded Sandy of green lawns and white dresses.

"No. The usual. Guy fingerfucks his stepdaughter, a dirty house case, a couple of 'under the influence.' "

Sandy sighed as she stretched across the table to pick up some of the forms. "Same here, it looks like."

"You must be real disappointed, Walker." Allan Cooper scooped up some declarations and passed them to Sandy. He was new. He needed to develop a sense of humor and a stronger stomach. So far all of his development was muscular, a point he accentuated by wearing clothes that looked like they had been spray-painted on him. Today he was dressed in an unbelievably bright orange suit. "I heard about that case you had last week with the Mexicans who had their daughter tied up and locked in a closet. I heard you got a dismissal."

Christ, Cooper was stupid. The county had to dismiss because the kid died. Before she could suitably respond the judge entered and took up his place on the bench.

"Rosas."

No one answered.

Greg Herbert tittered and rolled his eyes. Wanda pointed her finger at Sandy, who stood up, hastily clearing her throat and asking for second call. This must be the special case they were talking about. All Sandy saw was a short Latin woman with long black hair who was squinting at her as though she were nearsighted.

After first calendar call, the attorneys followed their clients back out to the hall to finish interviewing and getting the cases ready. Sandy interviewed the Swanson woman, whose baby had been born suffering from drug withdrawal related to phencyclidine. A straight plea. There was nothing she could do with the medical records. The next case was a mother driving under the influence while her child was in the car. The woman's entire arm trembled as she clutched a coffee cup and a cigarette simultaneously in a hand with artificially long coral lacquered nails. This woman will love AA, thought Sandy, whose own headache had receded after taking four aspirin. Nothing to do but plead her. Ms. Butler decided she wanted a trial. At least she had one person with a case to try, even if it involved the demeaning act of cross-examining a child.

By the time she went to interview the Rosas woman the sun was high above the three large window panels that faced south down Broadway toward First and the *Los Angeles Daily*, which was located directly across from the court building. The temperature was continuing to rise, bleeding the colors from the flag on top of the news building and blurring the edge of a weather vane so it appeared stark as a cross. Heat ascended in waves from the streets. She saw men had removed their jackets and slung them over their shoulders. Women dropped the straps of their dresses. There would be a violent red-and-purple sunset that evening on the beach where she lived.

She called the Rosas woman again. As she rolled the name in her mouth, she wondered where the woman was from. The woman was dark skinned with huge almond eyes. It could be Campeche, Veracruz, possibly the Yucatán. Sandy glanced down at the papers she was holding. The information sheet stapled to the top of the file said West Covina.

The Rosas woman was insisting in Spanish that the two women accompanying her come to the table with her. They were telling her to go on alone.

"Ustedes puedan acompañarnos, si ella quisiera," Sandy said formally, indicating for them all to follow her. The women looked suspiciously at her, then reluctantly walked over and sat down at the table.

Sandy took a cigarette from her coat pocket as she began her routine about the court process. The woman

21

looked at her blankly, as though she were speaking a foreign language. She hated it when they looked at her like they couldn't understand what she was saying. After all, it was their language. She had connected the nuances and found her voice softened when she spoke. Of course they understood her, just as she understood them. The relatives gazed out the window. Sandy fumbled for a match.

"*¿Fósforo?*" she inquired of the trio.

The Rosas woman looked at her oddly, smiled, and took a book of matches from her purse, which she then closed hurriedly.

Sandy struck a match and began to read aloud, translating English to Spanish. "This petition alleges that your three children, Miguel, age four, Alejandro, age three, and Flora, age one and a half, normally live with you at this address in West Covina. That on or about July twenty-eighth you started a fire in your house and threatened to kill all of your children." Sandy let her voice trail off, allowing the woman time to deny the allegations.

Silence.

Reina Rosas, her mother, and sister-in-law were staring at the glowing tip of the cigarette.

The sun crept across the floor toward their legs. A breeze poked the lifeless flag. The three women sat motionless and heavy lidded, watching Sandy.

"I'm reading the police report to you now. It says your sister called the police because you set fire to a pile of red clothing."

In the silence, the sun bathing them in scorching direct light, Sandy saw Reina Rosas for the first time. Reina Rosas was a pragmatic saint, face painted with cheap tropical colors, a promise of redemption curled in smoky geranium lips. She had arteries like Sunset Boulevard, tattooed like La Maravilla project walls. A tear was painted under her left eye. She wept tamarindo and guayabo. Reina Rosas, the queen of angels, worked at Third and Vermont in an herb shop filled with tiny green bottles of good luck oil and plastic crucifixes blending mango clouds with the essence of the promiscuous eucalyptus in red rituals for women with bruised hips and broken faith. Her husband had left. *Nuestra señora reina de los angeles* burned carnation scented candles under the bed. She said bombs exploded in the closet. She said the devil lived in the color red. She smoked yerba buena and consulted *curanderas*. She gave her children to her *cuñada* in El Monte, locked all the windows, and set fire to a pile of red clothing. She expected saints, salvation, a crimson judgment. The police arrived.

The report said she'd been on a seventy-two-hour hold at Metropolitan State Hospital. Sandy imagined Reina Rosas leaning forward in a gray room, forearms on thighs, skirt caught between parted legs, restless fingers weaving the story of a small town unknown in the mountains south of the capital where time was measured in distance. She saw Reina Rosas as a girl leaving her parents' house, crossing miles of an ancient valley up into the mountains, sleeping curled beside volcanic rocks, watching the moon grow fat in the southern sky, the sun spill *sangre de cristo,* eating herbs and flowers, guided by lizards who talked to her in the language of unbearably hot afternoons, climbing along the bed of a sylvan stream, bathing naked, calling fish to her. She discovered pyramids overgrown with vines. A rain forest grew between her legs. She made love with jaguars who laid her in the ocher dirt and sang with the rhythm of wild grasses. She learned to disguise herself as a tree, a serpent, the wind. She rolled the night in her hands like dice carved from teeth. Reina Rosas expected the sacrament and they gave her Thorazine.

Reina Rosas, her relatives, and Sandy all watched the burning end of the cigarette in Sandy's hand, the long ash

23

curling over, balanced as precariously as Reina Rosas's fate at that moment. Sandy saw it would be a long time before Reina Rosas got her children back. A *curandera* would have prescribed a poultice of iguana oil, powdered teardrops, and three Hail Marys. But this was Los Angeles. Sandy wrote "plea" on the paper and dropped her cigarette into an abandoned cup of sticky cola.

Michael Fillipini was trying to rub an orange stain off his tie when Sandy wandered into the courthouse cafeteria and pulled up a chair next to him. A man and woman one table away were saying something about a probation report; lowering their voices, they bent toward each other. She glanced briefly but without any real interest in their direction. "So, where's everybody else?"

"Everybody else? Everybody else went somewhere decent to eat. How come you always want to eat here?" he complained.

"I'm a creature of habit, I guess." She dropped her purse on the table and brushed off the seat of the chair she was about to sit on. "Did I ever tell you about George Barker? When I was a corporate attorney they had a free cafeteria for the employees because they didn't want anyone to leave and not come back."

Michael returned his attention to the plate in front of him. He speared the last of a burrito with his fork, using it to mop up the remainder of the offending orange sauce.

"They used to tell the attorneys to eat together. It was seven married men and me. All they could talk about was cars and football and putting new sod in their lawns. I hated them, all of them, but there was a guy named George Barker who was the worst."

Michael pushed the empty greasy burrito plate aside and hunkered down on a piece of apple pie.

"George Barker had the biggest dandruff in the world. He wore green suits with short socks so his ankles always showed. I tried not to sit across from him because I didn't

24

want to see him while I was eating. One day, I was trapped next to him and he sneezed without covering his nose and blew it all over my cottage cheese."

Michael dropped his fork. "Jesus Christ, you're really getting disgusting."

Laughing, she snatched the pie plate off his tray.

"Go ahead. I didn't really want it. I was just eating to keep my strength up."

Innocently, she let her eyes travel slowly down toward his waist. According to the actuarial charts, he was at least forty pounds overweight.

He sucked his stomach in self-consciously. "Okay. You want to play dirty? I got a case today with a girl who drank bleach."

She grimaced as she took a sip of water from his glass. "Sounds like Ripley's Believe It or Not. Is this a bizarre custom somewhere?"

"Got me. The girl's from Jamaica. I didn't even know there were any people from Jamaica here." He tapped a pack of unfiltered cigarettes against the table, took one, and lit it, inhaling deeply. "This is the second time she tried to commit suicide. The first time she took a bottle of her mother's sleeping pills." Michael stopped and looked around the cafeteria, which was full of jurors, primarily elderly people wearing plastic badges who were reading paperback books and working crossword puzzles. "We ought to find out where that new court reporter in Department Twenty-five eats lunch," he said gloomily. "This is depressing day after day."

"I thought you wanted to tell me about your new girlfriend."

He brightened perceptibly. "She's a real estate agent in Brentwood and she gives great head. Her name's Phyllis."

Sandy dragged her purse toward her and fished in it for another pack of cigarettes and a pocket mirror, which she used to verify that she didn't look hung over. "So what's going to happen with the Jamaican girl?"

"You're not interested in hearing about Phyllis?"

She shrugged. All his girlfriends gave great head.

"Are you serious? You want to hear about the kid? I'd rather talk about Phyllis and her gasoline ass and long fingernails. That woman could . . ."

Impatiently, Sandy drummed her nails on the table. She was becoming obsessed with the details about the children.

"Who knows what the kid is like? They're all alike. Shit, I can't even remember their names. I can't even figure out what they're talking about half the time and this one was speaking English."

It was hot in the cafeteria. It was hot everywhere. In Bolivia forty thousand adobe houses had simply melted in the heat. There was flooding in the Caribbean. Fifteen people, including a teacher, a dentist, three children, and a diesel mechanic, had drowned in Cuba. All the vagaries of human behavior were being conducted through the air like electricity, like thunder crashing in the distance and growing closer. Sandy Walker fanned her face with her hand as Michael Fillipini talked.

"The kid got left in Jamaica with her grandparents when she was five and the mother took off to New York to look for work. Then, after eight or nine years, the mother sent for the girl."

As he spoke she saw the mother and the girl quite clearly. They were in a small room. It was growing dark, the windows were open. It was hot and muggy. They had been arguing. The mother hit the girl with a belt many times, the buckle catching her above the right eyebrow once, cutting her, leaving a scar like a crescent moon that reminded the girl of the summer sky above Ocho Rios and the August nights she had played in the yard of her grandparents' house before her mother sent for her. The

26

mother sewed canvas curtains in a factory on the lower East Side. She was ashamed and angry that she had hit her daughter. Nothing in her life was working out as she had expected. There were rats in the apartment; the rent was late; it had been three weeks since she had heard from Seymour, the elegant black prince from Belize who worked as a doorman over on Sixty-eighth Street; and last night someone had lifted her wallet out of her purse on the subway. She decided she would take the girl and move to California. To Los Angeles.

Sandy blotted her mouth carefully with a napkin, wanting some physical reality, no matter how small, to connect with. She was starting to get used to the fact that these images appeared out of nowhere. This had been going on for a few weeks. It had been going on almost as long as the strange winds and the bad weather. It was probably because she couldn't sleep at night, she told herself. If it didn't stop she'd have to go to the doctor for some sleeping pills. "So what's going to happen to the girl?"

"She doesn't want to live with her mother and her mother doesn't want her. They'll have to put her in Mountainview or some other group home with a structured environment." He paused, then continued in a professorial tone. "Persons such as this sometimes accidentally have a successful suicide attempt because their judgment is so poor."

"Maybe you could take her home," Sandy said, outlining her mouth with a half-used tube of flame-colored lipstick. "I bet she could learn to give great head."

A woman jostled Michael's arm as she squeezed between two tables. The trial courts were going into afternoon session. A group of four old men Sandy recognized as courthouse regulars stood up from their nearby table. They folded newspapers, stuck cigars in shirt pockets, and stretched.

"I'm going back up to Division Forty-three, where that

27

drug smuggler murder trial is," announced one of the men.

"Sounds good," agreed another, "but I'm going back to Fifty-two. That's a rape trial. You see there was this young gal who . . ."

Michael trailed the men wistfully. "I wish I was in real court today. A nice burglary. A little assault with a deadly weapon. Friday I'm going to be in Compton on a robbery prelim, so do me a favor and take my pickup day, okay?"

"Two arraignment days this week? Are you crazy?" She held open the door to the stairwell for him.

"Come on. I need a favor and you probably need money if you're still supporting your little amigo Jose."

"Manuel," she corrected him automatically. "And stop talking about him like that."

The hall outside Department 28 was still crowded but it had become very quiet. The waiting women were drained. They drooped noticeably. Voices had become hushed and secretive. The Rosas woman was standing in front of the window, staring blindly ahead. Her relatives had withdrawn to the shade along the wall; periodically they glanced over at her, then spoke briefly among themselves before returning to a listless half sleep. Only the Swanson woman, whose baby was born in the midst of withdrawal, still seemed awake. She sat in the chair closest to the courtroom door, neck bent, shaking her head slightly from side to side.

All the children were detained. The Butler boy was going home with his father. The woman who had been driving under the influence of alcohol called her sister, who then failed to appear. The Swanson woman's baby would be transferred to a foster home when it was able to leave the hospital. Only Reina Rosas did not cry.

Sandy drove south down Broadway toward Washington Boulevard. Tall, tightly packed gray buildings with carved cornices and vaulted doorways blocked out the sun. These structures had lost their individual identities and the scope of their original design as the city cracked and spread like roots of a tree pushing through concrete. Dry winds scraped the edge of the city. Broadway was the one fixed point along the sifting border between north and south.

She drove past the jewelers, clothing stores, *farmacias*, and movie theaters hung with posters of blazing red gun battles and big-breasted women. She drove past the Latin women tottering in high heels, clutching babies and grocery bags overflowing with tomatoes, peppers, squash, and cilantro. Past the vans and stands of the money-changers from Tijuana, Mexicali, and points south who overnight set up *casas de cambios* selling pesos for dollars. The working men who bought these pesos would send the money to women waiting on the other side of the parched Rio Grande, to children who would study black-and-white photographs to learn their family histories. The men who sent money back to Mexico managed to save enough to pay for their rented rooms in shabby hotels on Central or Alameda. They avoided the missions on the Nickle between Second and Fifth because they feared the contagion of failed dreams. The lucky ones saved enough for a couple of beers at the Club Jalisco, or the fights at the Olympic Auditorium, enough to go to a dance hall on Saturday night.

She glimpsed these lives like the shadow of a cheekbone of a man passing, his head bent to the sidewalk; in passing, the cheekbone appears iridescent for an instant and periphery vision is lost in the slope and hollow of the cheek. A man stood in the window of a building at Broadway and Washington and slipped off his shirt revealing a tattoo of some intricate design and meaning that told the story of his life. The traffic light changed.

The Spanish conquest of this area had been virtually bloodless in comparison to the rest of Mexico. Boundaries

29

had simply been effaced by heat. The priests had come, then the ranchers and farmers. Almost no one remembered the names of the tribes who had lived here. They had just disappeared. On Washington, she turned west toward the beach and her apartment. The oldest human life in Los Angeles was a woman who had been excavated from the tar pits near Wilshire Boulevard, her head caved in millions of years ago by a blunt instrument. Now, as the day was ending along a row of run-down stucco motels and fast food stands near La Brea, the hookers were coming out.

Sandy Walker did not make it to the beach for the red-and-purple sunset; instead she parked the car outside her apartment, went in and double locked the door. She took off the new silk suit and hung it carefully in her closet. From the unmade bed she picked up a thin white cotton nightgown and pulled it on. She got a bottle of Greek brandy from the top of the refrigerator, a glass from the sink, and went back into the living room, which was simply furnished in black and gray. Books crowded shelves that were bracketed to the wall and painted white. A large oil painting hung over the couch. It was an abstract assemblage of oranges, greens, yellows, and blues. She stopped and looked at it, straightening it slightly, and stepped back. The smeared and irregular blues were like bruises on the canvas. Pouring a drink, she walked over to the window that faced east toward Los Angeles.

"I'm not going to get drunk tonight," she said out loud.

The unnatural heat was having an effect on people all over town. Seventeen miles away, Jesus Velaria, who was twenty-eight years old and born on the outskirts of Mexico City, was in a bar called Noches Tampicos on Sunset Boulevard having a beer with four of the men he worked with. Ordinarily he went straight home from the body shop but it had been been an unusually hot day and he wanted to kill the taste of paint and metal in his mouth.

He was telling them about a class he was taking at the Socialist Alliance School near his house. Of the four men with him, only Raul seemed vaguely interested in what he had to say. The others kept interrupting him and telling dirty jokes. They yawned loudly in his face. Finally they began to tease him that he was becoming too serious. "Man, is your brain going soft from getting too much pussy?" one of them poked at him with a finger. "If it's too much for you, just say so and I'll come over and fuck your old lady for you a few times." Jesus Velaria shook his head in exasperation as he glanced around the table. Sometimes he wondered if he had ever been like his friends. Raul lounged next to him, lazily drawing circles and curves in the wet pools made by the beer glasses, a crude black tattoo that said EL MEXICO running down his forearm. Sighing, Jesus Velaria straightened himself in the chair. He was medium height and slender with light, coppery brown skin. His wavy black hair was cut short and he had a widow's peak. The waitress gazed in his direction. Someone bought him another beer and he looked quickly at his watch. His wife would be home by now and she would have picked up Soledad, their nineteen-month-old daughter, from the old lady down the hall who was their babysitter. They were waiting for him now so they could eat dinner. He tilted the glass to his mouth and said it was time for him to go home. The men laughed and made fists, which they moved back and forth as if they were masturbating. That made him laugh. It was three days since his wife had spoken to him.

The last bit of mauve faded from the arid sky. Sandy Walker, a glass of brandy held against her breastbone, watched the lights go on in the house next to her apartment. In the backyard of the house a dog barked happily. The woman who lived there opened the back door and let him in. The light fell across her hair and face as she bent down to pat the dog who wagged his tail and fell upon himself with pleasure. The woman's husband would be home soon. Sandy knew this because she often watched from her window. They had an outdoor barbecue, two bicycles chained against the fence. Sandy took a drink as she stared into the yard. They probably used a food processor and were happy.

All down the block, lights were going on. Doors opened and shut. Someone in an apartment across the alley turned on a stereo. A saxophone began to cry. The high notes made her nervous, so she shut the window and turned on a fan she had placed in the middle of the floor. It was dark now. The only light she had turned on was in the kitchen and it made a small path into the living room. Sandy Walker was restless.

She poured a little more brandy into the tumbler. From the chrome-and-glass table next to the couch she picked up a book of aerial photographs taken by Saturn 7.

The earth was thin and flat. Mountains were stretched across the page and the oceans were shallow. It was difficult to identify anything. The sliding forms lacked organic connections or definition.

Impatiently, she tossed it aside and took another book, which she quickly discarded. Sandy Walker had trouble sleeping. She looked through the remaining pile on the table. Even the book on Marxism and literary criticism that usually put her out did nothing. The night was hollow and loose. She took another book, which contained photographs of the great Mayan pyramids. Uxmal. El Tajin. Palenque. The remnants of apocalyptic civilizations based on fear and the adherence to natural laws. She sat down in front of the fan so that the air picked up the front strands of her hair and danced them around her head. There were drawings of the reconstruction of Teotihuacan, which had been laid out along an immense north-south avenue bounded by the Palace of the Sun and the Palace of the Moon. This simple unity of dark and light had been directed by ancient codices printed on parchment. The fan ruffled the edges of the pages. Before parchment they had been carved in stone. Before stone there had been shamans and priests charged with negotiating the weather and protecting the people.

And before that everything had been dark.

Closing the book of pyramids, she poured more brandy and put the bottle next to her. The moon had become a reckless guide. She lay on the floor, letting the fan travel up and down her body, and closed her eyes to try to sleep.

She had the feeling something was in the room with her. It was like a child breathing. Perhaps it was only the wind.

2

"You're a glutton for punishment," Cynthia, the red-haired bailiff of Department 28, said when Sandy announced she was picking up for Fillipini.

"She's getting it on with Fillipini." A loud whisper drifted from the direction of Wanda's desk. The clerk snickered, swiveling slightly in her chair, hoping to catch some stammer of admission. How this rumor had originally started Sandy had no idea. Wanda was humming innocently, reviewing the mound of papers on her desk.

Sandy returned her attention to the bailiff, who was standing next to her. They were the same height but Cynthia was flat everywhere and had a tiny waist.

"You still getting up at five to go swimming before work? That sounds like punishment to me."

"Punishment, discipline, water sports," moaned Greg Herbert as he slouched in. He threw his battered briefcase down and slumped in his chair at the end of the table closest to Wanda's desk. "God, everyone who works here ends up getting crazy and perverted."

Cynthia blushed, as she did frequently, and reached for Sandy's purse to store it behind her desk. "Good heavens, what do you have in here? Rocks?"

Sandy wondered if she looked hung over. When she woke that morning her skin looked pasty, her mouth sunken and hard. She had put on a lot of blusher and stuck a half pint of brandy in her purse.

"Did you see how many people are out there today?" asked Sonia Perez, the Spanish-speaking attorney working that day as she came in the door waving a handful of petitions. Like Sandy, she was thirty-two but she was married and had a seven-year-old son. "Remember when Wednesday used to be the biggest day? Now it's like that every day."

A kid would get beat up at home on the weekend, his teacher would notice it on Monday, report it as required by law and it would land in court on Wednesday. There were two thousand juvenile cases a month. That was a conservative estimate. No one could guess how many went unreported, Sandy thought as she studied the files she had been assigned.

Victor Rodriguez was eight months old. He had been taken into custody as an abandoned child, then hospitalized for medical treatment. He was severely handicapped and suffering from malnutrition, anemia, and a salmonella infection. Although he hadn't been tested yet, he was probably retarded as well. He had been left carefully wrapped outside the downtown bus station before dawn. His abandonment had been thoughtful and premeditated. His mother must have held the little feet, brown and smooth as pebbles, in her hands for the last time. She kissed each one and put white socks on him. The woman held the tears inside, although they threatened to burst from her like a flash flood in a dry arroyo. She smoothed the thin layer of black hair across his scalp and wrapped him in a red blanket she had bought the day before on Seventh Street. It was all she could give him, a red blanket and the chance to be discovered by someone who would call the police.

The Morales children had been observed going through a trash can looking for food. The officers who searched their apartment found half a package of tortillas and arrested the mother for being drunk. The woman told Sandy her husband was in Mexico looking for work when the children were detained. He'd been unable to find any in Los Angeles. It was the Salvadoreans and Hondurans, she explained bitterly. They were taking all the jobs. She drank some tequila and tried to cook some mussels one of the neighbors had brought her from the Santa Monica Pier. The man sat on her couch and told her she was beautiful, she didn't have to be alone, he would help her, that her husband was never coming back. He touched her hair. She drank more tequila. When she awoke on her bed it was with the sense of having been violated. Her children were sitting on the floor looking at her. The mussels cooking in the pot had burned and the house had a terrible, poisonous smell. She thought it was the man who called the police.

Lifting her hair up from her neck, Sandy mopped the damp skin, thinking, I'll bet everyone here drinks.

Lashanda Simpson was a nine-year-old girl from Culver City whose mother had spanked her with a belt on Sunday for saying bad words. There were abrasions and contusions on her face and body. Her tooth had been chipped. She told her teacher at summer school alternately that she had been hit in the face with a softball, that she had fallen on a metal sprinkler, that she tripped on the sidewalk.

The changes in the weather seemed to be having a disorienting effect on everyone. Besides the rains and scorching heat, El Niño had warmed the ocean. Sweat beaded up on Sandy's forehead.

She dropped Lashanda Simpson's papers on the yellow wood table. "Hey, Barbara," she called across the room to the court reporter, "you have some more aspirin?"

Sandy stared at the paper again without seeing it. She was fifteen years old. She had a broken front tooth. She had told her teacher she fell down by the swimming pool.

Lashanda's teacher called the police. During the interview, Lashanda told them her mother's boyfriend sexually molested her. Bad words, sighed Sandy, the kid was probably trying to tell her mother the guy was dicking around with her.

She wondered if it was too early to go get her purse.

The last case was a woman who had slapped her teenage daughter during an argument in the front yard of their house. Her name was Jeanette Ray. She lived in Long Beach, was unemployed and devoted herself full-time to the service of the Church of the Blinding Spirit and Redemptive Word located on Cherry at 78th Street. She said her daughter was a whore. She deserved it.

"Look, Ms. Ray, 'she had it coming' is not a valid defense in this court. Let me look at the police report."

Although the hall was crowded and they were seated next to each other, Sandy avoided looking at the woman who was irritating her. The heat in the hall was overwhelming; there was a dying hurricane off the coast of Mexico; and she had a headache. Surely this woman must have a better explanation. However, Jeanette Ray merely rearranged her purse, a straw-and-cloth basket, setting it carefully between herself and Sandy. Jeanette Ray patted the purse several times and turned it slightly from one side to the other until it was centered, then, apparently pleased with the symmetry and artistry of this composition, she looked up as though Sandy should have had time to comprehend the simplicity of the situation.

Jeanette Ray had brought her two younger children with her. A girl and a boy dressed in Montgomery Ward Sunday clothes sat sweetly next to their mother holding Bibles in their laps.

"Do you want to ask the kids to wait at the end of the hall or go to the cafeteria for Cokes?"

Jeanette Ray gave her a small beatified smile tinged

with sadness, as though the painful secrets of the Lord's work had given her gas. "We don't drink Coca-Cola, smoke cigarettes, or buy products from mainland China," she explained patiently.

Sandy made a point of lighting a cigarette while she started to read the police report. She smiled uncomfortably at the boy and girl and rubbed the palm of her hand on her black linen skirt.

"You sure you want these little kids to stay here while we do this? I don't think that's a good idea."

"My children are staying right here with me." Jeanette Ray put a protective arm around each child, pulling one into each tiny, pointed breast. "They know everything. They are simple and blessed. They are my jewels. They will tell you that Julie is a whore. Besides . . ." she said, dropping her voice and glancing up and down the hall, "there are a lot of bad people around here."

"It's up to you."

Jeanette Ray released her grip on the children and replaced her Bible, which had started to slide off the lap of her pink-and-white gingham sundress.

Methodically, Sandy made her usual diagram and explained the detention hearing as she watched a woman on the other side of the hall rocking a baby.

"The girl's no good," Jeanette Ray was saying. "She whores around with those niggers in the neighborhood. Lays in the park with them. I found her myself once in the schoolyard across the street from my house, laying on a lunch table with her skirt above her waist."

The two small children nodded thoughtfully as though called upon to testify to the veracity of this.

"I want her home with me so I can watch her. She's not going to run wild in the streets or go to one of those homes where they smoke marijuana and listen to rock and roll."

"Ms. Ray, this is a detention hearing." Sandy pushed her jacket sleeves up around her elbows. "Your daughter told the police she doesn't want to go home with you. She's afraid of you—"

"Praise the Lord."

"—and she doesn't like you. The police report says that a couple of years ago you cut all of her hair off."

Whatever Jeanette Ray said evaporated in the terrible heat. Again Sandy saw herself at age fifteen. Her father slapped her. They were in the wood-paneled living room of their house in the San Fernando Valley. It was one of those unusually warm January afternoons when Los Angeles stretches out in the sun and tans. She was wearing a bikini. Her father told her to cover her breasts. Called her a whore.

Now Jeanette Ray was saying something about her daughter not coming home from school on time. The words were peripheral, for Sandy was sitting in a wooden chair in the backyard of her father's house. The camellias were in bloom, their waxy red petals scattered on the grass. Her father was cutting off her long blond hair. It fell around her. On the ground the hair lay, iridescent and shimmering like skins shed by snakes.

Unsettled by this remembrance, Sandy stood, awkwardly moving away from the woman and toward the courtroom. "I'll argue that she should be released."

Inside Department 28 Greg Herbert was waiting for her. "Here's a couple of papers for you."

She took the proffered documents. "What are they?"

"Supplemental petitions. We're filing on the other two Ray kids."

"I can see that, but why?"

"Sibling filings. We're alleging that the abuse of the older minor endangers the physical and emotional well-being of the other minors."

"But she's never hurt them. They're fine. You can see for yourself. They're outside with her."

"I know. We want to pick them up and detain them

40

today." He sat down again, rearranging the papers in front of him. "We're going to do it now. We don't want her to have the opportunity to leave the building with them."

"I think I should have time to prepare her for what might happen." Sandy started for the door.

"Forget it, Sandy. If you didn't mention the possibility to her, that's your problem. It's too late now. Your job's to think of these things."

Through the partially opened door to the judge's chambers, she could see the judge putting on his robe. He paused once and ran his hand over his nearly bald skull.

"Ray. Persons on the Julie Ray case," the bailiff announced over the loudspeaker.

Motioning Jeanette Ray forward, Sandy showed the two children a chair where they could sit near their mother. The judge asked the parties to identify themselves; Jeanette Ray nodded cordially to the judge and the court personnel. The door to the shelter-care area opened and Julie came into the courtroom. Mother and daughter glared at each other from opposite ends of the table. Jeanette Ray turned away, directing her attention to the judge as she folded her hands and rested them on top of the Bible.

Without looking at her brother or sister, Julie Ray turned her swivel chair away from her mother and flung her long brown hair over the back of the seat.

Greg Herbert informed the judge the department had just filed two new petitions and wanted to arraign the mother on them as well as the older girl's. Jeanette Ray, who didn't understand what was being said, continued to smile pleasantly at the judge.

Sandy leaned toward Jeanette Ray to explain what was happening. Out of the corner of her eye she saw two deputies who had just entered the courtroom move

41

slightly closer. Jeanette Ray interrupted her by placing her hand on Sandy's forearm and standing up.

"Your Honor, there's nothing wrong with my two little babies. They're my jewels. You can see for yourself. They're perfect, just as God created them. It's Julie. She's a whore."

"Ms. Walker," the judge ordered, "would you please speak to your client? Ms. Ray, you may be seated. If you have anything to say, just tell your attorney."

Jeanette Ray sat down and opened her Bible.

"Your Honor, we're asking for the detention of the two younger children as well as the detention of Julie." Greg Herbert arched his eyebrows as he glanced at Sandy, as though asking what she was going to do.

Jeanette Ray looked suspiciously from Greg Herbert to Sandy. Without waiting to hear what Sandy was going to say, Jeanette Ray stood up again. The two younger children stirred uncomfortably. The little girl's petticoat rustled as she started to get up from the chair in which she was sitting.

"Your Honor," Sandy put her hand lightly on Jeanette Ray's shoulder and pushed down so she would get the idea to sit.

The deputies edged closer.

"What's happening here?" Jeanette Ray yelled, looking wildly around the room. "What are you doing? Those are my babies. My perfect jewels. I'm not going to let you take them. They belong to me."

"Counsel, can you control your client or am I going to have to ask my bailiff to do it?"

Sandy moved her hand to Jeanette Ray's upper arm.

"Please sit down." The pink-and-white material was thin. She could feel the muscle in the woman's skinny arm as Jeanette Ray leaned over the table in the direction of the judge.

42

"Those are my babies. God's babies. You can't have them."

"Bailiff. Detain those children."

The boy and girl began to scream. Cynthia, her service revolver bumping against her flat hip, came up fast behind the children, grabbing them around the waist and dragging them toward the shelter area before they had time to clutch their mother. Wanda leaped from behind her desk in a surprisingly sprightly way, took the little girl in her arms and carried her toward the shelter. Julie Ray jumped up and ran through the open door, shoving her younger sister in her haste. Jeanette Ray, her hands transformed into angry claws, lunged at Cynthia who still held the boy and scratched her across the cheek. The boy squealed in terror. The other two bailiffs grabbed Jeanette Ray from behind as she was pulling her son's arm. One chopped her in the soft inner part of her elbow to break the hold on the boy. Jeanette Ray's purse flew through the air and fell to the floor as she kicked her chair over. The purse opened, scattering its contents across the floor, and a cheap Japanese tape recorder rolled across the rug.

Attorneys who had been standing in the courtroom pressed against the wall. Sonia Perez climbed over the wooden railing that divided the counsel table from the empty rows of benches. Sandy hurried to the end of the table, where she ducked down beside the court reporter, who was still trying to transcribe all that was being said in the noise and confusion.

Jeanette Ray howled as the deputies tried to take her down. She fell, striking her head on the oak table. Blood dripped from her forehead. On her back, arms pinned on either side by a deputy, legs furiously kicking in the air, Jeanette Ray rolled and heaved from side to side as she thrashed at the men. The pink-and-white gingham skirt lay around her waist. Her legs cut wide slices through the air and everyone saw that from the waist down, she was naked.

The phone rang before she wanted to get up. Her head hurt. She tripped over her black suit and high heels, which lay in a pile beside the bed as she stumbled to the phone.

"I hear your client gave Judge Stevenson a beaver shot." It was Michael Fillipini.

The light coming in around the edges of the thin metal blinds made her head ache. "Something like that. Did it make the news?"

He giggled.

She realized her stomach didn't feel very good and that he sounded ridiculous when he giggled.

"It didn't make the papers but it was a hot item at the Lucky Ring last night."

Closing her eyes, Sandy Walker slumped against the thigh-high red lacquer dresser that ran almost the length of one wall. She could imagine Greg Herbert holding forth at the bar in front of the social workers, court reporters, and other lawyers. The Lucky Ring was always busy after work. He must have been delirious with joy as he told how she had lost control of her client and the situation. He must have positively pranced. The prick.

"Oh, that," she fumbled through the top drawer, hoping to find a pack of cigarettes. "You think it's a bad sign if a tape recorder drops out of your client's purse while she's wrestling with a bailiff?"

There was another giggle from the other end of the line. "Maybe she wanted to listen to some country-western music. I heard she was wearing a square dance dress."

"Texas," Sandy said absently, still rummaging in the drawer. "I think she's from Texas."

Michael turned serious. "She probably taped the whole

fucking conversation with you. Jesus Christ, Sandy, how did you manage to get those kids detained without at least preparing the woman for it? That's malpractice, live and on the air."

Sandy slammed the drawer shut and kneaded her temples with one hand. "I don't know. I guess I didn't think it was a serious enough case for the county to file on."

"You know, at least you ought to know, they automatically file on the siblings just for being in the same house. What's going on with you lately? You're getting sloppy. Like a week or so ago when you forgot to show up for the trial in the Payares case. It's a good thing I was down there and able to cover for you."

"I didn't forget. I wasn't . . ." she paused, searching for the right words. "I wasn't feeling well." She brought up one cough to emphasize this statement. In fact, she had been too hung over to get off the bed. "Must have been a touch of flu."

"Sandy, don't bullshit me. You didn't even call in. No one knew where you were. I told the judge you asked me to appear for you."

"I thanked you for that. I'd do it for you." Sandy squinted toward the window. She wondered where Manuel had been last night.

"That's not the point. You're not working up to par lately and I'm trying to ask you what the problem is because I know you're a pretty good trial lawyer." Michael Fillipini hesitated, but then blurted out, "Is it that wetback you've been going around with?"

"How many times do I have to ask you not to call him that? He's an undocumented worker."

"Get off it, Sandy. He's an illegal alien and that's not the only thing illegal about him."

She jerked the drawer open to look for cigarettes again. "It's a little early for this. Am I going to have to listen

45

again to the lecture about how stupid you think I was to bail Manuel out of jail?"

"No. You want to throw your money around, you want to pay for a twenty-three-year-old kid so he'll come around and bang you sometimes, that's up to you. You just better watch it or you won't have a job much longer."

"I'm not paying him, and he's twenty-four. . . ."

"Twenty-three, twenty-four. What's the difference? He's a moron. Guy gets arrested for grand theft in a surfboard shop. For Christ's sake, Sandy, couldn't you at least pick a guy smart enough to commit an adult crime? What is there to take in a surfboard shop to push it up to a felony?"

"I told you, they dropped it to a misdemeanor. He's going to trial in September. It's a case of mistaken identity." Irritated, she stopped rummaging. She pulled a large silver-and-onyx bracelet out of the drawer and put it on. It was cool against her skin.

"Fine, whatever you say."

Sandy Walker turned the onyx bracelet. It was carved with primitive faces and facets of coral. It reminded her of the mysterious jungles and dark cenotes that kept appearing in her dreams.

"So, what are you going to do about the lady with no bloomers? She sounds like a pretty hot little number to me. Want me to take care of her, since I seem to be doing your work these days anyway?"

She stopped stroking the dark stone face. "They gave her five days in SBI for contempt. I thought I'd give her time to cool down and then go to see her." With that she said good-bye and hung up quickly because she didn't want any more questions.

Being vertical made her head hurt. It was too early. Sandy lay down on the bed, again wondering where Manuel was. It was true he was unreliable. He didn't have a telephone. It was also true he was twenty-three. Sandy thought about these things until it became obvious her head wouldn't stop aching unless she had a drink.

A stale breeze wafted in from the east as she looked up and down the narrow sliver of sand that separated Los Angeles from the sea. It was the end of the afternoon by the time she had straightened herself out with brandy and a hot bath. In this light, her hair, which was usually a pale, bleached ash, turned gold. She was barefoot. Small pieces of broken shells churned in the swirling water. Following the ragged trail of foam that burrowed its way into the wet sand at the edge of the low-tide line, she headed north toward the Venice Pier.

Manuel might be there. He might be in the large parking lot trying to buy a dime bag of marijuana, which he would smoke greedily after haggling with the seller. He would insist sadly that it was not real Acapulco Gold or real Colombian; he would regretfully point out the numerous stems while empathizing that one had to make do. He would call the seller *mano* or dude. He might be playing soccer on one of the grassy knolls along the beach. He might be in the arcade playing video games. He might be anywhere in the crowd that milled around the pier. Foam wrapped around her ankles in white rings. White is for the north, the land of thorns, so it said in the myths and *leyendas* of Mexico. Manuel had been working his way north for some time.

She had watched him all one afternoon as he dove again and again under the breaking waves. He was young. She was looking for something pure, less changeable. She had invited him into her apartment for a cold drink. He had asked for a glass of water with ice. Amused that he couldn't see through this elemental deception, she took off her bikini and stood before him.

Now he appeared with increasing frequency in the middle of the night dressed in denim pants, carrying a black leather jacket he had saved seven months to buy. He

47

was a carpet layer's assistant, lived near Western and Beverly, had crossed the border at eighteen with a coyote from Tijuana, and sent money to his mother and brothers in the state of Chiapas. He spoke mostly in Spanish and of his former life said only, "This process takes time. I depend on the god of the near and close and an occasional novena to the fertile Mary Magdalene."

Rock cod, sea bass, an occasional bonito swam off the end of the pier. Since El Niño had altered the composition of the water and air, there had been marlin. Hundreds of miles north of their usual waters, the marlin had survived while other species of fish had vanished from existence as streams of warm water along the South American coast overrode the Humboldt current and blocked the surge of cold, nutrient-rich water from the bottom of the ocean. People were clustered intermittently along the pier fishing. Their excited voices shouting *"mira mira"* or something comparable in oriental languages punctuated the lapping of the surf and the jumble of transistor radios.

"Sandy."

Shielding her eyes from the sun, Sandy saw Manuel leaning against the railing of the pier, his mouth forming other indistinguishable words, which the breeze carried away. She climbed a steep abutment of packed sand up to the concrete ramp, which was the pier entrance, and had to pause to catch her breath.

He turned so his elbows were propped on the railing behind him. He was about three inches taller than Sandy and very dark skinned. The summer sun had turned him nearly black. He was broadly built through the shoulders with thick muscular arms from carrying rolls of carpeting. Michael Fillipini thought it was a joke when Sandy said Manuel was so solid his nipples didn't move when he ran, but it was true. He wore his hair straight and long, cut in layers that he pushed back. The abrupt angles of his face were relieved somewhat by broad lips and thick eyelashes.

48

Each time she saw him she was surprised by these details and by his youth. As usual he was dressed in tight pants that accentuated his stocky legs, a sleeveless white T-shirt cut under the arms down to his ribs, and a pair of white tennis shoes.

Sandy stood next to him studying the backs of the waves that were breaking beneath them. Eventually she turned with deliberate casualness to face him. "I haven't seen you for a few nights. ¿Que te pasa?"

He twisted around to avoid the question, leaned his forearms on the railing again and scrutinized the ocean. "They say there is a storm building off the coast of Mexico. The waves will grow large. Tomorrow I'll go surfing." His speech was slurred, the whites of his eyes veined and red.

In the three months they had known each other, Sandy had not decided whether Manuel understood any of the things she talked about. She told him about her work, her father; she showed him the books she read. Sometimes he regarded her blankly when she spoke to him or stood and paced around the room when she asked him a question. Eventually she decided he selectively ignored those things that did not interest him.

"Where have you been?" she repeated, stepping closer to him.

"Around." Manuel glanced over Sandy's shoulder at two teenage girls who were walking by. "My friend Guillermo," he added hurriedly, "he lives near here. I stayed at his house."

"Is there something wrong with you lately?" Sandy frowned. A deep vertical wrinkle appeared between her eyebrows.

"I'm just trying to stay loose, not worry about anything." He smiled ingratiatingly and put one arm around her shoulder. "I've been thinking about you."

Sandy was aware of the deepening crow's-feet around

49

her eyes and an imperceptible but certain slackness in the skin of her throat. If she had it to do again, she would lie. Say she was twenty-seven, a secretary. "What about me?"

"How good you are. How good you are to me." There was a trace of anger, though he nearly erased it from his voice when he spoke. Although he had spent less than four hours in jail before Sandy bailed him out, he had been distraught, then sullen. He was afraid of being deported.

"I've told you a million times they're not going to put you on trial. They're going to offer you a lesser charge for a plea. You're not going to jail again." Although Sandy knew he was innocent, she realized his story was so unreasonable and convoluted no one could possibly believe it.

Manuel pulled slightly away from her and stared out at the ocean again. "I should just disappear. There are hundreds, no, thousands, of guys right here in Los Angeles who fit my description. I could go to a new neighborhood, a new job, get a new name, a new life."

Michael had warned about this.

"*Callate.* Don't be silly." Sandy wrapped her arms around his neck, kissing him because she was afraid of being alone at night.

Manuel parted his lips and pressed against her.

"You want me to make everything all better for you, don't you?" she teased.

They walked back to her apartment. Turning on the radio, Manuel changed the station to rock and roll. He cranked up the volume and drummed his hands against the shelf, lazily fondling her butt as she moved past him.

"Look, I'm going to show you that you don't have anything to worry about, that everything is going to work out fine."

She motioned him to sit on the floor.

"I'm going to tell your fortune."

Sandy went to her desk, which was two black file cabinets with a sturdy board painted black laid across the top. Smiling over her shoulder at him, she searched in the bottom drawer of one of the cabinets for a minute before pulling out a deck of tarot cards. She had never used them before. When she worked at the insurance company, a woman who had drawn her name at the annual Christmas party gave them to her. Sandy had considered the cards an odd gift, something banal for the truly bored, nevertheless she had examined the cards and studied their meanings before consigning them to the drawer.

"These cards," she intoned in an artificially deep voice, "tell the future." She waved the cards in front of his face.

Manuel stopped drumming to look at her skeptically. He crossed his arms across his chest. "Those are games for old women and *brujas*. Leave them alone."

Her curiosity aroused by the strength of his protest and the relative fluidity of speech it provoked, Sandy sat down cross-legged on the floor.

"Are you chicken? They're only cardboard with pictures printed on them." She smiled up at him, tossing her hair back over her shoulders.

The music vanished as he snapped off the radio. He sat down across from her.

"Pick them up with your left hand."

Manuel hesitated but picked up the cards. She mimed the action so he would shuffle the cards and put them down in three piles as she directed. Then she indicated for him to reassemble them in one pile.

Satisfied and waiting briefly to allow for suspense, Sandy took the cards into her hands. Laying out the cards in a series of parallel lines, she smiled at him again before looking down at the cards.

The walls became clammy and the cards began to breathe.

Seduction, deception, cruelty, doubt, and desolation,

the possibility of civil war. Tears, separation, banishment, and degradation.

Her hands hesitated above the cards.

The metamorphic figures with bent necks and flying robes whispered back frivolity, cunning, malice, prejudice, and suspicion.

"What is it, Sandy?"

"Nothing." Her hands were wet.

"You don't know how to read them?" Manuel yawned and looked at the construction on the floor without any real curiosity.

Sandy patted the cards gingerly. They spoke of dissipation, folly, an overwhelming past, but none of it was about Manuel. They were for her. "You will have a long and happy life," she said finally in a small voice.

He straightened his legs and stretched, knocking over the pile of cards. "Let's go in the other room."

After Manuel had fallen asleep, Sandy got out of bed quietly. She carried the bottle of brandy into the living room, where she turned on the light and began to gather the cards. They fell from her hands, scattering around her as she knelt on the floor. Unfortunate combinations, lack of vision, the possibility of a shipwreck, decadent desires, and suspended decisions, figures falling and settling upon themselves.

3

Nowhere was it recorded how many times El Niño had altered history. It was said that the Incas were conquered during El Niño, that the boats of Francisco Pizarro were pushed along by the erratic southern-bound current so they arrived suddenly and without warning. The scientists insisted there was some rational order to this phenomena but their explanations were hesitant. They had failed to predict the arrival of El Niño and were unable to say when it would end. The fishermen off the coast of South America who had been the first to notice these changes were forced to sail closer to the edge of the horizon. There was chaos in the air and Los Angeles was smoldering.

Mary Lou Watkins beat her son with a belt. He was six years old and had come home late from school. When the belt broke, she beat him with an extension cord.

Belt. A defined linear bruise. Extension cord. A distinctive loop-shaped, striated pattern. On some black children these marks are particularly virulent and purple. It has to do with the amount of melanin in the skin.

Mary Lou Watkins was arrested once and jailed in Sybil Brand Institute in 1978 for assault with a deadly weapon. She said a woman who was under the influence of some drug attacked her with a knife during an argument. Mary Lou had a knife, too, and there was a fight.

Such fights take place in laundromats, outside corner grocery stores, during very hot afternoons in the middle of July on streets with cool placid names like Acacia, Cotton, Myrtlewood.

Sandy was in Department 19 dealing out clients and fanning herself with a yellow legal pad. Department 19 was the courtroom where parents entered pleas and admitted they had abused their children. Mary Lou Watkins admitted it all. She was contrite. But then she had been in 1978.

It was the courtroom where defaults were taken against those parents who, for one reason or another, failed to show up to claim their children. Feliciana Barrera came to the United States when she was eight years old. Her mother had died in Chihuahua of kidney failure. Feliciana crossed the border at Juárez with her uncle and his family. An elderly woman relative she had never met came from Los Angeles to El Paso on an airplane to take her away. Feliciana Barrera had never been on an airplane. They lived together for five months in Chatsworth out near the county line. Feliciana Barrera had never heard of Los Angeles. The old lady threw her out of the house one night because she thought Feliciana had stolen some perfume. It was Evening in Paris in a midnight-blue bottle shaped like a heart stretched vertically. She was found asleep behind a trash can by some neighbors.

Sandy had also been appointed to represent two sisters, a thirteen-year-old named Yolanda and Linda, who was a year older. When the petition was filed, their mother appeared in Department 28 in the morning, then disappeared over the lunch break. Now there was a warrant out for her arrest.

The girls had been living with relatives and friends for most of their lives. Their parents had long histories of narcotics addiction and incarceration. Their mother, Peggy Cazuela, had been at CRC in Norco for three years because of heroin. When she got out she took Yolanda from her mother's house in Whittier and Linda from the home of Maria Elena Fuentes, who had been taking care of her on and off since she was three months old. Peggy took them to a place on Via de los Santos where a man named Johnny was waiting for her. It was a small, one-bedroom apartment in the area that runs east of Hollywood and north of the Pico-Union where the Salvadorean refugees concentrated in run-down brick buildings and men sold mangoes on the street corner. Johnny was the brother of a woman Peggy had met in prison. He was dark and handsome and had an evil-looking Pancho Villa tattooed on his left shoulder blade. The first time the girls looked at Johnny they knew he would die young and a lemon tree would grow on his grave.

For some time the girls watched silently as Sandy, in a beige silk dress and a coral necklace, searched uselessly in her briefcase for their file. They were seated on a purple vinyl couch in the deserted jury lounge off Department 19. At last Sandy pushed the briefcase aside, lifted her hair up with both hands, shook it out to try to cool off, then let it fall back around her shoulders.

"So, where did you go after your mother left Johnny?"

The girls rolled their eyes at one another.

"Hey, don't you read the police report?" snapped the one she thought was Yolanda. "It's in there."

She couldn't remember which girl was which. Linda, she decided, must be the one dressed in dark-blue pants and a yellow blouse with her hair parted down the center. Sandy raised both hands helplessly and dropped them into her lap.

"I forgot to bring my file. Remind me."

The girls looked at each other and shook their heads.

"I don't even know what we're doing here. We were

55

okay until you people started messing with us." Yolanda scuffed her tennis shoes along the floor.

"I want to help you," Sandy tried to soothe the girl, although she lacked conviction about her ability to do so. "Why don't you try to help me? All I can remember is that you were with your mom at Johnny's and then she took you to some woman's house to stay."

"She took us to her friend Lupe's house 'cause there was a party going on at Lupe's for her *sobrino* Carlos and then, when the party was over and the people left, Lupe told our mom and us that we could stay there and live with her. So we did," Yolanda recited while poking at the couch with her fingernail.

Most of the benches in the hall had been pulled apart and were missing their foam stuffing so they were actually only wooden benches covered by pieces of deflated black naugahyde. She always wondered what happened to the stuffing since she never saw any of it littering the floor. It was one of those things that just disappeared into the air.

"I still don't understand," said Sandy as she watched Yolanda picking at the vinyl. "Where was your mother when the police came to get you?"

"I don't know. She was probably with Johnny."

"You mean while you were at Lupe's your mom just disappeared one day? Didn't that make you mad? Or scared?"

Yolanda jabbed the couch angrily. "She didn't disappear. She went to the store."

"And didn't come back?" Sandy probed.

"I don't know. The police came before she got back."

"How long was your mom at the store before the police got you?"

"Three days."

The explanation hung in the air and the three examined it silently for a minute like a cloud passing on the horizon.

56

"Your grandmother was the one who called the police. Don't you know she was worried when she found out you were gone? Don't you want to go back and stay with her?"

No. The girls wanted to live with Lupe.

"Yolanda, Linda, you can't stay there. She doesn't have a foster license. The judge can't let you live with a person who doesn't have a license. It's against the law."

"She can get one," Yolanda insisted stubbornly.

Lupe, according to what the woman's landlady had told the police, frequently harbored runaway girls. There were often men at the apartment who drank and used drugs. The landlady had seen couples lying together on the floor. It made Sandy sad that the girls had been robbed of their childhood.

"How about your dad then?" Sandy asked with a half-hearted sense of duty. She couldn't even remember if he'd been mentioned in the police report.

"He don't want us," Linda exploded bitterly at her. "He's got a girlfriend. They're going to have a baby soon."

Yolanda yawned, examining her nails. "Get me a foster home then. I'm not going to my grandma's. She don't let me wear makeup."

As the day wore on, Sandy found herself by the pay phone several times but she didn't want to make the call. She didn't like the woman. Finally and reluctantly, she punched in the phone number, then her credit card number. It wouldn't do any good to put it off. Jeanette Ray must be out of jail by now.

The phone was answered on the first ring.

"You're coming to my house? Good. I have so many things to tell you. I can show you her diary and the letters I've found. I'll play tape recordings I made of her on the phone."

Place must be like a stereo store, thought Sandy glumly.

Jeanette Ray gave detailed instructions on how to get to her house. As Sandy wrote them in her calendar, she remembered her father finding her diary. The afternoon he found it he read it aloud to her. He told her he would tell her mother what a tramp she was. He said he'd been looking for some paper to write on. He had gone into her room and looked through her dresser drawers, took the blue-and-white drugstore notebook from among her pajamas and nightgowns. He sat on her bed and read it. Read the parts about smoking cigarettes and going for a ride in a car with a seventeen-year-old boy whose family owned a Corvair, about the place the boy had put his hand. This would kill your mother if she knew. Then he slapped her.

The phone clicked as Jeanette Ray hung up. It was too hot to eat. There were too many anxious-looking people in the hall. Dazed, Sandy wandered into Department 21 for some quiet place to wait for afternoon. Tricia Spivey was sitting in the back of the empty courtroom with her briefcase open beside her, adjusting a machine that rested on her lap. Tricia's enormous platinum-and-diamond wedding ring flashed as she uncoiled a wire and plugged it into the machine.

"New dictating machine?" Sandy asked as she slid in on the bench next to Tricia.

"No. Look. It's a little television my husband bought me so I can watch the soaps."

Sandy picked the machine up, examined it, then handed it back. "Why?" With one hand she gestured around the room and toward the door. "This is the soaps. In three-D."

Tricia Spivey adjusted a dial on the television.

"The soaps are believable. This place has absolutely no connection to reality as we know it. Thank God."

Dropping her chin slightly so that her hair fell around her face, Sandy studied Tricia, whom she had known for a couple of years. "You mean this work doesn't get to

58

you? Doesn't keep you awake at night sometimes? Make you have an extra martini when you get home, perhaps?"

"You're kidding me. You come down here, you get paid, you go home. I got enough to worry about. The Guatemalan housekeeper put my new cashmere sweater in the washing machine. I have to lose fifteen pounds by next week because I'm going with my husband to his annual sales conference in New Orleans. My daughter calls me 'the other mommy' because I'm gone all day."

Tricia was interrupted by the shrill voice of a woman in the hall yelling, "Get over here or I'll spank your butt good. Get over here now."

Sandy glanced uncomfortably at the door.

Tricia turned the volume of the television up.

"Relax. Have you seen this show? It's one of my favorites." Tricia Spivey tapped the television screen with her fingernail as the credits rolled by in infinitesimally small print.

"I'm telling you, Sandy, it's not our responsibility. You can't do anything for these people. Forget it. You'll just drive yourself crazy if you try. They're hopeless. They're scumbags."

Sandy wanted to talk to someone about how much she was troubled by the cases but Tricia Spivey was focused on the television. The show was beginning. Sandy leaned over Tricia's shoulder so she could see the small picture. Tiny figures of men and women moved through black-and-white space.

"Con permiso." Someone coughed loudly once.

Sandy looked up from the television as a woman's voice continued in beseeching Spanish.

"Can I talk with you now?" It was Mrs. Lopez, one of her afternoon cases.

She took the woman back out to the hall, where at least twenty families had already congregated to wait restlessly. A fat woman in a long, nearly see-through gauzy print dress was brushing a little girl's hair and tying ribbons with plastic flowers into it. Sandy leaned against the wall, squeezing in beside two flamboyantly attired black men arrayed in sharp greens and yellows.

"They sent me this *SOPENA*," one was saying, "and I don't even know the bitch. Ain't seen her for three years and she trying to say I'm the father. Sheeeeit."

Mrs. Lopez, who held a pink sweater in her arms, turned her back to the men. "I didn't know how long I'd have to wait this time." She sounded apologetic. "My husband didn't come. I heard he was living with some woman over in Montebello. Does that mean I'm going to get my daughter Malver back today?"

Sandy tried to remember the case. It sounded like a molest. The woman interrupted her as she was explaining that the judge had first to decide if the petition was true or not.

"If my daughter said he did it, he did it. She's a good girl. I don't know what happened. I was at work."

Malver told her mother that while she was alone, her younger brothers and sisters playing outside, her father had felt her breasts and put his finger in her vagina. As soon as Malver told her mother what had happened, the woman confronted her husband. She told him to get out of the apartment. He left without taking any of his clothes with him. Two days later he was back. First he was angry that his wife would believe such a story. It was a lie. Then he told her he'd leave without giving her any money and they would all starve. Finally he said it was an accident.

An anonymous neighbor who heard the yelling and screaming called the police. When they arrived, Malver told them what her father had done to her. Mr. Lopez, who was pacing the sidewalk with his hands in his pockets, was arrested 288 Penal Code for lewd and lascivious acts against children. Malver was twelve.

It had been the beginning of July. The twisted rains had

stopped beating against the windows. Smog lay heavy and malignant upon the city. During the daytime he followed her from room to room asking, "Have you made love with a boy yet, my daughter? *¿Puedo besar tus pechas?*" He slipped into the room where she pretended to be dreaming. Time in the various heavens stood still. The room was black as obsidian. It was nine steps to hell. He stood above her bed and felt the bitter wind, an arrow pierced his heart, and he knew there was no turning back.

The girl lay silent as death, afraid to breathe. She imagined she was in the land of the fleshless. Her hair became long grass. Her eyes became caverns, wells and fountains. Seed-bearing plants grew from her ears, from her nostrils sprouted an herb that is good for curing fevers. She felt his hands upon her, lifting her nightgown.

This is the mythology of ordinary lives.

She felt his finger prying the lips of her vagina. It hurt but she was afraid to move.

"We don't need to wait," Sandy said to Mrs. Lopez. "Your husband's not going to show up for this trial, but I don't think I'll be able to convince the judge to release Malver to you while you still live at the same address. Mr. Lopez could come back any time."

"He is either in jail or gone. He will not come back." Her voice was hard, a knife of stone.

Yet the police report contained page after page of domestic violence incidents. The couple had separated on at least eight different occasions. In the summer of '79 he had beaten his wife, breaking her arm. Four months later he had given her a black eye. The following year he bruised her ribs and the year following that he loosened her jaw.

The girl was seated by the social worker's desk. She was chubby with a dark, heart-shaped face; her long hair was caught up at the temples in two ponytails. The woman at the foster home had bought her a navy-and-white sailor dress with a large collar and a red tie. Sandy knew as she was talking to Malver Lopez's mother the girl would not be released. The court would decide Malver Lopez's mother had failed in her duties.

Sandy remembered her own mother, who had locked herself in the bathroom and run the water in the tub so she wouldn't have to hear what was going on in the next room. Yes, Malver Lopez's mother had failed in her duties and it was that failure that poisoned and stung the air like ashes.

The judge told them to go into chambers. Malver Lopez took the chair closest to the window overlooking First Street. She didn't cry. Tears were common magic for rain in the New World. She stared out the window while reciting her story. When the girl finished speaking, Sandy sat heavy, motionless, hypnotized by her frankness and the unrelenting heat. She did not feel like ripping into her with cross-examination. As Sandy looked at Malver Lopez she saw herself. Malver Lopez's voice was her voice. Malver Lopez's story was her story. There was no need to look for the flaws in her recounting of those events. It was all true. Impulsively, Sandy reached out and hugged Malver Lopez as she was being led away.

The Gonzalezes were waiting in the hall for Sandy. Mr. Gonzalez nervously smoothed his hair back from his forehead. His wife sat rigidly by his side. After she had been appointed to represent them they had come together to her office, making the long bus ride from La Puente carrying a small manila envelope full of their son Roberto's third-grade records. The reports said he didn't do his homework, he had trouble sitting still, he hit children who were smaller. Neither of the Gonzalezes ever finished school.

Roberto told the teacher his mother burned him on the back when he lost his books.

Sandy had the color photographs the police had taken

of Roberto's back and showed them to the Gonzalezes. They held the pictures delicately by the edges, examining them with grave attention.

Mrs. Gonzalez handed the photos back. "Those are bug bites."

As they passed the pictures back and forth Sandy became aware that a man sitting by the door of the next department was watching. He was probably in his mid-twenties, six feet, tall for a Mexican, with a classically handsome face. He had the generous Olmec mouth, the carefully sculpted Totonac nose. Sandy looked over at him several times while she was talking. He was wearing a stylish sports coat of pale cotton and a knit tie. Must be the doctor, thought Sandy, turning to give him a better look at her profile. She imagined the kind of conversation they could have about the photographs of the boy's back. Innocently, she would twist the top button of her silk dress as she talked to him so that it came undone.

"We brought Roberto's report cards for you to use in court."

The judge just wants to know if you burned the kid or not; Sandy stopped herself from telling them this again. She took the small dog-eared manila envelope offered by Mr. Gonzalez because it was easier than formulating another explanation of the judicial system and shook out its contents. A green disposable lighter fell from the envelope, clattering and bounding across the floor. Sandy jumped after it. The man, who had been following this transaction, rose and bent gracefully to retrieve the lighter. As he handed it to her he smiled, bowing slightly as though it were a rare orchid.

Blushing, she took it quickly from him.

"What is this thing?" she hissed at the Gonzalezes, drawing closer to them so she stood between them and the man, who had returned to his place further down the hall.

63

They returned her look evenly, glanced down the hall at the man, and shrugged their shoulders.

"Whatever it is, put it away. Don't you understand we're going to trial?"

"Yes, you explained that to us," Mr. Gonzalez said politely. "You told us that if we wanted to we could tell the judge our story. That's what we want, to be able to tell our story and show the judge Roberto's report cards."

Their conceptualization of their defense was so ridiculous Sandy stopped listening. It was too late. She stepped aside so she could see the doctor again. Pouting slightly, she gave him a long stare that she hoped conveyed animal magnetism. The bailiff paged the case on the loudspeaker. Sandy let her tongue flick the corner of her mouth as she turned slowly from the man and went inside with the Gonzalezes.

For the first witness the county counsel called Roberto. Then, the expert from County General Burn Unit. Sandy stretched, sat up, and waited for the chicano doctor to come in. A prematurely balding intern in a badly fitting seersucker suit testified that the red-and-brown marks on Roberto's back could only be the result of direct application of intense heat. There were no further witnesses for the county.

The Gonzalezes decided not to take the stand after all. Glumly, they followed her out into the hall. Other women and men waiting for their cases to be called stared at them with curiosity. Mr. Gonzalez straightened his shoulders.

"Is it over?" The tall latin stood discreetly by the side of the door to the courtroom they had just exited.

Sandy nodded. The Gonzalezes shuffled uncomfortably as they waited to find out what would happen to them next. They looked apprehensively at the man.

"I guess they don't need me then." He put his hands in his pockets.

Sandy considered the drape of his trousers now that he was standing. "Who are you?"

"Officer Gomez."

"The arresting officer?"

Sandy Walker didn't like cops. The young ones were nervous but earnest in court; the older ones were constantly perfecting their ability to lie under pressure. Her first experiences with them had been during Vietnam—the headbanging at the march on Century City, their unwelcome presence on campus when she and the other students had closed the law school during the bombing of Cambodia, their brutal eruption in East LA after the murder of Ruben Salazar. It was particularly hard to understand why a chicano would want to be a cop.

"Yeah, it's over."

He gave her a candid up-and-down appraisal. "I thought you were the social worker."

She started to turn to the Gonzalezes.

"I won't need to come down here again?" he interrupted with some apparent regret.

"Talk to the county counsel; he's your lawyer," she snapped.

The Gonzalezes appeared oblivious to the details of this conversation. She turned to them, dismissing Officer Gomez from her vision, but he continued to stand beside them. She could smell musky after-shave.

"Is there something else?" she asked.

A dimple appeared at the corner of the left side of his mouth. "I thought I'd stay to see if you wanted me to help you."

"Help me what?"

"Talk to the Gonzalezes. Interpret for you. I could do that since I'm not on the case anymore."

What the hell did he think she'd been doing? Miming Beckett? "Great, that would be very helpful. Tell them exactly what I'm saying."

He nodded agreeably.

Sandy smiled reassuringly at the Gonzalezes. "You'll have to come back to court in three weeks. A social worker will be out to talk to you. Officer Gomez here wants you to know he's very sorry you've missed two days of work and he believes, as you do, that the system is biased and unfair in its treatment of latinos."

They all stood there.

"*Pues,* aren't you going to translate for me, Officer Gomez?" Without waiting for his reply, she touched Mrs. Gonzalez lightly on the arm. "*Adiós, nos vemos en tres semanas.*"

She took a firmer grip on her briefcase. "Why don't you just shove off and mind your own business, Officer."

He sauntered beside her as she walked. Her cheeks were hot. They walked to the ground floor in silence. She hurried out the south exit of the building and turned right on Broadway. Her heart was beating faster as she stepped off the curb and watched the approaching traffic.

"Are you going to jaywalk here?" he inquired politely.

Tossing her hair over her shoulder, she looked at him coolly and with disdain.

"Yes, Officer, I am going to jaywalk right here, in the middle of the block, in the middle of the traffic. There doesn't seem to be any clear and convincing danger at this particular moment and I'm in a hurry to get home."

"I could cite you for an infraction."

"You could, Gomez. Vehicle Code Section 11128. My defense would be that I was trying to escape your advances when I was forced out into traffic; so I don't think you'll try that."

She strode deliberately into the street. He followed her.

"You don't mind me walking with you, do you?" he asked with the smile that produced the small dimple.

Sandy ignored him. She started to open the door that led to the underground parking structure.

He reached out and held the door open for her. "You should be more careful. There are all kinds of people around here. These parking structures can be very dangerous."

"It doesn't make me feel any safer to be with a member of the LAPD. I bet more people have died in custody this year than in one of these parking structures."

There was no sound except for the muffled roar of a car starting and the click of Sandy's heels on the concrete. She stopped by her car, a white '63 Porsche. It was gleaming and had new tires; the engine was rebuilt and had almost a hundred thousand miles on it.

"Good day, Officer."

"You obviously have some very negative feelings about law enforcement officials. That's a very unfortunate attitude and I think that it would help us both in the performance of our duties and responsibilities if we discussed this in some depth." The dimple reappeared.

Sandy opened the car door, threw in her briefcase, and whirled angrily to face him. "I wish you had been called as a witness, Officer. I think it would have been a lot of fun to cross-examine you."

"I'm really very charming. I make a good impression. Women judges always like me. They find my testimony honest and compelling." He leaned against the side of her car with his hands in his pockets.

"Oh, and do women lawyers always like you? Is this your routine?"

"No, actually I've never tried it before. I was watching you, you were watching me. I wanted to ask you out."

"You've never done this before? Well, you picked the wrong person to try it on, Officer. And get off my car."

"My name's Frank. Sunday's my day off. I could come over to your house in the afternoon."

"I'm not interested. I don't like cops and I don't like you. Good-bye."

67

He stood up. They were very close.

"You sure I can't talk you into it?" He put his hands on her waist and pulled her toward him. He leaned down and kissed her, pushing his tongue into her mouth. He was the color of Oaxacan clay and she felt him pressing into her, the gun at his waist cold against her hip.

After he had gone she drove aimlessly through downtown trying to decide where to go. She considered various bars—bars in J-Town dark as caves with jukeboxes playing the top forty in Japanese, or a couple of sloppy bars on the east side of Alameda where the downtown artists hung out, out Beverly to the geisha bars where Tokyo businessmen in heavy gabardine suits smoked and drank with women whose faces were powdered like white porcelain. There were always the bars of the big downtown hotels or out Seventh Street to the Tango Room, a little hole in the wall by MacArthur Park. Finally she turned the car back toward Chinatown to the Lucky Ring.

The place was packed. She had to push her way to the bar. The red flocked velvet wallpaper and plastic Tiffany lamps lent a false respectability to the gossip being passed around and the propositions being made. Ordering a double brandy, she surveyed the crowd.

Allan Cooper, in a shiny green suit and his breath reeking of gin, tottered toward her. "Well, it's finally driving you to drink. We don't see you here often."

"I got delayed stress syndrome." She dabbed at her mouth with the cocktail napkin. "So what's happening tonight?"

"You mean besides Pattie Robertson?" He nodded over at a tall brunette with a tight beige skirt cupped around her fanny and slit up the side, flame-colored silk blouse unbuttoned to the middle of her bare chest and ankle-strap high heels. "I've been meaning to tell her that

68

I love her, that I respect her as a social worker, and invite her to open a case file on me beginning with a home interview. You think that would work?"

Sandy saw Michael Fillipini talking with Pattie.

"It's probably as good as any of the lines she gets."

Michael glanced up at that moment and winked salaciously in their direction.

Allan appeared cheered by that idea. He loosened his tie.

"So what are you doing tonight? You're looking real good. Nobody could guess that you'd just spent the entire day with perverts and child molesters and most of the niggers in town."

He sidled closer, dropping his voice, whispering in her ear. "Maybe you're looking for a little action yourself, a little slippin' and slidin' to help you forget the cares of the day. Help you block out the nasty memories of guys who like to lick baby cunts and jam their dicks into little butts."

Then Allan Cooper stumbled, leaned across the bar, and shouted at the bartender for another martini.

"Looks like you're out to have a good time," observed Sandy.

"Have I propositioned you yet?" he wondered, picking the olive out of the drink the bartender pushed toward him and dropping it in an ashtray.

"I think you were working your way up to it. I was going to say no."

"Ah ha. Well that saves me a lot of time, not to mention a lot of money trying to get you liquored up. I am grateful." He lifted his glass unsteadily to toast her. "I intend to do a lot of drinking this evening and I will probably need all the paltry change I have with me."

"You haven't bought me a drink yet tonight." She leaned on the bar and signaled the bartender with a wave of her hand.

Allan Cooper shook his head dumbly. "I haven't? That

must have been some other tart then. I wonder if I had the common sense to proposition her?"

"Probably not or you wouldn't be here trying to hold up the bar by yourself." God, there are a lot of sloppy drinkers, Sandy thought as she watched Allan Cooper.

Michael came up carrying two empty glasses. "Look out, you two. I'm hot tonight."

He ordered two Black Russians and put an arm around Sandy and Allan, drawing them into a conspiratorial circle.

"I think Pattie is getting ready to invite me to see her etchings," he chortled, patting them each on the shoulder several times before releasing his bear grip.

"What can I do?" he gurgled as he held the drinks above his head and twisted away from the bar. "When you're hot, you're hot!"

"Imagine that, not only is she beautiful, she's an art collector. Talk about class," said Allan, sorrowfully staring after Michael's back as he worked his way through the crowd.

It was funny that Allan Cooper, even if he was bombed, couldn't see through Michael. Maybe only women noticed things like that.

Impatient, restless, Sandy dropped her head forward so that her hair streamed out, then flung it back so the hair fell in a line down her back. She stamped her feet in time to the music and did a few steps in the direction of the packed dance floor. "Come on, let's dance. Give me some change."

Shuffling her feet, she searched the song titles of the jukebox next to the tiny dance floor. "Goddamn, not a thing with a beat," she complained, tapping a quarter against the glass.

"Sandy," Allan Cooper said suddenly, "do you ever wonder why you're doing this kind of work?"

"Sure," she shrugged without looking at him, keeping

70

her face from him. "I just look at my bank balance and the answer becomes very clear."

"No, I mean really, Sandy. No joking around. Don't you ever wonder what we're doing here?" He lifted his somewhat stupefied gaze from the jukebox to face her.

Every night. I can't sleep. If I go to sleep I have terrible dreams. When I'm awake I see things like dreams. I hear things, voices. But she didn't think she could tell him this. Startled, she inserted another quarter into the machine to avoid looking at him. "I don't think about it very much."

He took her by the hand and led her into the dark alcove where the pay phone hung. Turning his back to her, he leaned his forehead against the wall. She could barely hear his voice over the music.

"I saw something so horrible today. I got a case where the guy must have been trying to sodomize a sixteen-month-old baby and the baby died during it. . . ."

She stared into the drink she was gripping. Jesus Christ. At that age, they weigh about twenty pounds. Like fucking a turkey.

"I got the photos of the autopsy today. Beautiful baby girl, face like a little angel, brown curly hair, big eyes. There she was, laid out on white sheets with blood smears on the corners, her butt bruised and all torn up around her little asshole."

Allan made a gurgling sound, his shoulders slumped forward. "They had photos of the top half of her skull cut off exposing her brain like a cantaloupe in a goddamn coffee shop."

Finally he pushed himself up, fumbled in his pants pocket and took out a small amber-colored bottle and a tiny spoon, which he used to pack his nose with cocaine. Without saying anything further he passed the vial to Sandy.

Back at the bar they found Michael perched forlornly on the last stool nursing a watery Black Russian.

"Where's Pattie?" Sandy sniffed, wiping her nose with the back of her hand.

"She left. She said she didn't want to mix business with pleasure."

"She was going to charge you money?" Allan danced around Michael, apparently recovering from his earlier mood.

It was hot in the bar. Extremely hot. Suddenly Sandy was very tired of the Lucky Ring.

Night rushed in the open car window as she pulled onto the Harbor Freeway south through downtown blazing beneath a cloudless, starless sky of carbon paper. In the distance the Hollywood hills were charged with radiance. She remembered once her father had taken her to Mulholland Drive on top of those hills and parked the car facing into the San Fernando Valley on a clear night. They sat for a long time in the dark without saying anything. He seemed sad. He lit a cigarette and put his arm around the back of her seat. The heat from his arm scorched her neck. His hand dangled from where it rested and brushed against her shoulder. Everything stopped. His hand on her bare shoulder, the darkness, the smoke from his cigarette. Finally he lifted his hand and pointed out into the valley. "Nothing ever changes. Each one of those lights is an unpaid-for television set."

Fern Street in Long Beach was a lower-middle-class neighborhood in what had once been a booming development at the end of the old Pacific Electric trolley lines. All the houses crowded in tight rows were painted the same muddy yellows and corals. Front yards were simple but redundant arrangements of hardy perennials, succulents, and a few overexposed rosebushes. Sandy drove slowly, looking for Jeanette Ray's address. It was Saturday afternoon. It would have been a hundred in the shade if there were any trees on Fern Street.

Jeanette Ray stood in the doorway watching as Sandy parked the car.

"I was just making some herb tea for you. Come on in."

Sandy regretted she hadn't thought to buy a cold drink at the liquor store she had just stopped at.

"You didn't have any trouble finding the house?"

Without waiting for an answer, she beckoned Sandy to enter. Jeanette Ray was dressed in a loose orange sundress, her feet stuffed into a pair of fluffy blue bedroom slippers. Her long reddish-brown hair was pulled back from the sides of her face, ratted high at the crown, the back set into a stiffly curled flip. Wispy bangs fell in points above her rigid plucked eyebrows. Sandy realized for the first time they were the same age.

The living room was small and overcrowded. The sagging green-and-white plaid couch had lace doilies on the armrests and an afghan of baby-blue-and-pink squares was folded neatly over the top. Above the couch hung a rug woven of shiny blacks, reds, and midnight blues depicting a catatonic-looking Christ at the Last Supper with his bored disciples. A red easy chair took up one corner of the room and a rocking chair sat by the window facing the street. Numerous wood tables of varying sizes and heights cluttered the room and were covered by nylon scarves imprinted with pictures of the Garden of Gethsemane and other knickknacks. There were plates painted with the raising of Lazarus from the dead, a trivet of tile and wrought iron advertising Bibleland in Odessa, Texas, and a plastic pair of deathly white hands that were plugged into an electrical outlet so they glowed like a dismembered apparition.

"Come on, come on, right this way. We'll sit in the kitchen so you can use the table to make notes."

73

Sandy was troubled Jeanette Ray had not yet said anything about jail. She followed Jeanette Ray down the hall.

The kitchen was tiny. Jeanette Ray gave a quick swipe with a dish towel to the top of the formica dinette table, which was shoved up against the refrigerator. There was a vivid scarlet-and-blue painting of the Sermon on the Mount and the multiplication of bread and fish. Scattered glitter highlights made the fish appear to glisten with slime. Bell jars of brown water-soaked beans and seeds gave off a faint sour smell. On the table was a large, expensive-looking portable radio cassette player with police bands. Several cardboard boxes with photographs, pieces of notebook paper, and letters peeking out the top were stacked on the floor.

"Now you just sit right down here and make yourself at home."

Sandy removed a handful of religious tracts bearing the legend ARE YOU READY TO MEET THE LORD? from the indicated chair and sat down.

"How about a nice cup of chamomile tea?" Jeanette Ray gestured toward a pot on the old stove.

"Not just now, thank you." Sandy grasped more tightly her purse, which held an unopened half pint of brandy.

"I tried to get all the papers about Julie in some kind of order." Jeanette Ray sat down and pulled a cardboard box on the table toward her. "I first started having trouble with her when we lived in Texas. As a matter of fact, I had so much trouble with her that I took her out of school and we moved here to California. Something got into her, just like the devil or the wind."

Jeanette Ray took a stack of documents from the box and removed the two thick rubber bands that bound them together. "These are Julie's report cards. You can see she was an excellent student in the seventh grade." Jeanette Ray laid the school records down like a hand of cards.

74

"But in the eighth grade she started to go wild and run after boys. See here . . ." Jeanette Ray tapped one of the papers. "She started to sneak around with some older girls when their mothers weren't there and they'd let boys come over."

"Ms. Ray, you don't know that she was doing anything wrong," protested Sandy. She hated the way this sounded. It was already conceding to some uninspired definition of sin.

The red highlights in Jeanette Ray's hair seemed to smolder.

"I know what they was doing. I found notes boys wrote Julie; she carried them around in her books and in her wallet. She got a smart look in her eye and started thinking she could come home any time in the afternoon she wanted. She started buying lipsticks from the dimestore." Jeanette Ray slapped the table. "What she was doing was bad. Fornicating. Like a dog. I almost died bringing that girl into the world. I gave her everything. A roof over her head. A Christian upbringing."

She rummaged through the box again. "Look at this, look at it," she demanded. "What did I tell you?"

Sandy unfolded a piece of notebook paper. The handwriting was thin and shaky and juvenile. It made Sandy remember again her father reading her diary. She put the letter down angrily.

"Ms. Ray, this is hardly what a court would call conclusive evidence. Why are you showing me these things?"

"Because she's a whore." Jeanette Ray kneaded her hands together. The knuckles turned white.

"She's your daughter. She's fifteen years old."

"She has no right to do what she wants."

"You're only going to make things worse."

"The Lord says . . ."

"I thought you were interested in getting her back."

Lips pulled tight and triumphant, Jeanette Ray smiled

brittlely. "Exactly. That is your job, isn't it? To protect my interests."

Sandy tossed her head irately. "My only job is to represent you before the Superior Court. This isn't the kingdom of heaven; it's not the promised land. It's Los Angeles. You're going to go to trial and you're going to lose. Then I'll do everything possible to get the judge to send your children home anyway. Do you understand me?"

The two women glared at each other.

"Now, if you'll excuse me." Sandy pushed her chair back clumsily so that it squeaked across the floor. "Where's the bathroom?"

The door didn't lock. Sandy pulled out a drawer adjacent to the door to jam it shut. She dumped the contents of her purse, found the bottle of brandy, and took a long drink. More relentless Christs eyed her from the wall.

When Sandy strolled back into the kitchen, Jeanette Ray was in the same place; she had poured herself tea, which was steaming in a dainty yellow cup in front of her. She had neatly piled the letters and report cards on the table.

"I have the tape recording," she announced.

The tape of their first interview? Sandy's heart skipped a beat. No, that would have to be in the Sheriff's Department. It would be Julie talking to some pimple-faced boy.

"No, I'm sorry. It won't help." She placed one hand down on the table in a small, deliberate effort to comfort the woman. "The court is going to order you to get into therapy."

"What's that? A psychiatrist?" Jeanette Ray sneered. "I won't go. There's no reason."

Turning away from the table, Sandy walked over to examine the Sermon on the Mount. The fish floating in the air made her think of the marlin who had unexpectedly found themselves off the coast of Southern California

76

rather than Mexico. "Okay, we'll look for some kind of program connected with your church."

Jeanette Ray seemed somewhat mollified by the reference to the church. "Are you a Christian?"

Sandy debated a reply. She had been one of two Episcopalians in a Catholic girls high school in San Fernando Valley. Mother Adrian, who was eighty and deaf as a doorknob, had been assigned to teach them remedial religion. The class was a year long; they had gone through the catechism book nine and a half times with Mother Adrian giving special attention to the mortal sin of gluttony.

"Does God love you?" she would ask, reading aloud from the catechism.

"He loves us, yeah, yeah, yeah." They sang Beatles songs, told jokes and talked about their Saturday bus trips down Ventura Boulevard, which turned into Barham, then to Hollywood. Ratting their hair, putting on lipstick, eyeliner, walking down Hollywood Boulevard, smoking, shoplifting, drinking chocolate cokes with cream, eating french fries with mustard, flirting with black guys, and putting their feet in the footprints at Grauman's Chinese Theater.

"I'll show you the girls' room," decided Jeanette Ray after a moment, when it became obvious nothing more was going to be said.

The girls' room was cotton-candy pink. Some grimy sad-eyed stuffed animals and a few unattractive dolls, their legs sticking out straight and pale beneath crocheted dresses, sat on the twin beds. A particularly gaudy and effeminate Christ hung on the wall between the beds.

Jeanette Ray smoothed a chenille bedspread. "Isn't this sweet?"

A little water glass on the chest of drawers held a handful of vivid begonias.

1964. The colors that year were hot pink and orange.

77

Sandy had hot-pink-and-orange flowered bedspreads in her room and large baskets of straw flowers so that it looked like a Mexican motel. The walls were covered with collages of bullfight pictures she had cut from magazines and a large poster of Manolete dying in Seville. She and her father belonged to Peña Taurina Seda Sañgre y Sol, which met once a month in a drab community room in Cahuenga Pass.

They would go on Friday evenings and sit in a hot, poorly ventilated room to watch black-and-white films of famous bullfights. At first she had gone without enthusiasm, dreading their evenings together. He said he wanted company, that her mother was too tired. Later she became fascinated by the elegant composure and handsome faces of the matadors. They would arrive as the films began, after the cocktail hour of sangría made with cheap Spanish wine and slices of lemons and oranges the members brought from their backyards in North Hollywood and Burbank. Potbellied men in elaborate embroidered shirts spoke atrociously accented Spanish with their sun-baked wives who had skin like leather, orange hair, and stiff, heavy fiesta dresses edged in silver and sewn with sequins. Her father got two metal chairs and set them apart from the group.

The movies began, jerking and flickering, the matador passing a large dark cape around himself in the center of the arena. The bull charged from a tunnel into the sunlight. Apprehensively, she would study the courage and stamina of the bull. Rarely was there a bull strong enough to survive. The matador made wide passes, testing the bull to see which way he hooked his head. Picadors entered the ring on horseback. Their horses, sides and flanks heavily padded, stood and waited for the bull to rush them. The picadors stabbed their lances into the muscles on either side of the bull's neck, wounding him severely enough to subdue the twisting and force him to drop his head. Although she had no maudlin pity for the bull and understood he was going to die, she was very still. The matador exchanged his cape, crimson on one side, gold on the other, for a smaller scarlet cape and signaled the picadors to leave the ring. In the black-and-white film his suit of lights was flat and opaque. He paraded to the center of the ring and began the slow, arduous passes that brought the bull closer and closer to his body. Her father's breathing seemed louder than the shaky soundtrack and undulated in time as though synchronizing itself with the movements of the cape. The matador dropped to one knee, threw away the cape, and raised his arms above his head; he pulsed his chest out at the bull. Then he rose, picking up his cape, hiding a long sword within it.

She could feel her father moving slightly beside her. His arm slid around the back of the chair. His breathing was ragged now, his fingers stroked her sleeve. The matador pulled the bull closer to him. Wrapping the bull around him, they moved in slow circles. They were locked together. Sandy leaned forward to get away from her father as the matador raised himself to the balls of his feet and shoved the sword downward behind the neck toward the heart.

"I've been keeping their room just so, until they get home," Jeanette Ray said.

He's got his own fucking wife. Why doesn't he . . . Sandy touched the begonias carefully.

"Real pretty, aren't they?" Jeanette Ray nodded proudly. "You see, everything I've done was for my children."

4

In the morning Sandy told Manuel she was going to visit a friend. This was a lie. She was waiting for Francisco Gomez. She didn't know why she had said he could see her again. Earlier she had called the operator for his telephone number so she could tell him not to come, but she hung up when she realized she didn't know what part of town he lived in and that there were a lot of men named Francisco Gomez. She was waiting on the balcony and dressed in a loose white shift tied at the shoulders so it revealed the top of the curve of her breasts. In ancient times the sacrificial victim was stripped naked and painted blue. She colored her toenails the lurid magenta of an August sunset and frosted her mouth to resemble a ripe plum. At low tide the pilings of Venice Pier stood out like bones of uncovered skeletons. It was already three-thirty and he was half an hour late.

Many people on their way to and from the beach used the alley called Speedway below her balcony. Washington Street was two blocks away. It ran from the neighborhoods and barrios of central and east Los Angeles to an abrupt end at the Pacific Ocean. As she smoked and glanced at the newspaper, she poured a brandy and contemplated the seemingly placid lives of the passersby. She would often sit on the balcony or walk along the beach imagining these people were the same people she had seen in court. Or would see next week. Their voices drifted across the alley. There were families, teenagers, two women leading a group of children, even a man walking slowly as he held the hand of a very small black-haired girl dressed in red shorts. As they passed under the balcony Sandy imagined the man called the child Soledad.

"Soledad."

Jesus Velaria held his daughter by the hand.

The girl looked up at him, then danced away, pulling him toward the beach.

He was not yet accustomed to taking her places by himself. He still couldn't believe his wife had left him. It had been nearly five days. Had he brought enough diapers? Was she old enough to eat a hot dog? His wife would have packed everything; there would have been no question about their preparedness for the day. A fire, a tidal wave, an atomic bomb and his wife would calmly pull out a plastic bag with the correct number of safety pins or cookies. Where was his wife?

The sound of the waves crashing against the shore filled him with dread. Should Soledad go in the water? His father had thrown him into the river when he was barely four years old. He remembered the terrible sinking, the moments of being unable to breathe, his father's laughter from the riverbank before he was finally pulled out by his uncle. His father and uncle argued briefly. His father said he didn't want his son to be a sissy. *Maricon*, faggot, was the word his father had used. Then the men drank a beer together and embraced. Jesus Velaria shuddered seeing himself again as a wet, skinny boy huddled in a small, dirty white towel.

Soledad was fearless. The first night her mother had

not come home Soledad cried all night. The second night she went to sleep with the light on and so it had been for the last three nights. Now that the ocean was in sight she laughed with delight and tried to run on her short fat legs.

La viva es pesada, thought Jesus Velaria. Then in English, because he was always trying to practice, he repeated the life is a motherfucker. How could she have left? He scooped the child up into his arms.

"Soledad."

Solitude. What a blessed idea. The constant movement of people on Speedway was like the constant surge of humanity in the halls of the courthouse. She could never get away from them. Malver Lopez and all of the other little girls who had been molested were her constant companions. She poured more brandy. There was no escaping it. The people, the stories, the fear.

It was almost quarter to five by the time Francisco Gomez arrived and she was moderately intoxicated.

"Sorry I'm late."

Handing her a cellophane bag of oranges he had bought at a freeway off-ramp, he laid his sports jacket across the black vinyl couch, sat down, and looked around the room at the books and pictures.

Her curiosity was aroused that he offered no explanation. She fixed another drink for herself without asking if he wanted one. He picked up a magazine from the table next to the couch and flipped through the pages for several moments before dropping it back on the table. If he had made any field sobriety observations, he didn't say anything about that either.

"Nice afternoon," Sandy suggested. She waited for him to make up some story about where he had been or how difficult it had been to find a place to park.

"What's that thing?" He jerked his chin in the direction

83

of the wood-and-metal painting placed against the raised black tile fireplace.

"A *retablo* from northern Mexico. They were painted by the devout as payment for answered prayers. Usually they're figures of saints or scenes of accidents," she added, picking it up to show him.

Instead of examining the *retablo*, Francisco Gomez got up and crossed the room to search through her record collection. He took albums, turned them over, read the liner notes, then replaced them while whistling tunelessly. She noticed for the first time how carefully he was dressed, the khaki slacks with sharp pleats, the freshly pressed black T-shirt. Sandy replaced the *retablo* and stood by the window as though she were looking out. She peeked at her watch. Her grandmother had always said it was twenty past the hour or twenty of the hour when a conversation fell dead.

She snapped the blinds shut and turned to look at him. In the shadow Francisco Gomez turned to smooth mahogany.

"Why did you want to come over to see me?"

"I don't know." He grinned, making the dimple appear. "I guess I have a real affinity for blonds."

"That was it? Because I have bleached hair?"

"What do you want me to say? I saw you and I was attracted to you. I ran a felony warrant check on you and it came up clean."

"You ran a make on me?" she erupted in disbelief.

Christ. That called for a drink. Abruptly she stalked out of the room and into the kitchen, where she grabbed the bottle of brandy, which she carried by its neck back into the living room. Francisco Gomez had seated himself again, casually, in the middle of the couch. She stood over him, the bottle on her hip.

"Why didn't you just ask me?"

His eyes rested briefly on the awkwardly executed Saint

84

Jude in the *retablo* before he spoke. "Okay, what's a *güera* like you doing hanging out downtown?"

Sandy stiffened. "Maybe you can tell me why a kid from East LA would want to join the police department."

"Alhambra, and it was the best living I could think of," he replied evenly, although he stopped smiling. "The pay's regular, the work's exciting, there's a sense of accomplishment, and we get uniforms to wear. That's pretty good for a guy whose father was a farmer." His black leather shoes, perfectly polished, reflected the last light of the afternoon, which seeped into the room.

"So how about you? How'd you get involved in child abuse cases?"

Fate, ritual. Memories bubbling at night like lava. Tossing her hair, she laughed in his direction. "You're a rookie, aren't you?"

"I been on the force a year and a half."

She drank from the bottle. "A year and a half. Well, well. You must know everything by now." She laughed again at him, swaying slightly.

He put out his hand to help steady her.

She slapped it away. "You don't know anything, you badge-heavy son of a bitch. They taught you how to shoot a gun, how to jump out of your car, how to put someone's arm behind their back and break it. You think that's all there is?"

The afternoon light faded from the room. His outline was blurred and silent.

"You got a lot to learn, rookie. There comes a day when you won't be able to take one more person telling you they just got raped or robbed or their old lady just locked them out of the apartment. You go home, but you find it eats on you at night when you want to sleep. You get a call late at night to go out to a house and when you get there it's some sad soul who's blown their brains out. There's shit dripping down the walls. You get sick to your

85

stomach. You feel sorry for the poor bastard and at the same time you're already thinking about what doughnut shop to go to so you can write your report. While you're writing the report you're figuring again whether you're going to have enough money to make your car payment this month. You learn about being tired. About being split in two by what you're doing."

He shrugged noncommittally. "I like to help people."

Sandy centered the bottle on the table and collapsed heavily on the couch next to him. It seemed pointless to explore the nuances of right and wrong, the ambiguity of morality, the slender threads of circumstances.

Neither one of them moved to turn on the lights. She dropped her head onto the back of the couch.

"As long as you're here, Officer, and you've been able to simplify things so, I feel inclined to make a confession."

Francisco Gomez laid his arm along the back of the couch. It brushed Sandy's hair.

"This isn't going to be incriminating, is it?" he chuckled.

Sandy closed her eyes. When she spoke again her voice was tired. It had become barely a whisper, so he had to incline his head slightly to hear her.

"It's a long, long time ago. I was about five years old and I lived in a big apartment building. There were two other girls who lived in the same building. One of them was my best friend. The other one we didn't like. I don't know why. She was different from us; she went to a different school. One afternoon she was going to a birth-day party and we weren't invited to it. We didn't even know the kid who was having the party but we were angry. I can see that girl so clearly, all dressed up in a stiff pink organdy dress with ribbons in her hair. Just as the car that was going to take her to the party pulled up, we sneaked up behind her and dumped a bucket of mud over her head."

"That's not funny," he cautioned.

"No, it's not. That poor woman has probably spent the rest of her life in therapy." Opening her eyes, Sandy gazed at the hazy Saint Jude. "I can't remember what happened to me for doing that. All I remember is the mud falling as though from the sky." Memory, like superstition or the belief that words can be connected to perceptions, is learned. It is not punishment but the betrayal of trust that defines memory.

Furtively, Sandy wiped at her face in the dark. Then she sat up and turned on the light. The bottle was empty. There were only two choices, said the Mayans—ritual purity or the elation of alcohol. She got up, returning to the room this time with a pair of white sandals dangling from her hand. "Let's walk over to the liquor store."

"I don't want any and if you'll excuse me saying it, you look like you've had enough."

She lifted her head as she finished tying the sandal. "I have a lot to forget. Now do you want to accompany me or not?" In the dry season victims were captured for sacrifice to the rain gods and no one ventured out alone.

"I guess there's not much choice."

It was the only thing he'd said all evening she agreed with.

Country blues poured from one of the bars on the corner as they walked toward Washington. Globes of light strung above the water illuminated the pier. Sandy wondered if Manuel was there. There were still some roller skaters on the boardwalk. Small groups of people burdened with poles and plastic buckets of fishing gear moved toward the pier. A gang of bikers lounged in front of the bar with the band. A languid breeze rustled the trash filling the gutters. The sidewalks were littered with dog shit. A wild-eyed woman with spittle running down her chin panhandled them for a quarter. This was the end of the world. During the storms that had lasted all winter and all spring, it had been flooded for blocks by the pounding rain and relentless sea. A group of *vatos* and their girls in the parking lot turned up the volume of a portable radio; the sound of heavy metal crashed around them like an accident. The bikers looked toward the latins as though a fight was inevitable but it was still too early in the evening.

The same lanky junior college student in a yellow Hawaiian shirt who had been working behind the counter the last several times Sandy was in the store shoved a bottle of Greek brandy in front of her. While she was paying for it, Francisco Gomez browsed through the magazines. Two dark-haired women came through the door laughing. They stopped at the refrigerator case and pushed back the top, bending their heads down into it, giggling in the escaping cold air as they picked out ice-cream bars. The one closest to the door glanced over at Francisco Gomez and winked as she nudged her friend. He didn't notice. Sandy looked over his shoulder at the magazine. It was a picture of a naked airbrushed blond holding a kitten and looking coyly into a mirror.

Sandy widened her eyes and pouted slightly, imitating the photo. "Is this what 'affinity' means?"

He stuffed the magazine back in the rack.

The sand glistened like silver under the arc lights at the edge of the parking area and then receded into darkness. He hung half a step behind her as though counting the people grouped around iridescent sedans in the parking lot. The volume of the radio dropped and the *vatos* gave them room; they had spotted him as a cop. Embarrassed that it was so obvious, she walked toward the lifeguard tower at the southern end of the lot without saying anything. The old tower had been destroyed by the storms. At the beginning of summer the county had hauled out a new one and attempted to secure it with cement posts buried fifteen feet in the sand.

"Do you come out here often?" he asked, watching her climb the wooden ladder.

"Yeah, it's one of my favorite *lugares*."

Pulling her dress above her knees, she knelt in a corner and rummaged for four tiny stones she had placed there several weeks ago. Manuel knew about the pebbles and would sometimes rearrange them as a message that he had been there. Satisfied they were undisturbed, she pulled the bottle out of the paper bag and sat down, leaning against the backboard. "I like to sit up here and have a drink, watch the sunset, see the lights when it's dark."

Francisco glanced toward the parking lot. "Alone?"

She started to say yes, but looking down and seeing his expression, she merely averted her eyes, looking past him at the ocean.

He shook his head as he climbed up the ladder. "You must feel like you don't have much to lose."

"What do you mean?"

The lifeguard tower shook slightly as he stepped onto the platform.

"You hang out in these dangerous places, drunk maybe, and you act like nothing will ever happen to you."

"Those aren't the kinds of things I worry about," she shrugged.

"You should. Why are you so fascinated by this *vida loca* stuff, anyway?"

Turning away from him, she drew her knees to her chest. The heat had made the air stale. It was cloudless, a few stars showed themselves. Above them was the Big Dipper. The Mayans said they were not stars but the eyes of animals thrown into the sky to watch over the night and protect its drunkards. She put the bottle between them.

"Go ahead," he said. "I'm sort of curious to see how much you actually do drink."

"I only do this on weekends sometimes," she lied. The simple fertility rites had become so complicated.

She pointed along the coastline, expecting he would ask names of buildings or towns or beaches, but he did not follow the movement of her hand. He was watching her profile and the twitch of a nerve at the base of her throat.

"You want to know what I worry about," she asked finally, addressing the horizon. "That we all come from pasts we will never understand. Or even remember. I worry that I've forgotten the special name of the moment that precedes dawn. That my language is foreign. That my body is a tropical tree with sap the color and density of blood. And the rain is turning to resin. That the ocean is a volcano of water. And that all we can rely upon is the manipulation of existing images. The past shifts and changes constantly. Our lives are hidden from us like layers of sand and silt laid down on a beach."

She turned quickly to face him. "Right now I'm worried that I've talked too much and I'm not going to get laid tonight."

He stood. "Let's go then."

In the partially darkened bedroom she started to undress, slipping the slender ribbon ties off her shoulders. Francisco dropped his sports jacket on the bed, drew off his T-shirt and folded it. The white dress hung around her hips in soft folds.

"Put on those black high heels I saw you wearing the other day," he said.

As she took the heels from the closet, she remembered a time the year before when she had picked up a carpenter in a bar in Hermosa Beach and taken him to her apartment. She was drinking brandy and water tall. She had poured out her life story like she had almost done with Francisco Gomez. He had fucked her hard, stuck a popper of amyl nitrate under her nose and left in the middle of the night. Sometime later her apartment was burglarized.

Pushing her white silk bikini down to her ankles, she sat up on the dresser and kicked them off. She leaned against the wall, spread her legs and made a slow show of putting on each shoe, holding her ankles with her hands, stretching her leg out.

Seated on the bed, Francisco Gomez watched intently. Was he wondering how many men she'd been to bed with? She stared back at him. He glanced around the room for a place to hang his pants, then stood and withdrew his service revolver from a holster at the back of his waistband. After he had folded his pants neatly, he took the gun, examined it, and laid it under the bed.

"Aren't you going to get out the handcuffs?" she asked, her voice bored and whiny.

He sprang from the bed. In a single motion he grabbed both of her wrists, which he held tightly above her head with one hand.

"I don't think we'll need the handcuffs." With his other hand he pushed hard on her breastbone, pinning her to the wall as he shoved in between her knees. "Did you want me to screw you like that?" he breathed in her ear. "Is that what you expect? Or are you so burned out and fucked up you don't care what happens?"

"Hey, you're hurting me." She bent forward, trying to pull away from the wall.

"That's what you're looking for, isn't it?"

"No," but her legs wrapped around the back of his thighs.

"You crazy *ruca*. What's with you?" He dropped his hand from her breast and shoved a finger into her vagina. "Sometimes you act like a kid and sometimes you act like a whore."

Sandy tried to twist away from him.

Loosening the grip on her hands so they slid down the

wall and rested on the crown of her head, he pressed against her, kissing her. For a moment longer he kissed her, then abruptly he pulled his finger out of her and forced it into her mouth. The salty taste was like tears. He brushed her hair away from her face.

It was five in the morning and he was getting dressed. She must have dozed. He bent over, his back round as he tied his shoes. There was a Mayan lord who had carried mountains on his back. The books that contained this story delineated days of ceremony, cataloged dreams, and described the way children were created. However, she had realized the evening before that Francisco was not interested in cosmological concepts; he was probably wondering if his partner was going to let him drive that day. Sandy turned her face into the pillow, pretending to sleep.

After he kissed her on the cheek and closed the door quietly behind himself so as not to disturb her, she lit a cigarette. The sun was starting to rise. It would take twenty minutes under the shower to feel even half decent, she calculated. The morning was already hot and sticky. It would take an hour to drive downtown because the freeway would be littered with cars that had overheated.

Over on Seventh and Valencia in downtown Los Angeles the sun was beginning its long arc across *Varrio Loco Nuevo*. Jesus Velaria stood in the window of his small apartment considering the gutted building opposite him. It was over-grown with vines and grasses and inscribed twice with the number thirteen. The *Botanica La Ayuda* across the street began to glow in the early morning light, became pale pink and chartreuse.

This was the time of year when it was not much cooler at night than in the day. Perhaps that was why he was unable to sleep. Last summer it had not been so hot but that was before El Niño and the random winds. Now Zamora's market on the corner opened at five in the morning. Recently they had started to sell ice cubes in plastic bags. He remembered summer in Mexico City when he was a boy and his father and his uncle Arturo would take him to the baseball game in Parque Seguro Social on Avenida Cuauhtémoc over by the Viaducto Piedad. Jesus Velaria took a child's plastic cup decorated with cartoon characters from a cupboard and ran water in the sink. They would always stop to buy him *horchata* from one of the vendors clustered around the entrance to the ballpark. It had been sweeter and colder than any drink in the world.

The *botanica* was a strange place, he thought as he returned to the window. Of course he had gone to church when he was young but he could not understand the continuing, willing devotion to saints and images who were so mercenary. He had seen many of the neighborhood women going in and out of the *botanica* accompanied sometimes by small children or reticent-looking husbands. He had refused to be married in the church and supposed this was a major reason why his wife's relatives didn't visit more frequently. But the *botanica*, despite all its Catholic appurtenances, was really a herb shop where the legendary and common cures of the people were sold. He was able to accept this quite readily. Chickweed for headaches, sage for sore throats, mugwort for disturbed dreams. The *botanica* straddled the thin line between convention and history, between fate and acceptance. What he found unbelievable was that there could actually be herbs for securing a better job, herbs for falling in love, herbs for picking the right horse in the third race. Why not, he wondered, herbs for a real social purpose. Herbs for a successful revolution, herbs for urban rapid transit, herbs that could be placed on a glass plate in the center

93

of a room and would cool the air without the necessity of electricity.

Watching the play of light and deepening colors, Jesus Velaria shook himself from his silent sentry position. It must be time to go. He took a peach-colored shirt that had been hanging in the open window, put it on with his jeans, and went to look in the next room. His daughter, Soledad, was still sleeping in her crib. At that instance he was struck again with amazement at how small she was. Then he wondered where his wife was and if she was ever coming back.

By the time Sandy arrived, the courthouse lobby was full of hot and irritated pimps, hookers, gangbangers, lawyers in seersucker suits, and police officers in a variety of uniforms and ineffective disguises all waiting impatiently for elevators. Usually she had coffee in the cafeteria with Michael Fillipini. He was entertaining three women with a story that seemed to involve much poking and gesturing. She couldn't remember if she'd eaten dinner the night before so she ordered three scrambled eggs with hash browns, refried beans, and a large coffee. Alfredo behind the counter had mastered the egg-to-oil ratio so the eggs were always greasy and soothing to an agitated stomach. As she passed the service counter she grabbed a bottle of tabasco sauce, which was her favorite hangover remedy. Without breaking his monologue, Michael pulled up a chair for her; she greeted everyone with a nod, sat down, and poured tabasco sauce all over the plate.

"How can you eat that stuff first thing in the morning?" Michael asked as he finished his story to a round of laughter. "You're going to turn black if you keep doing that."

Lacey Potter gave him a disgusted look. "You know I hate it when you do that."

"That's not racist," protested Michael. "Look around, all the people dumping tabasco on their food, except for Walker here, are black. It's like barbecue. It's genetic. You know what I mean?"

He looked around the table for someone to agree with him. "You want real barbecue you go out Slauson or to South Central. You don't go to Glendale or Sherman Oaks."

Lacey Potter took out a cigarette and looked away.

"Since we see so many poor people down here in this system it stands to reason that most of them are black or latin," Sonia Perez intervened.

"Mexicans got absolutely no sense of humor," Michael said.

Tricia Spivey giggled and Sonia Perez gave Michael a light but quick punch in the arm.

"Hey, come on, Lacey," Michael cooed, leaning forward to light the cigarette for her. "Let's jump into your Mercedes at lunchtime and go out and get some barbecue. I'll show you a terrific place. Right in your old neighborhood."

Lacey Potter blew smoke in his face. "Maybe some other time. I'm going to the Black Women Lawyers luncheon in Chinatown today."

"I've made some observations about child molesters based on ethnic groupings," announced Sandy, looking up from her plate for the first time. "I'll give you a quiz."

They looked back at her skeptically.

"What group is most likely to orally copulate a child?" Silence.

"Latins. What group is most likely to sodomize a child?"

More silence.

"Blacks. What group is most likely to be involved in incest as compared to step-parent molestation?"

"It must be American Indians," said Michael.

The silence continued uncomfortably so she put the fork down. "Oh come on, you must have noticed some patterns. There's no negative connotations involved. It's not saying one group's better or worse. It just refers to cultural taboos and the amount of time it takes for one culture to assimilate another. . . ."

"Hey, Sonia, is it true Mexican guys don't eat pussy?" interrupted Michael.

"You're perverted." Sonia gave him another punch in the arm before turning toward Sandy. "I don't know if you can make such generalizations, but I have noticed that most of the Mexican molesters come from the state of Jalisco."

"Is that based on personal observation?" inquired Michael.

"The only observation I've made," added Lacey Potter, "is that the hardest people to work with are the drunks and the PCP smokers."

Tricia Spivey nodded her head in agreement. "You get those Shermheads with breath like dry-cleaning fluid, you don't know what they're going to do."

"I got a woman today for trial who's been committed to Camarillo seventeen times since she got out of high school and she's only about twenty-nine years old," bragged Michael.

Sonia Perez rolled one of her long filigree gold earrings between her fingers. "What's she here for?"

"Filthy house. She and her kids were living in a shack in the middle of an auto wrecking yard."

"You'll do a brilliant job, I'm sure," said Tricia Spivey as she stood and brushed invisible crumbs off her new ivory gabardine suit from Beverly Hills. Lacey Potter picked up her briefcase. It was time to work.

Sandy stood in the middle of the hall staring at the name written in her calendar. Taylor. It meant nothing to her. She looked around to see if any of the women looked familiar.

Tall, short, thin, fat, black, white, brown. They were all garishly dressed. The hall was a riot of sordid hues. Sandy imagined the failure to grasp the concept of the primary colors had led each of these women to progressively graver errors in judgment.

A woman approached her.

"Ms. Taylor?" Sandy frowned as she tried to place the woman.

"No, but I need a lawyer."

The woman began telling her story before Sandy could stop her. The story was long and involved. Several drops of perspiration glistened on the woman's upper lip. Sandy looked past the woman's shoulder, barely listening. There was a certain poetry, a litany of images. The baby had a burn on its thigh, the father was gone, she was raped three times, her mother wanted money, somebody had been smoking Sherm, who called the police?

Sandy heard only some of the flow of words that flooded her. Inside, something was stirring, swirling. Abruptly she excused herself as she felt come falling from her vagina onto her panty hose.

The bathroom door creaked on its hinges. Paper towels were thrown on the floor. The sinks overflowed. A fat black woman pulled the pants off a little boy, scolding him for having messed in them. Sandy tried to catch a peek of herself, but a couple of tough-looking latinas wearing heavy rouge and pale lipstick stood in front of the mirror combing and recombing their hair.

In one of the gray stone stalls carved with graffiti, she sat carefully on the edge of the toilet and examined the spreading wet spot between her legs. Tentatively, she touched the glossy area of her inner thigh.

When she was fifteen she had been raped by two boys who lived in her neighborhood.

This memory was unexpected. Unexpected as the winds shaking the city. She was able to forget about it for long periods of time. It had happened at her best friend Lori's. Unexpectedly, Lori's mother had gone out to dinner with some man. Half an hour later, she remembered the time exactly because they'd been watching Lloyd Bridges in "Sea Hunt," the two boys showed up with a bottle of bourbon. Then the boys had her in the bedroom.

I didn't know this would happen. Daddy. Help me.

Lori locked herself in the bathroom and wouldn't open the door even when she began to scream. The bigger of the two boys hit her and that was the last thing she remembered until she woke up in the middle of the night alone in a pool of vomit.

Of course her father found out. Told her she was a whore. And an alcoholic. While rampaging through her room looking for other evidence, he ripped up all of her underwear. After that he looked at her differently.

Carefully, Sandy cleaned herself and stuffed a wad of toilet paper in her panty hose.

Michael Fillipini was smoking and pacing outside the third-floor courtrooms. It was the only form of exercise he indulged in other than regular Sunday strolls through Palisades Park, where he went to boost his cardiovascular capacity by talking to women wearing skimpy nylon jogging shorts. Sandy almost bumped into him as she rounded the corner coming out of the bathroom. He fell into step with her. Two little boys were wrestling on the floor by the water fountain as Sandy leaned over and took a drink.

"Did I ever tell you you got a nice butt?" Michael inquired in a loud voice.

She straightened quickly, brushing her jacket down. "I thought you had a trial this morning."

"Two of them in Department Twenty-seven. I'm going to be here all goddamn day; I'm waiting for a sign-language interpreter," he said sadly. He probably wanted to get home early so he could relax before the Mets-Pirates game he had fifty dollars on.

Three uniformed policemen strode past them toward Division 20. A burly red-faced detective carried a shotgun with several white identification tags hanging off it. The two little boys leaped up from the floor to ogle the gun.

"County this size and they only got two goddamn sign-language interpreters," Michael snorted, his eyes following the cop with the shotgun.

"I got a gun like that at home," bragged one of the boys.

"So? I'm going to be a policeman when I grow up," retorted the other.

Sandy pictured Francisco Gomez in his blue uniform cruising through downtown Los Angeles past the walls and garages, spray-painted by Mr. Baby, Pantera, El Loco, and Spyder, past Thai restaurants, past union halls, past Chinese acupuncturists, past faded tropical-colored cafés with names like Mi Ranchito, El Payaso, Corazón de Merida.

With what he considered to be a fatherly expression, Michael bent down to the little boy and asked, "Don't you want to be a doctor or an astronaut? Wouldn't that be fun?"

"No," persisted the boy, who jutted his chin out and stuck his hands on his hips impatiently. "I'm going to be a policeman, like that man," he said, giving particular emphasis to the last word.

Michael Fillipini placed his hand on the boy's shoulder and tried, "How about a lawyer? Do you know what a lawyer is?"

The boy nodded his head. "Yeah. An asshole in a suit." The kid threw himself into a convincing feet-spread position, with his hands together at shoulder level, pointed his

99

index fingers at Michael as though taking aim, and screamed, "Freeze, mother-fucker!"

"You see that," Michael observed as the two boys ran away shrieking and people in the hall turned to look at them. "That's what's wrong. Not enough of these little bastards being seriously abused by their parents."

"What's the interpreter for?" she looked at her watch, wondering if she and the Taylor woman had missed calendar call.

"I'm representing a deaf guy who supposedly molested one of his daughters. Look back over there." Michael jerked his thumb over his shoulder. "See that girl over by the pay phone, the fat dumpy one with the bad skin, in the orange blouse? Okay, see the little muffin with the tight jeans and the long hair. Those are the daughters."

She glanced over at the girls. "So which one did he molest?"

"Jesus Christ, Sandy, he's deaf, not blind. Which one do you think he molested? You been reading *Popular Lobotomy* lately or what? I wish I'd had the chance to molest that little nymphet."

Sandy flushed, annoyance creeping into her voice. "You're really a sexist, you know that, Fillipini?"

"Oh, bullshit." Reluctantly he pulled his attention away from the girls. "That's the real trouble down here. Everybody tries to pretend they're some kind of liberal, like they're shocked. Hey, she's probably spreading her legs for every high school boy who spends five bucks to take her to a movie."

"What's that got to do with anything?" Sandy snapped. Rape victims in a criminal trial were entitled to the privacy of their sex lives, why not high school girls? None of the judges would inquire into the girl's delicate First Amendment rights, except possibly Judge Hillary, who wanted to tell everyone about birth control.

Michael smirked and made a grand gesture of poking

her in the ribs with his elbow while winking lecherously. "Admit it. She was probably thrilled to be getting plugged regular. Once they get a taste of it, they can't get enough." He took a pack of cigarettes from his breast pocket, shook two out, lit them and handed one to Sandy. "That reminds me, did I tell you my ex-wife called me the other night?"

Sandy had heard the story about how women pursued him a million times, more if variations of the theme were counted. Sometimes it was a well-dressed woman in the supermarket, or the girl behind the counter at the dry cleaners, or the lady next door who needed help getting something down from a high shelf. For a moment she wondered if this was why his second wife left him.

"I got a case today," she said, wanting to change the subject from the uncomfortable mood that was settling about them. "I represent a woman where the father molested the two kids, a girl and a boy."

Michael pretended to shudder. "An incestuous bisexual! Is nothing sacred?"

"Apparently this woman knew when she married him that he'd had a history of molesting children." Sandy shook her head in disbelief. "Who on earth would get involved with a man who's supposed to be a child molester? I mean, what kind of guy goes around putting his hand in little girls?"

"What did he do?"

"You need three guesses? The usual stuff. Oral copulation, fondling, simulated intercourse, hand jobs."

Michael looked rapturously at the ceiling. "Oh, I love the part about blow jobs. I always get excited about cases that have blow jobs."

Beseechingly, Michael shrugged his shoulders as one of the other men who worked with them joined them. The man looked cautiously up and down the hall before announcing in a stage whisper to Michael, "I got this lady who molested her daughter."

"Oh stop it," Michael groaned. "I love that mother-daughter stuff. It makes me want to touch myself right here in front of everybody. What did they do?"

Sandy turned away to find the Taylor woman. The heat wafting through the building made her feel heavy and somnolent. Her skirt clung limply to her legs. The hall was full of women—black, latin, white, and an occasional oriental—all trying to control and hush restless children. Like the Mayans, they were interested in miracles. It was hard to tell whether the air-conditioning was working or not. She was slowly examining the many faces when she recognized the woman sitting by herself at the end of the hall.

Nadra Taylor was dressed in a tight rayon dress of hot pink, slit up both sides. She sat slumped on the wooden bench, legs crossed, swinging one exquisite black calf encased in a white vinyl boot. She had been walking up Gower, one of these bleak repetitive streets of half-dead palm trees and crumbling stucco perpendicular to Sunset, with her two little boys when she lost track of time. Outside a coffee shop, she stopped in confusion, waited in front of the newspaper vending machines as though reading the headlines, and asked a man who was passing by to watch her children while she went in to use the telephone. She didn't come back. Finally the man called the police. They found her two days later in Metropolitan State Hospital, where she was waiting to be released from a seventy-two-hour hold.

"Hi, Ms. Taylor. How are you feeling today?" It was more an announcement to shake Nadra Taylor out of her listless reverie than a question.

"I feel just fine," she beamed. "It's a lovely morning."

The heat was breaking records. The sky was heavy and smoggy.

Sandy gave her a quick once-over to determine if she was oriented in any of the three conventional spheres. "Did you remember when we met before and we talked? I explained you were going to have a trial today for the judge to decide if you left your children in Hollywood and if it's true you have a drug problem and certain mental problems?"

"Certainly. Right as rain. Those are all lies." Nadra Taylor bobbed her head agreeably.

Sandy leafed through the red folders she was carrying. "It's the job of the county to prove what it's saying about you."

"That's a nice suit you have."

"Thank you," Sandy faltered, tugging at her skirt. "You look very nice today, also." Nadra Taylor wore fuzzy three-inch eyelashes, the crooked space between her own sparse lashes and the randomly applied false ones glazed with thick chunky black eyeliner.

"Thank you. I'm an entertainer. I got beautiful clothes." Nadra Taylor looked contentedly at her feet. "I got alligator pumps and a fox coat."

"I imagine you do," Sandy said in a consoling voice. "Now, let's review the police report again so you'll understand what the police are going to testify." She flipped to the back of the file. "First of all, it says that on July eighteenth, at about seven-thirty in the morning, you were walking down Gower . . ."

Nadra Taylor stopped picking at her cuticles, puzzlement on her face. "Where's that?"

"In Hollywood."

"Right," she relaxed. "I live there. I just forgets the name of the street all the time."

"And that you stopped in front of the Silver Nickle coffee shop."

"That's right. We was going to eat breakfast. My boys

103

love, love, love pancakes. We eats pancakes all the time," Nadra Taylor crowed happily.

"And that you asked a man named Delmore Williams—"

"Who? I don't know no Delmore Wilson."

"Williams."

"William? I don't know no William neither."

"Delmore Williams. Anyway, you asked this man to watch your boys. . . ."

"That's a lie," she shrieked, her face contorted with rage. Her eyelashes flapped erratically. "We was going to eat breakfast, pancakes with lots of syrup, and these two men kidnapped me, right there on the street." She dropped her voice to a near whisper. "They forced me to prostitute for them."

Sandy sat down next to her and folded her hand over Nadra Taylor's. "How did you get to Metropolitan State Hospital in Norwalk?"

Nadra Taylor lifted her hand, waving it dismissively. "That was so long ago, more than a year ago. I don't remember how I got there. I guess somebody gave me a ride."

"No, I mean how did you get to Metro last month?"

"I wasn't there." Nadra Taylor was talking to the wall now. "It's just like I told you. These two men kidnapped me. They took me to a motel somewhere. Wouldn't even let me out of the room. Wouldn't even give me anything to eat. I had to do whatever they said."

Sandy was momentarily intrigued by this new detail Nadra Taylor was creating. "Are you telling me you weren't in Metro last month?"

"That's right. It was way more than a year ago."

The police report was five weeks old. "Okay. How did you end up there a year ago?"

Nadra Taylor sighed and dropped her hands in her lap.

"It was terrible. I got kidnapped by five men and they made me take PCP. They blew it up my nose."

"The two men in Hollywood kidnapped you last month, were they the same ones who kidnapped you last year?" Sandy asked gently, closing her file.

"No, they was all different ones," Nadra Taylor shook her head sadly. "Men like me. These two men who kidnapped me, they was out to get me because my boyfriend, Mr. Larry Samson, got arrested on some phony cocaine charge and they must have heard about it."

Her client wouldn't understand any of the testimony, wouldn't understand where she was or what was happening. When it was over and Nadra Taylor was alone, she would create a plausible legend for herself and the streets she lived on to explain the disappearance of her children.

"Do you know where the boys' father is?"

"Which one? Terry's? I'm not married to him. I heard we was divorced."

"How about the other boy's father?"

"I was waiting till Ronnie got a little older so I could see who he looked like," Nadra Taylor smiled.

"What about your mother then? Could she take care of the boys for a while?"

"My momma lives in Chicago. She's been taking care of them almost all the time anyway. I just went there and got them from her a little while ago." She stopped brokenly and poked at her eyelashes. "What's going to happen to me?"

"I don't know." It was true. Sandy didn't know. In ancient times there were people who could transform themselves into balls of fire or eagles or leopards. There was some transmutation of glandular secretions or arcane ritual that permitted them to transcend personal history. Lacking these abilities, Nadra Taylor would return to Hollywood; she would buy more bad dope and meet more bad men.

When Sandy arrived at her apartment that evening, she was still thinking about Nadra Taylor. She left the door ajar to lure in any ocean breeze that might spring up during the night and kicked off her shoes. She couldn't stop thinking about Nadra Taylor. Peeling off her hose, she caught the fabric on the slender silver chain she wore around her left ankle, ripping the nylons. Barefoot, she went into the kitchen, opened the refrigerator door, surveying the limp celery and a half-empty carton of some strange brown noodles Manuel had bought at a health food store. She let the door slam shut and took the bottle of brandy down. Exhausted, she remembered the sacrificial victims were often beaten with the thorny *pochote* branch. After the second drink she noticed that it wasn't really hot, that the air and the temperature of her skin were the same, so that she was merging with the night. She wondered how Nadra Taylor was spending this time. Did Nadra Taylor realize her children were being held somewhere in Los Angeles and that the details and inventions of her life were beyond her control?

It was late at night when the phone rang. Startled, she imagined it was someone calling to tell her that her mother had died. She had missed the call when her father died. She had been gone, coked up and laid out for three days in Silver Lake with a guy from the Department of Water and Power. When she finally got to her mother, it was over. The house had been stripped of everything that belonged to him. It was as though he had never been there.

She stumbled in the dark and answered the phone warily.

"Hello, blondie, *mi rubia.*" It was Francisco Gomez. "Sorry to be calling so late. I just got off duty."

There was a clock on the dresser. Two in the morning. "Is this an emergency?"

"I wanted to tell you I was thinking about last night."

106

"What about it?" She picked up the phone, carried it to the bed, and crawled back under the sheet. "If you're calling to find out if I have some sexually transmitted disease, you should have thought of that last night."

"Don't you take anything I say seriously?" he asked somewhat peevishly.

"Sure. Last night you were talking dirty to me in bed. You seemed serious about that." The Yucatec term for sacrifice was *p'a chi*, meaning to open the mouth, but they were referring to blood, not these awkward attempts at communication. As her eyes grew accustomed to the dark, she would make out the shape of her body.

"I want to see you again."

Sandy paused, watching the illuminated second hand moving around the face of the clock. As she took the empty pillow next to her into her arms she wondered where Manuel was. "I don't think so."

"How about if I come over one night after I get off duty?"

She fell back against her pillow again, still sleepy and half dreaming. She wondered why she was doing this, why she had let him come over, why she was talking to him on the phone. In pre-Columbian times human sacrifice had been sporadic and voluntary. Nudity was considered degrading.

"You acted like you liked me," he said finally, as though his feelings were hurt.

He was asking too much of her, expecting normal responses from the circuits that had shorted out. She wanted to be kind but felt it would be both beyond her abilities at the moment and useless.

"I did. You were great in bed, but I don't want to see you again."

"Why?" he asked in surprise. "Because you're older than me?"

Silently she counted to ten.

107

"Is it because . . ."

She pulled down the pink nylon nightgown that had bunched up around her waist. "It's because you're a cop."

He sounded relieved. "Is that all? I'm not always assigned these hours. I have days off. We'll work it out."

"That's not it."

"Would you worry when I was out working?"

"What?" she exclaimed in surprise, her voice rising in the dark.

"Would you worry that something might happen to me when I was out on the streets?" he asked hopefully.

The gravity of her mistake in letting him near her was apparent. "You've been watching too much television!" she snapped.

"I don't understand." His voice was warm and coaxing.

Annoyed, she sat up, switched on the light next to the bed, and poured three fingers of brandy into the glass on the bedside table. After she was raped, she had expected her father to call the police. He had not.

"I don't like what you represent."

"I don't understand why you feel like this."

No. And it was none of his business. "Perhaps I just need to resist authority," she answered glibly.

"You weren't resisting too much last night."

"Francisco Gomez," she drew his name out, exaggerating the pronunciation. "You must have been dreaming."

"Don't play with me."

"You're mistaken. Last night never happened."

"You should think about this some more," he said finally.

"There isn't anything to think about."

"Wait a minute." He was angry. "You act like you're a real tough broad, don't you? Don't care about anything. Drink your brains out. Screw everybody in the world.

Real tough all right. Down in those crummy halls all day defending a bunch of perverts and child molesters. Some kind of big liberal, huh? Take care of everybody but yourself. Do you think you're fooling anybody?"

"Thanks for your concern, Officer. It's been lovely." Sandy started to put the phone down.

"You want to hear about last night? You should. Do you remember anything after all the drinking and fucking and sucking?"

Sandy lined the glass up on the edge of the table.

"You cried in your sleep all night long. You were clinging to me like you'd never let go. I don't know how you feel about that. Maybe you do that with everyone you rub your pussy on. But for myself, I felt something. It's a rotten world, *chingado*, but you do the best you can and sometimes it's just with one person. Think about it. I'll call you in a couple of days."

He slammed the phone down.

Sandy couldn't sleep. She didn't want to. There was too much chance she would have another terrible dream, one of the ones that had her moving through an intricate pattern of chambers and corridors.

5

Michael Fillipini looked as though he'd had a rough night, too. He was wearing a gray pinstripe suit that pulled slightly at the waist and the red Italian silk tie Sandy had given him for Christmas. He wouldn't buy a summer suit; he was waiting until he lost weight. His usual broad smile was replaced by an abnormal puffy earnestness.

"Sandy, what do you think of getting married?"

"This is so sudden. I mean we've never even . . ."

"I don't mean you and me. I meant me."

"By yourself? Can that be done in this state?"

It was noontime and he had insisted they walk to J-Town for lunch. It would be the usual twenty dollars of sushi for Michael, a California roll and two beers for Sandy. They were moving slowly. The palm trees wilted under the scorching sun, their serrated shadows split across the sidewalk.

"I've been considering getting married," he said with a touch of hurt in his voice, "and I thought you would want to hear about it."

"I do. I do," she volunteered solicitously. "Who's the lucky girl?"

"My ex-wife."

"Which one?"

"Mariam. The first one, of course."

A tall, skinny Japanese boy, Nisei probably, pushed an orange mimeographed advertisement from the restaurant he was standing in front of into Sandy's hand, but she shoved the paper in her purse without looking at it. She was staring at Michael Fillipini in amazement.

"What do you mean the first one? You haven't seen her in almost twenty years. You haven't even finished getting divorced from the second one yet."

"I've been talking to Mariam on the phone a lot lately. Seven hours last night. Seven hours long distance." He lifted his sunglasses and squinted. "See these bags under my eyes. This is the real thing." He dropped the sunglasses back into place, apparently very pleased with himself.

"This doesn't make any sense," Sandy exclaimed. "In all these long conversations, the subject of your abandonment of this woman has never come up? You mean to tell me she has no hard feelings that you told her in sixty-two you were going to the store and instead of coming back with a paper, you hopped a bus to LA?"

"We have discussed that," he replied assuredly.

Sandy was skeptical. "What'd she say?"

"She missed me." He added a roguish grin.

They ducked beneath the white-and-blue cloth banners that separated Sushi Tokai's door from First Street and exchanged bows with Hiro, the bespectacled chef behind the counter. *"Buenos dias,"* Hiro called to them in an effusive round accent. The busboy hurried to get a beer for Sandy.

"She's always been in love with me," Michael said nostalgically, settling himself comfortably in a pale-wood-and-leather chair at the nearly deserted counter. "She never stopped thinking about me, even when she was married to her other husbands. She told me so."

"I'm sure that's true," Sandy said, directing her attention to the act of angling the beer into the glass so it

112

wouldn't foam up. "But how do you know you're still in love with her?"

Michael seemed to be giving the question an unusual amount of thought, but then he tapped on the counter in front of him, indicating he wanted some fresh tuna.

"She was my high school sweetheart. Don't you understand what that means? A time of innocence and hope before Vietnam, before double-digit inflation, before I lived in Los Angeles, before I became a criminal attorney. She's all that's untainted in my memory," he sighed theatrically.

How come, if it was so great, you left? Politely, Sandy avoided this question by finishing what was left in her glass. "What makes you think she hasn't changed?"

"I guess that's what I want to believe. Everyone needs something to believe in. You just hold on to your dreams and go for it." Enthusiastically as a cheerleader, he jabbed the air with his chopsticks for emphasis. "You have dreams, don't you?"

The dreams she had were horrible. Averting her eyes, she turned from the tuna, yellowtail, and eels in wet piles behind the counter to look for the busboy who could get her another drink. She fought a sense of panic as she thought about the horrible figures that wrapped around her in her dreams. And how was one to say with any certainty what the difference was between dreaming and waking? Forcing herself to breathe slowly, she knotted one hand in her lap and, with the other, signaled the busboy. "I like to dream about living in Mexico," she said finally, "at least that's where I think it is. It's sort of a jungle, lots of sunlight, miles of trees and vines, flowers." Her voice trailed off. Michael Fillipini stared at her in bewilderment.

"You know," she struggled. She wanted to be able to explain what she felt. That was all that was important; the offering of one's own blood, the blood falling on sheets of bark paper. "I used to live in Mexico. It was beautiful. I

113

was away from my family for the first time. I spoke Spanish constantly, and as my vocabulary changed, my perceptions did also."

Michael hoisted another piece of sushi with the chopsticks clutched awkwardly in his big hand.

"What are you talking about? Changing perceptions! I'm talking about the winning touchdown, the malt shop after school, necking in the back of your old man's Ford. Getting to feel tits."

"It sounds so simple, so long ago." Where was the busboy?

"It was a long time ago. It was also Pittsburgh and not the Tropic of Cancer or wherever you were." Michael paused for discretion. "Is that why you only make it with latin guys?"

"It has to do with color, with certain rhythms of language, what the air in the tropics smells like at night, a sense of history, a vision for the future."

"I should have known it was too hot to walk over here," he complained.

She folded her paper napkin as though to demonstrate to him she was in complete control of herself. She said, "In South America, they are making the man of the twenty-first century. Imagine what it would be like to live without boundaries or preconceptions."

"Boundaries? You're pushing your luck. We're talking significant cultural achievements of knife fights in barrooms, illegal entry into the United States, maybe making it big and working in a gas station."

She closed her eyes. She understood that Michael was telling her he cared about her. As with the *evangelistas*, the men in small towns in Mexico who worked in public parks and central plazas writing letters for the illiterate, words sometimes created a gulf. The *evangelistas* set up rickety tables with antiquated typewriters under the trees where they prepared love letters, birth announcements, notices of death and messages of grief. If a lover lacked an adequate vocabulary, if the indebted sought reprieve, or the errant forgiveness, the *evangelistas* embroidered appropriate and poetic phrases like a flawless fabric to swathe the mute. In the beginning, however, there had been but one tongue and all speech was urgent, insistent like the reverberating hum of insects.

"What do you expect to get from one of these guys?" Michael Fillipini reiterated, nudging her.

Sandy opened her eyes. The crab meat wrapped in sheer shiny seaweed he had ordered for her lay untouched on the wooden tray in front of her, a full glass of beer by her right hand.

"Someone who speaks the same language I do," she answered.

He laughed. "You mean you're going to become a Mexican now?"

Someone opened the door. There was a surge of voices and a blast of heat from outside.

"What I want," continued Sandy, over a woman's high-pitched tones lingering in the air, "is either someone who understands me completely, or who understands nothing." She stood, finishing what was left in the glass. "Come on, let's get back to work."

First Street was quiet in the incredible heat. They walked several minutes without speaking. The gasoline haze of passing automobiles contributed to the somnambulant feeling. Cartons of leafy green vegetables and twisted black roots were stacked on the sidewalk in front of the greengrocer's, but even the women shopping and comparing stalks of bok choy did so in heavy silence. As they passed Ben Kikutu and Son's Jewelry Store on the corner Michael was moved to announce, "I've decided to have Mariam come out here to visit me. Yesterday I sent her the money for a plane ticket."

They cut through the park in front of City Hall. A

115

group of school children were playing tag in slow motion, hiding behind the palm trees and running through the puddles created by the erratic sputtering lawn sprinklers.

"Is she going to stay at your apartment?"

Michael pursed his mouth slightly in a prim way. "Of course not, this is my ex-wife we're talking about. I'll rent a hotel room for her. Start out slow."

Sandy looked doubtful, the corners of her mouth twitching as she fought to prevent a silly grin.

"I have it all planned," he reported seriously. "The ultimate in spontaneity. Take a week off work, meet her at the airport with some long-stemmed roses, check her into the hotel, go for a little drive down the coast, have a nice dinner, give it time. That's the way, Sandy. I'm through with one-night stands. I want to establish rapport, mutual respect, build a relationship, let it grow into something lasting and decent."

"You couldn't get laid in China with that line," said Sandy as she opened the Temple Street door to the court-house.

Esperanza Rivera had been waiting over an hour on the bench outside Department 26. She was in her early thirties, hair cut short and curled around her face. Slightly overweight, she was dressed in a blue-and-green floral blouse with a brown skirt and a pair of scuffed pearlized white high heels. Her black patent purse was placed care-fully next to her.

"Mrs. Walker, here you are."

All of her clients seemed to want to have her married, as though it would give her some additional strength or credibility.

"I've been waiting for you. Am I going to get to take Maria home with me today?"

Sandy recalled the woman and her painfully slow polite cadence from the arraignment. "No, but you'll be able to

116

visit her in the building this afternoon when the trial is over. Where's your husband?"

She had been appointed to represent both of them because they said there was no conflict in their positions; neither of them claimed to have any comprehension of what had happened.

"I don't know if he's coming."

"Want me to discuss the police and medical reports with you again while we're waiting?" Sandy offered.

"No, not really." Esperanza Rivera shook her head sadly. "I have been thinking about them ever since the first time we talked. Trying to imagine what could have happened. You explained that in the girl, the vagina is like this." Esperanza Rivera held her hands up in front of her like an arthritic praying, the fingertips and the heels touching so they created an oval space. "And you said that in the vagina hangs an invisible curtain called the
. . ." She changed languages and said, "Hymen, that's right? And that this invisible curtain or wall is very thin and that in most of the girls who are virgins, they have this thin shield of their own skin. The doctor who looked at Maria said hers was torn, no longer in one piece. So I am thinking, what could have happened. I think maybe the doctor when he examined her, he used his finger, and of course, it was an accident, he didn't mean to do it, but he tore it a little bit, maybe with his fingernail."

Esperanza Rivera lifted her face hopefully to Sandy.

"It doesn't happen that way," Sandy shook her head, hair veiling her face as she bent toward Esperanza Rivera.

Remember the first time you had sex? It hurt, but you didn't want to cry, at least until it was over and you were alone. It felt like something inside you was ripping apart. The man you were with had to keep pushing because it was tight. There was a barrier and he pushed through it. You knew the exact moment when the wall was broken.

117

Sandy's mouth was dry. "There's only one way it happens."

Esperanza Rivera's lips trembled. "My God, I have prayed and prayed and tried to imagine all of the ways an accident could happen. Riding a bicycle. Falling off the swing in the park. One of the other children hitting her in the stomach. But, I really knew there was only one way."

Sandy and Esperanza Rivera looked at each other shyly, each remembering a past, each seeing their knees bent above them like distant and foreign mountain ridges.

"What's going to happen with you and your husband?" Sandy asked both out of curiosity and to break the tenuous silence between the women.

A flicker of suspicion crossed Esperanza Rivera's face for an instant; she glanced quickly toward the elevator. "I will divorce him, of course, as soon as I can get the money. Until then, I will just have to live with him. He is in and out of the house. I haven't seen much of him lately."

"He's probably afraid the police are looking for him."

The elevator doors opened and a group of people pushed their way out.

"Are they going to arrest him?" asked Esperanza Rivera, forming the words cautiously as she watched the disbursing group.

"They should, but they won't be able to." Sandy moved so she could block Esperanza Rivera's view of the elevator. "When you took Maria to Queen of Angels Hospital, they did a pelvic examination of her. They thought she'd been sexually molested, but she wouldn't say anything to the doctors or the police about what had happened. They asked her many times if anybody had touched her, but she wouldn't talk."

"So my husband won't go to jail?" Esperanza Rivera seemed uncertain whether she was pleased or displeased with the information.

Sandy folded her arms tightly across her chest. "She won't tell who did it to her."

"She is only five years old," said Esperanza Rivera, as though by way of explanation or apology.

"You think your husband is the person who did this to your little girl, don't you?"

"I keep thinking that somehow, it is my responsibility. That I should have known." Large tears began to roll down Esperanza Rivera's fat cheeks. Sandy searched in the messy clutter of her purse and found a used kleenex with lipstick on it, which she pressed smooth and gave to the woman.

"I wonder if maybe one of the men in the neighborhood where we live could have done it." Esperanza Rivera blew her nose loudly. "Perhaps she was playing in the front yard. I turned away to look at the television, to stir something on the stove, or to put some clothes in the closet. I was not looking. Perhaps in this moment, a man came to her, took her down the block with him, or took her into a car."

Sandy placed her hands on Esperanza Rivera's shoulders. "The police can't prove anything against your husband. The little girl won't testify; they can't bring a criminal case against him without a witness. So all that's going to happen is that the county is going to take your daughter away from you unless you figure out what happened to her, and how to protect her in the future."

Esperanza Rivera stood without moving. Her body was rigid, tense, as though she had to use all of her control to keep from falling. Sandy felt an inexplicable, overwhelming need to push her.

"You knew. That's why you took her to the hospital." Sacrifice took many forms. She dropped her hands from Esperanza Rivera's shoulders and walked briskly into Department 26 where another sexual molestation trial was already in progress.

In the last row of benches, Lacey Potter was absorbed in making notes on a file. Sandy sighed as she looked around the familiar room. Over the bailiff's desk, the deputy had hung a new poster depicting a family of orangutans sitting around a dinner table.

"I don't believe it," whispered Sandy, as she sat next to Lacey Potter. "That's disgusting. A functional family unit."

"The daddy ape is probably diddling the baby under the table," Lacey whispered back with her hand over her mouth. "Girl, I can't take much more of this. Things getting weirder and weirder down here every day. Right now, I got a loony redneck outside who's just gonna do something crazy."

Sandy lifted the file from the lap of Lacey's green-and-white silk print dress, to look for the name on the file.

"This guy's a real loser." Lacey shook her head. "And you should hear the things he has to say about me. He already told me he didn't want no nigger bitch for a lawyer."

"Sounds like you have a client control problem."

"It's not enough we have to figure out the defense of these cases, we have to put up with shit from these people."

"What's he so hot about anyway? This court can't put him in jail." Tucking her hair behind her, she opened the file. "So, what did he do?"

"Had his kids working in porno movies."

Sandy whistled under her breath. "Mondo playground."

"You got that right." With one large hand, Lacey Potter adjusted the strand of pearls she was wearing so they fell discreetly into the cleavage her dress suggested. "Of course, the county's going to take his kids. It's just a question of whether I can work a deal to get him some visitation, and the asshole keeps telling me to figure out some loophole."

"Full split kiddie beaver movies?"

Retrieving the file, Lacey Potter unstapled an envelope of photographs, which she handed to Sandy. Lacey closed her eyes wearily, dropped her head back for a moment, and then peeked over Sandy's shoulder. "You're holding that one upside down."

Sandy flipped her wrist to examine the photograph again. "Holy Christ. I didn't know anybody could do that." Gingerly, she handed the photographs back, holding them by their white borders. "You explained to him there are no loopholes in kiddie beavers?"

Lacey Potter sighed, nodding her head as she resealed the envelope. "He's going to do something. I can feel it."

The case being tried ended and the judge announced a five-minute recess so she could smoke. The clerk took a drink of coffee, the court reporter stood shaking out her hands and cracking her knuckles. The Mayans had worn their hair long, pierced their ears, and sacrificed humans and dogs. The bailiff opened the bottom drawer of his desk and took out another sports magazine.

"Next," the county counsel called in a bored voice.

Esperanza Rivera was still seated on the bench, watching the elevator. She had carefully braided the old kleenex; it lay in her lap like a dead lily.

"Did your husband show up?"

Lighting a cigarette, Sandy looked away without waiting for an answer. He wouldn't come. He was probably in Tijuana by now. He would stay a week or so with some distant cousins who lived near Teniente Guerrero, the main square. He would reappear when he felt like it. This would be easy. There were at least eighteen million border crossings last year, and those were only the ones that were reported. The border fence was ten feet high, topped with barbed wire, cut or trampled in places by Mexicans,

Hondurans, Salvadoreans, Chileans who wanted to go north. Some of them would stay in Tijuana, which had the highest per capita income in Mexico, but most were on their way to Los Angeles. They crossed illegally at night, in the last instant before dawn, across the last arid peak of the Baja Peninsula into the gentle, green, rolling hills of California without looking back.

Tears had again formed in Esperanza's eyes. Or perhaps it was the heat which was making everything melt.

"Everything's going to be okay," Sandy hastened. "You're here and that's all that matters."

Esperanza Rivera looked up uncertainly, but with gratitude.

"I know this will work out for you and Maria." The bitterness of this lie swept through her like a sudden cold breeze.

In her entire life, Esperanza Rivera had never lived alone, until three days ago. She had always lived with her family, and then her husband. She was afraid. Sensing this, Sandy dropped her cigarette on the floor and guided Esperanza Rivera in the direction of the door.

It was a very short trial. Sandy made no objections to the introduction of the medical records. An interpreter sat between Sandy and Esperanza Rivera, who watched her hands the entire time, as though they were birds that might fly away from her. The judge amended the petition to reflect that some person had sexually assaulted the girl and that such a thing does not ordinarily occur unless the parent had been unreasonable or neglectful.

The interpreter led Esperanza Rivera, who was now sobbing, away; Sandy drooped against the clerk's high oak desk waiting for a visitation pass. The sobbing could still be heard after the door clicked shut, or perhaps it only seemed this way because the beer had given her a headache.

"Another satisfied customer," Lacey Potter observed, striding forward to take her place at counsel table.

Sandy gathered her papers and briefcase. "Break a leg. Why don't you give your guy something to really worry about, tell him Henry's the judge," Sandy tossed her head toward the county counsel, who was also black.

A sniffling Esperanza Rivera waited with chastened dignity. "Do you think my daughter understands what is happening?"

"You mean about court?"

Esperanza Rivera drew in a sharp breath. "About being sexually molested."

Sandy understood what the woman was telling her.

"Did this happen to you also?"

Esperanza Rivera appeared startled, as though Sandy were some kind of white *bruja* who could see through her.

"And you yourself were young?" Sandy probed. "It was someone you knew?"

"Twelve. My uncle."

"And you didn't tell anyone?"

Esperanza Rivera nodded her head and grabbed Sandy's hand. "I thought it was my fault. That there was something wrong with me. I was frightened. I feared that no one would believe me, or that no one would forgive me. Since that time, I have felt my life was hidden from me like the moon behind the sun, as sometimes occurs in one of those nights of great blackness."

She exhaled with difficulty as she took the visitation pass from Sandy. "I will see my daughter now."

The day ended slowly, badly. Traffic hadn't moved for ten minutes. The back of Sandy's ivory silk dress was plastered with sweat to the car seat. She pulled her hair up into a loose ponytail on top of her head and adjusted her yellow mirror-coated sunglasses. Black smoke rose from a bus broken down ahead at Washington and Vermont. She pulled over into the parking lot of a liquor store.

While a glass of brandy with three melting ice cubes made a water stain on the bedroom dresser Sandy rummaged through the closet for a white cotton dress from Tuxpan. On the riverbank fronting the working-class neighborhood of Santiago de la Peña a blind woman and her daughter had made the dress. The daughter carried the dresses across the river to the romantic old port where occasional German tourists or the timid wives of men who had come for tarpon fishing would buy them. Sandy peeled off the sticky silk dress, dropping it on the floor.

She put several albums on the stereo—Bach, too liturgic and dense. Stones, too jumpy. Coltrane, piercing. Sandy switched off the music. Listlessly, her hair sprawling, she lay on the black couch, leafing through old travel magazines. She wanted to be somewhere hotter, tropical, closer to the equator. The scorching sun would dull her senses, absolve her of responsibility.

Eventually, the magazine slipped from her hand. The dog in the next house barked and the noise seemed to come from very far away. The Mayans had set an ear of corn in bed to guard a sleeping child. In that particular blue blackness, that silence before haunted dreams, Sandy's head drooped, jerking her awake. Sweating, she sat up, lit a cigarette, and felt for the lamp switch. Michael Fillipini must be home by now, she decided, her heart pounding. They could talk about baseball. Or the weather. Anything. Her heart was racing and her mouth dry, so she poured more brandy as she automatically dialed his telephone number. An answering machine clicked on; she hung up after the first eight bars of Louis Prima and Keely Smith doing "That Old Black Magic." Flipping through the pages in her phone book, Sandy came upon Lacey Potter's number. She answered on the first ring.

124

"Thanks for calling. I was just sitting here thinking about that insane case today." Lacey tittered, obviously embarrassed. "I bet you don't sit around and think about these people."

"Once in a while," Sandy replied evasively, straightening a stack of magazines. She couldn't imagine Lacey Potter three sheets to the wind like she was and desperately calling whoever might be home. "What was the outcome?"

"They're keeping the kids in detention out at MacLaren Hall until they can find a foster home."

"So did this come as a big surprise to your client?"

"No, that's not really the problem. He says no one has the right to tell him what to do. He says he's entitled to raise his children any way he wants."

Sandy clamped the phone between her ear and shoulder. "You're going to have a great time at the disposition." Her attention shifted to an annoying twinge beginning in her stomach.

"An impossible time. He's completely unmoved by convention, logic, or reason. He's amoral. He really doesn't think he's done anything harmful. He's beyond the reach of the law."

Sandy thought of her father. He pulled a chair into the center of the wood-paneled living room. He told her to sit down. She was fifteen years old again. He clasped his hands behind his back, bent his head and walked in circles around the chair, calling her whore.

"He's going to do something strange," Lacey Potter was saying.

"Don't worry," Sandy mumbled without conviction.

"I'm not," Lacey Potter laughed. "I'm just astounded that there are actually people like that in the world."

Sharp pain stabbed Sandy's stomach. She could barely hold the phone. "I have to go. I have to take something off the stove," she lied. As she hung up she could still see her father, his shoulders hunched in an old black sweater as he continued to circle her.

It was quiet as she hurried across Speedway to the beach. The moon was a thin slice of white laid against the sky. The lights curving around Santa Monica Bay to Malibu and south to Palos Verdes were like stars that had fallen to earth, shimmering translucent beyond recognition. She climbed up into the lifeguard tower, took a drink from the bottle she had brought with her, and settled back to listen to the waves.

"This is the tale of how all was suspended. Calm. Silent."

She didn't know how long she had been there when she heard this. She didn't know if she had been asleep. She didn't know her father knew this poetry.

"The heavens were empty. There was only the sleeping water."

Slowly, she opened her eyes and looked down. Manuel was standing at the foot of the tower. He had grown up with four generations of family under the same roof, people who could spin stories, who recorded time with myth, whose flow of words was like a channel of water cutting through a vast canyon, yet it was impossible to tell from his recitation what meaning, if any, the words held for him.

"I knew I'd find you out here," he said, scrambling up the ladder.

She held the bottle out to him as he sat next to her, draping an arm around her shoulder.

Manuel moistened one finger in his mouth and held it up to test the direction of the wind. "I never saw the sea until I left Mexico. Can you believe that?" he said, as he took the bottle and pointed with it out to the black water. "Where I was born was flat plain in the northern part of Yucatán Peninsula where it is always hot."

Tierra caliente. She moved closer to lay her head on his

126

chest. It was a jungle of rivers, lagoons, and swamps where heavy rains ran incessantly, pelting mahogany, ebony, rosewood, and Spanish cedar trees, forcing them to a breathtaking richness and a riot of stultifying wild tropical colors.

"All of my family lived there together, although a few went to the cities. I myself grew up in Mexico City before coming here to Los Angeles." He pronounced it slowly, endowing the very name with a moist eroticism.

It had always been unclear to Sandy what Manuel meant by this, since he had also told her that he lived in Mexico City for less than a year. Perhaps he was talking about the streets, the clouds of smoke and exhaust choking the sky, the petty thefts, lies, stories, inventions of a credible past, fights, the bravado of tight pants and nylon shirts with small neat half moons of sweat artificially smelling of lavender, black polished boots, standing on the corner to claim the attention of heavy-breasted women in tight skirts and red blouses who sauntered through the early evening heading for Chapultepec Park. Perhaps he was talking about careless remarks, white handkerchiefs pressed into a girl's hand after a frantic dance, a declaration of love to a slack-mouthed woman with worn lipstick, waking alone, instant coffee with boiled milk curdling across the surface of a chipped blue mug, or perhaps he was talking about the long hours of menial labor while listening to a radio station with American music and his longing to cross the border.

Sandy gave Manuel's hand, which dangled from her shoulder, a squeeze.

"What were you expecting to find here?"

"Beyond a job with decent wages," he shrugged, "perhaps I'd be lucky enough to meet a nice girl, get married, have a family. You think that's in the cards?" Manuel snickered at his joke then, tightened his grip around

127

Sandy's shoulders. "Don't you ever think of having children?"

"No." Sandy pulled the rubber band from her hair; the hair fell in one motion across her shoulders, curling over Manuel's hand and down onto her breasts. "I'd be afraid to."

"What's there to be afraid of, *niña?* You just like to practice making them?" Manuel dropped his gaze slyly. "That is good, too, if you do it with consistency, with just one man."

Startled, Sandy wondered if he knew about Francisco Gomez, but the breeze and the waves obscured the silence between them.

Manuel placed his hand between Sandy's legs.

A boat was passing in the distant shipping lane. Its lights moved slowly, shredding the invisible nighttime horizon.

"Don't you ever wonder what it all means?" she said, mostly to herself. She took another drink to enable her to decipher the tiny white dots.

Manuel's hand pressed into the mound of her vagina.

"All of this," she sighed, rocking back and forth. "The universe, that boat, the writing on hundreds of stone slabs, the wind and water."

"*¡Pendejo!* Those people you work with are making you crazy." Manuel took the bottle and screwed the top on it.

Sandy giggled uncontrollably, ending with a small belch. "I do seem to have a peculiar affinity for understanding the intimate details of the lives of others. That would be a nicer way to put it." She giggled again but stopped when she saw the look on his face. "Come on, didn't they have any crazy people in your town?"

He thought for a minute. "When I was a boy there was an old man with a she dog, a bitch. They would go everywhere in the town together. They went to the plaza and to the park where the boys were playing soccer ball.

They were always together. At first the people thought it was very nice to see the lonely old man with his dog. Then the old man became crazy, I don't know why, and he would fuck the dog."

"You saw it?"

Manuel, now interested in remembering the story, ignored her. "The people realized he was crazy, that something had to be done. There was a town meeting. Everyone went to it. They brought the old man and he became even crazier. He began screaming, 'You think it's wrong, don't you, because we're not married.' He even offered to marry the bitch right there to make the people happy. He had to be sent away to a larger city where they had a place for crazy people."

"What about the dog?"

Manuel looked at her, obviously puzzled that she had failed to understand the story. "They killed her."

"Why?" gasped Sandy.

"She had grown to expect the person who owned her to fuck her all the time," he said simply.

The boat had become a pinpoint of light north of the bay. Sandy closed her eyes again. Night was primitive, full of horror. The distinction between victim and perpetrator stretched thinner than the slender thread of moon high and inaccessible in the western sky.

6

Sandy stood in front of the mirror in the women's bathroom on the third floor, trying to smooth her upper lip and erase the bright pink lipstick that had run into the vertical creases. It made her mouth look like a carnivorous jungle flower. This provided a vivid contrast to the severity of her outfit, a navy-blue linen coatdress and a pair of Italian spectator pumps with a high arch. She looked tired. Maybe it was the booze. She ignored the thought and put on more lipstick. Women were waiting for her to give them structure and support. They were waiting for her to give them some news about their children. Straightening her collar, she paused to reread one of her favorite pieces of graffiti on the wall. "Tell a man Happy Easter and then say April Fool."

This threat of insanity was usually enough to get her on her feet in the morning.

Jesus Velaria straightened up from the Peugeot he was working on. His back was stiff and the air was dry. The torpid palm trees that lined the boulevard provided little shade. He turned off and laid aside his welding torch as he checked the bumper he had been installing. He was awake nearly all last night worrying about money. The ancient sacred numbers four, nine, and thirteen kept appearing. The rent, the baby-sitter, food. His wife had charged some clothing and turquoise-blue matching lamps for the bedroom four weeks before she left. He was saving to buy a van.

Formerly the people had traded among themselves brocaded textiles from the Yucatán, hatchets of yellow flint, duck feathers and salt from Isla Mujeres. They traded iguanas for medicinal purposes, tortoises, honey and wax, shells from the Atlantic, and green obsidian. A woman could be purchased for an amber nose ring or a small pile of cacao. Elaborate trade routes existed between the coasts and the highlands. Jade, pitch pine, and volcanic ash used in pottery-making were exchanged for lime, shark teeth, and pelts. The people felt they were in direct and emotional contact with the gods. The gods in return helped man with his work and provided him with food. Victims often represented the deities to whom they were sacrificed. Here they were all working for minimum wage in a shop that had secured licensing from the state by way of fraudulent application.

"*¡Despiertate!*" called Raul, gesturing toward Señor Aguilar, the boss, who was pulling onto the lot in his new black Cadillac. Jesus Velaria rubbed his tired eyes and returned to his welding.

Lourdes Mendoza gave Sandy a headache. Her story had the dismal certainty of dates of eclipses that had been foretold far in the future, obtuse as the movement of the planet Venus among the other heavenly bodies. To put it simply, Lourdes Mendoza had given her teenage daughter, a succinctly, ugly and graceless girl, to her second husband as a gift to keep him around the house. After her first husband died/disappeared/ran off, whichever was closer to the truth, Lourdes Mendoza, who was terrified

132

of being alone with middle age and an idiot child, had met a Vietnam veteran eleven years younger than herself. He was an alcoholic with a codeine dependency, which made him both irascible and unpredictable on Friday nights when Lourdes Mendoza brought home her paycheck from the electronics assembly plant where she worked in Carson. Sandy could imagine the nights Lourdes and her young spouse sat around the television set sharing a six-pack and a pint of tequila, the daughter lying on the bed in her room wishing that he'd get drunk fast, pass out and leave her alone for a change.

Lourdes Mendoza stopped her as she emerged from the bathroom. "What's going to happen today?"

Sandy repeated her prepared litany. "There's going to be a trial. They'll prove your daughter, Amalia, was raped by your husband, that you knew it happened and didn't do anything to protect her. You're going to lose. Then we'll come back here in a few weeks." Sandy wondered if it was possible that Lourdes Mendoza was an amnesiac.

Lourdes Mendoza's eyes narrowed to slits and she took a step closer. "What do you mean I'm going to lose?"

"I talked to your daughter's lawyer this morning. The girl's going to tell the judge your husband, Miguel, did it to her, she told you and you slapped her in the face." Sandy looked hopefully at Lourdes Mendoza.

The entire structure of the universe was built on these moments, on this one moment when Lourdes Mendoza could admit what happened and change the direction of her life.

"Santa Maria, how can she tell such a lie?" Lourdes Mendoza exploded.

"Just between you and me, Mrs. Mendoza, we know it's not a lie so let's try to think of some other tactic, okay?"

"She made it up," Lourdes Mendoza insisted.

"That's ridiculous," Sandy snapped impatiently.

133

"She's a fifteen-year-old with the brain of a third grader. Excuse me for saying this, but you realized a long time ago she was retarded. You knew and you let this happen to her. The judge isn't going to believe it either, that a retarded girl made up a story about being fucked by your husband."

"Don't talk to me that way. You're supposed to be on my side."

"I'm your lawyer. I don't have to like you. I'm telling you that your story stinks. However, if you're not able to think of a better one, then that's the one you're stuck with."

"I didn't know," Lourdes Mendoza whined.

"Fine. It's your life." Sandy turned to walk away, but Lourdes Mendoza's hand moved as fast as a lizard from behind a rock and grabbed Sandy by the elbow.

"Wait. It's your job to help me. You have to help me." Her fingers pressed into Sandy's skin.

"I have. I told you the choices and I spent a long time explaining the consequences." Sandy jerked her arm from the woman's grasp. "You know the choices. Now you have to decide."

"Choices? What choices do you think I have?" Lourdes Mendoza spat. "The devil has much to do with luck."

"You're her mother."

Lourdes Mendoza fingered the heavy, old-fashioned, gold-plated medal of the Virgin Mary that hung around her neck. "If I say that I knew, my husband will kill me."

"That's the choice. Him or your daughter." Blood was commonly drawn with the sting of a stingray.

"I need both of them." She twisted her necklace with great agitation.

Why would anyone want a man who raped children? Sandy shook her head with disgust.

"Just let me know what you decide to do," she called over her shoulder as she hurried away. Unconsciously she

134

put her hand to her neck and felt the hollow of her throat where a necklace would lie.

A silver-haired social worker coming out of Department 24 intercepted Sandy. "We got a girl down in shelter care who's going to need an attorney. Can you take the case?"

Sandy grinned at the woman, a soft-spoken grandmother of four who played the quarterhorses Tuesday and Thursday nights at Los Alamitos. "You know I'll do anything for fifty bucks an hour."

The social worker motioned her into the courtroom for the file. Michael Fillipini was in the middle of a trial. He stood at the sidebar with a police report in one hand, cross-examining a rookie cop a year or two younger than Francisco Gomez; it looked like Michael was explaining the case to him. A thin line of perspiration was beginning to form on the young cop's upper lip.

The file handed to Sandy was brief. Fifteen-year-old girl named Diane Lewis. Called herself Pat Answer, running the punk circuit, had been picked up last night outside a shooting gallery called the Paradiso Hotel on Santa Monica Boulevard. She had been voluntarily relinquished by her mother over a year ago and placed in a foster home out in Canyon Country, an isolated tract of ticky-tacky ranch houses and miniature golf courses at the end of the valley. Pretty damn dull for a girl who called herself Pat Answer, imagined Sandy. No wonder she had run away a couple of months ago.

As the electronically controlled door to the shelter area swung open, Sandy could hear the dissonant clash of two televisions tuned to different channels. Further down the gray carpeted hall a small child wailed. It smelled like it was beans and franks for lunch again.

"You got a Diane Lewis today?" she asked at the intake desk. Sandy glanced around the room, catching the attention of a pregnant girl who had been half dozing with her hands folded across her belly.

"Lewis, up front. Here's your lawyer."

Diane Lewis was tall and skinny with short brown hair cut so that it stood up around her face in spikes. The ends of her hair were platinum and a single long thin braid fell to the middle of her back. She had on a pair of straight-leg jeans and a grimy white T-shirt with the sleeves cut off, exposing pale arms that Sandy observed to be free of track marks. A needle-and-ink tattoo that said DESTROY ran crookedly across her right wrist. Sandy introduced herself and led the girl, who seemed annoyed at having been interrupted while watching television, into the interview room, a former storeroom with a table, three molded vinyl chairs, and an assortment of old and broken toys piled in one corner.

"You want me to call you Diane or Pat?"

"I don't care. Just get me out of here."

Sandy rarely took minors' cases. It was easier to work with the adults. On the infrequent occasions she did get a minor, she was solicitous, patted them on the head, and generally acted like she'd never been around children before. However, it was too late and too much had happened to Diane Lewis for her to be considered a child.

"Did you do this tattoo yourself?" Sandy picked up the girl's wrist and examined it. "You must be right-handed. Why didn't you put it on your left wrist so you could make it come out neat and even?"

The girl jerked her hand away from Sandy and sneered, "It's supposed to look like that."

"Why?" Sandy couldn't remember anybody like Diane Lewis when she was fifteen. They had all wanted to grow up to be hippies.

"Because. That's the way the world is." The girl slumped into one of the chairs and watched Sandy contemptuously.

"I just wondered. Isn't it a little difficult to pick up tricks in that outfit and with such a tacky-looking tattoo?"

"I don't know what you're talking about, lady."

Sandy sat on the edge of the table and lit herself a cigarette. She offered one to the girl, who took it without thanking her. "You were picked up last night by the police for prostitution. They brought you here instead of Eastlake after they ran a make on you and found out you were already a dependent of the court."

The girl stared at her defiantly. "I was just hanging around."

"If you were just hanging around, you would have been at TomTom's," Sandy said, naming a burger stand on Santa Monica frequented by punks, "not hanging by yourself up around Western."

"So what's it to you?" Diane Lewis stopped scratching her arm. "The question is, what are you going to do to get me out of here?"

"I'm going to tell the court they have to find you another foster home as soon as possible."

"I'm not going to no goddamn foster home," Diane Lewis sputtered.

Closing her eyes, Sandy placed her thumb and forefinger on her eyelids and massaged the pain that was beginning in the center of her forehead. "What's your suggestion? Your mom? She's the one who turned you in to the court to begin with. You don't have many choices."

She dropped her hand and looked at the girl.

"Let me put it this way. This is your last chance to make it. You blow this and you'll end up in a little uniform in a place where the lights go out at ten and there are bars on the windows. We don't want that, do we?"

The girl didn't say anything. She was staring at the dolls and stuffed animals that were shoved into the corner.

Sandy lowered her voice. She had no right to yell at the girl.

"Why do you want to live on the streets? You can get killed, or worse." Last summer a girl had been dumped out of a car with her neck almost completely sliced open.

Diane Lewis turned her face away from Sandy and bent down to retrieve a teddy bear that had been thrown on the floor. She carefully smoothed out the bedraggled red ribbon tied around its neck and retied it. She straightened the bow again. If she was going to cry, this was it, thought Sandy.

Diane Lewis flung the bear on the floor. "I'm going with my friends."

"What friends are those? The kindly old gentlemen who give you rides in their cars? Do you like doing that?"

"No! The friends I live with at the Paradiso."

The police report said she shared a single room with three young men who were reportedly gay.

"Are your friends here at court to help you?"

The girl shrugged.

"Are any of them over eighteen? Any of them have regular jobs or are they hookers, too?"

The girl pounded the table with her fist. "Shut up! They're my family and I take care of them."

"Is that right? You're out whoring to support three guys? I'm sorry. That has got to be the weirdest thing I've heard yet today." She put her face in her hands and made no effort to stop laughing.

"Hey, I thought you were supposed to be on my side. You're supposed to get me out of here," the girl protested.

"I'm sorry." Sandy wiped her eyes, smearing her mascara and eyeliner. "There aren't any places for kids like you. They don't exist. There's foster homes, jails, and the streets. That's it."

"I want another lawyer," the girl shouted, knocking over her chair as she jumped to her feet.

Sandy sighed unhappily. "I'm afraid this is as good as it gets." Opening her purse, she took out a large mirror, wet her fingertip with spit and cleaned the smudged mascara from under her eyes. She ran her finger around her mouth to smooth her lipstick.

"Look, Diane, Pat. Let me give you a little advice. You don't look that great. You're probably not getting more than twenty-five bucks, and you're going to have to do a lot of weird shit at twenty-five bucks a throw to support four people. I hope you'll give some more thought to the foster home."

The girl stood with her back to Sandy, her arms folded across her chest. Sandy watched the skinny shoulder blades rising and falling under her shirt. She was a child. Sandy knew she was gambling. The truth was she didn't know how to help her.

"Okay, don't listen to me. You're right; there isn't anything I can do for you but that's not the bad news. The bad news is that there are a lot of twelve- and thirteen-year-olds out on the streets. So if you're really set on doing this, I'd suggest you make your fortune now. . . ."

The Mayans had torn out the children's hearts and thrown their bodies into a cenote. The girl stood with her back to Sandy, the arms folded across the chest. Sandy waited, paralyzed. Finally, Sandy checked her makeup again in the mirror, then dropped it in her purse.

"What do you want me to tell the judge when they bring you upstairs this afternoon?"

"Fuck you."

"Come on. I have to take you back to the TV room."

"I'll run away again."

Sandy shrugged her shoulders. Perhaps it was the only solution. For Pat Answer, Sandy preferred that name, there were no other choices.

Lacey Potter was pacing the hall at the top of the stairs when Sandy reached the third floor after depositing her client in front of a rerun of "Happy Days." Lacey pushed through the swirl of activity accompanying the pat down of a woman suspected of carrying a razor in her purse. "Did you call me again last night around eleven?"

"No." By that time Sandy had been drunk and in bed with Manuel, who was continuously overjoyed to discover that North American women considered oral copulation a regular part of sexual activity. "Why?"

Lacey forced a weak, unconvincing smile. "I didn't think so. Someone called then and didn't say anything. I could just barely hear them breathing."

"You got an obscene phone call?"

"No," Lacey hesitated. "It was just a person checking up on me, letting me know he was out there."

Sandy shivered uncomfortably despite the heat. Menopause must be like this. "Lacey," she tried to quip, "I know you need the business, but you have to stop writing your name and phone number on bathroom walls."

"I think it was . . ."

"The guy you were telling me about yesterday?" Sandy finished.

". . . Harold Otis. Yeah. Yesterday I thought, now this is really crazy, but I thought I was being followed to my house." Lacey stopped talking as a woman edged toward them.

"Ms. Walker?"

Lacey bobbed her head and slipped away as Sandy studied the woman. It was a moment before she remembered. Yes, this was the woman who had tried to commit suicide while her children were asleep in their room. Her seven-year-old son had found her in the morning when he and the other two children woke up. He saw his mother unconscious, her breathing so shallow that the blankets seemed to have stopped moving. His brother and sister started to cry because they wanted their breakfast. He picked up the telephone and told the operator that his mother wouldn't wake up. The paramedics and the police arrived. The woman woke confused and angry in the

140

hospital, offended that her private ritual had been interrupted. She hadn't been able to understand why the police took her children away.

Sandy stifled a yawn. She was exhausted by all these people. They were unable to see any causal connection in their lives. It was as though they were stationary bodies in space around which revolved clouds and gaseous forms, some of them noxious, and they were continually buffeted by forces that were unseen and ungovernable. She looked at her watch. It was only eleven-thirty. As soon as she could finish work in the afternoon and get out of the building, she would head for the Tango Room, a deserted cheap bar on Seventh and Alvarado decorated with some remarkable photographs of voluptuous naked women printed in grainy black and white. The other patrons were too burned-out for conversation and it was only a twelve-minute drive from the courthouse.

Smiling, Sandy told the woman that everything was fine. The court was perfectly accustomed to working with young women who had only recently attempted suicide and certainly she would meet with remarkable luck in having the children back home very soon. Of course it would be necessary for the woman to agree to involve herself in a counseling program. Oh, no, she shouldn't worry that anyone would think that of her. It was just that being a parent was, after all, a stressful business and that it would be beneficial, even enjoyable, to meet with a group of similarly situated parents and share their experiences. Sandy was too tired of the smoky gray hall, the confused woman who stood before her, the screaming children, the sly, discomforted men who had been dragged unwillingly to court, and too thirsty for a drink to waste any time whatsoever telling the woman the truth.

Out of the corner of her eye, Sandy saw Lourdes Mendoza still stood outside Department 26 waiting for her. Sandy was about to sneak into the bathroom for a quick

141

drink when she saw Michael Fillipini emerge from the courtroom. He lingered for a second so he could saunter behind a statuesque black woman in a clinging cotton dress who was hurrying past him. He watched the woman's jumpy hips disappear around the corner by the elevator before turning to Sandy.

"You finished?" he asked, craning his neck after the woman.

"No, but let's get out of here a little early. I'm starving. There's something about attempted suicide that always gives me a terrific appetite."

"Chinese food?"

She wrinkled her nose. "You know I hate Chinese food. I want something hearty, filling, and with a full bar."

"We'll talk about it." Michael frowned slightly as he walked to the pay phone to call his office.

Sandy flushed. Michael Fillipini didn't drink, he didn't like the taste. Once a month he had a glass of red wine at the Italian-American Lawyers Bar Association meeting. That was it, marveled Sandy, once a month red wine with rigatoni. Discomforted, she followed his example and looked for change in her purse. It was time to call her office. She hated this. Only people with bad news called.

The receptionist had one garbled message. A girl named Malver had called. She hadn't bothered with the last name and wasn't even sure that she got the number correct because the girl spoke with a heavy accent. Sandy wrote the name down as it was spelled to her, then dropped more change in the phone and dialed. Someone answered on the very first ring.

"Mrs. Walker?" a little girl's voice inquired breathlessly.

"Yes, who is this?" The girl sounded uncertain and there was a lot of noise behind her. She was probably calling for someone who didn't speak English.

"Malver Lopez. You remember. You helped my

142

mother in court." The girl paused, then rushed on. "I ran away from the place in Panorama City where they were keeping me. I'm in Hollywood now. I don't know where my mother is."

Malver Lopez. Chubby, sailor dress, long black hair that had been pulled back by two blue barrettes shaped like butterflies. Sandy remembered Malver Lopez distinctly from a week or two ago when something had prevented her from cross-examining the girl. Sandy did not want to probe into the reasons she had stopped herself, why on that particular day at that particular hour she didn't feel like grilling one more little girl who said her father was a sex molester. Sandy did not want to reflect upon why her job was becoming increasingly difficult for her to do any more than she wanted to think about the overwhelming nightmares she was having.

"When was the last time you saw your mother?" Why was the girl calling her? She didn't know where Malver Lopez's mother was. It was impossible to keep track of the thousands of women she met.

"About a week ago she came out to visit me. She told me she was coming back to take me away."

"Wait a minute, you're not supposed to tell me things like that." Sandy glanced nervously around the hall as though somebody could have heard this. Did Malver Lopez have her confused with the county counsel?

"I don't know what happened to her. She said I should just wait for her, like nothing was happening."

Sandy was increasingly puzzled by the phone call and its disturbing undercurrent. "What makes you think you should call me? Why should I know where she is if you don't?"

Michael jostled her elbow. "Let's go," he mouthed.

"I think I can find her, but I'm afraid. I might . . ." the sound of traffic muffled part of what Malver Lopez was

143

saying. ". . . get picked up by *la migra*. I'm scared. Come get me."

Like Malver Lopez, Sandy had once been twelve years old, lying awake and vigilant in the dark, in the middle of the night. "Me?" she exclaimed. "You're supposed to be in a foster home. The judge said so."

"I don't have enough money to take the bus to my house."

"I can't come get you. That's impossible."

Malver Lopez's voice became so small Sandy could scarcely hear her. "I don't have anyone else."

"Look, Malver, no. It's wrong for you to ask me. Besides, I'm working. I couldn't just come over to wherever you are right now . . ."

"I'll wait."

There was a long silence between them. It seemed long and questionable, like the nights of silence when Sandy had listened for footsteps from her father's bedroom. Sandy shivered, hearing him approach. She turned her back to Michael to whisper, "Okay. Where are you? You'll have to wait until I finish work this afternoon."

Malver said she'd wait at the public library on Santa Monica and Marathon and then something big like a diesel truck roared by.

Hanging up the phone, Sandy wondered exactly what it was that she had agreed to do. Dazed, she saw Michael was leaning against the wall by the elevator waiting for her. She decided not to say anything to him. They might not find Malver Lopez's mother and if they did, Sandy would have helped to violate a court order. It was bound to end disastrously.

Surprisingly, the elevator stopped almost instantly when Michael pressed the button. It was jammed full but they pushed their way in, Michael's girth occasioning considerable pointed speculation among the other passengers. Impassively, she stared up at the licensing certificate, which admonished "weight limit not to exceed four thousand pounds." Her entire life was comprised of living dangerously.

"Ms. Walker, how nice to see you again."

The voice was familiar. In the back of the elevator, in full dress uniform, stood Francisco Gomez.

"Hello, Officer." Sandy had hoped she wouldn't have to run into him again in the court building. Michael looked at her so suspiciously that she blushed.

The elevator came to a spine-jarring stop on the first floor at just that moment and the passengers pitched forward, disentangling themselves from its claustrophobic confines. With a long easy stride, Francisco Gomez fell into step with them so that Sandy felt forced to introduce the two men.

"I had to come down to go over some testimony in a robbery case," explained Francisco Gomez.

Michael barely nodded his head in polite acknowledgment.

"I'd love to be able to stay and have lunch, but I got to get back on duty."

He sidestepped a bookie in a garish plaid jacket and waved pleasantly as he turned in the direction of the Broadway door.

"Who was that guy?" demanded Michael as they walked out the Temple Street exit toward Chinatown.

"Just a cop who was a witness on a case I did."

"He seemed rather interested in you." Michael let loose with one of his annoying braying giggles.

"Did he? I didn't notice." Sandy looked away, pretending to observe the traffic on Spring Street.

Sensing he was about to infringe on some sensitive area, he prodded. "What are you, a fucking cop groupie now?"

"Of course not!"

"On second thought, that might not be such a bad idea

for you, Sandy," Michael argued in a mock serious tone as they were passing the federal court building. "Guy with a steady job instead of your usual wetback felon. Upstanding, law abiding, keep you on the straight and narrow. Give a little discipline to your life."

Immediately she thought of Francisco pushing her against the wall of her bedroom, his hand flattening the curve of her breast.

"Piss off. Who are you to start giving me advice about how to run my love life? I'm not the kind of idiot who would send money to an ex-wife I hadn't seen in twenty years."

"Sandy," he said with hurt and as much gentleness as she could remember having heard him express, "I only do *silly* things. I don't understand you sometimes, like the guys you pick up. You do things I worry about. And you're drinking too much."

Flustered, she objected. "I show up to work."

"Most of the time."

"I get the job done."

"You got a bleeding heart. Why do you worry about these people? They're scum. They're here to pay our rent. They're not worth worrying about."

They were on the Hollywood freeway overpass. The sound of hundreds of passing cars should have been deafening but she could hear the radio in her father's bedroom turned down low on an all-night news station. She heard him get up, go into the bathroom, water running from a faucet, a glass being placed down on the counter. Probably taking more Miltown to try to knock himself out. Heard him go back into his room, the bed squeak when he lay down. She stayed awake as long as she could. It was impossible to tell whether he was awake or asleep with the radio going all night.

The sounds receded as they passed the plaza at Olvera Street. The heavy oak trees blanketed the noise and a

146

sudden warm and capricious wind, which was El Niño, rustled the leaves. They didn't say anything more. Without protest, she followed him into a restaurant that served only dim sum, although she hated Chinese food.

"It's not going to be a problem if I order a beer, is it?" she inquired in an artificially sweet voice.

"Make an effort. Get some food to go with it." Michael had one of everything and two of the things he particularly liked. Sandy tried to avoid looking at the slimy white balls of dough with their oily gray insides, which she believed to be the ground-up parts of undesirable animals.

When they returned to the court building at one-thirty, the courtrooms were being unlocked. The hall had grown filthier. There was a slick, spotty coating of spilled cokes and crushed potato chips. Waxy, crumpled orange papers from the burgers and tacos people brought upstairs to eat littered the floor. Lourdes Mendoza was still standing next to the courtroom. Rather than looking angry, as she had in the morning, an unusual tranquility had settled upon her. These unexpected mood changes before trial were always troublesome.

"Have you decided how you want to proceed?" Sandy waited for Lourdes Mendoza.

"Yes, you will speak to the judge. Explain that it was all an accident. You will arrange it all." This was said simply and without affect.

Sandy felt like punching the woman. She wanted Sandy to intercede for her like a saint painted on the glass containers of candles sold in the *botanicas* and herb shops some of her clients went to for spiritual guidance. It was as though Lourdes Mendoza believed there was some kind of higher order that they could plug into, like electricity, and the solution to her problems would be illuminated in a clear and convincing way.

"I'm going to tell the county counsel to get their witnesses here," Sandy snapped with exasperation. She shifted the strap of her heavy purse, which was cutting into her right shoulder. "We're ready."

Lourdes Mendoza sat like a catatonic during the entire trial. When her daughter was brought in as a witness, Lourdes Mendoza looked at her blankly and without recognition as the girl was led quickly away to the judge's chambers to give her testimony. While the court reporter read the daughter's statement to Lourdes Mendoza, Sandy stood in the hall smoking a cigarette and thinking about what Francisco Gomez's body looked like without the uniform.

After the trial was over and the court made its decision that the girl had been sexually molested with the mother's knowledge, Sandy tried to lead her client out to the hall for the usual discussion of the disposition process. Lourdes Mendoza, her face ablaze with a magnificent rage, pulled away.

Again, Sandy started to explain the next part of the proceedings. Lourdes Mendoza stopped her. "You don't need to tell me what will happen. I know what will happen."

Frustrated and angry, Sandy walked away. At her back she heard the low but urgent voice of Lourdes Mendoza. "Cat's eyes, black nights, whore with a sorrow in her heart worse than the sores between her legs."

7

This goddamn heat must be making me crazy, Sandy thought as she stepped off the curb in front of the courthouse on her way to meet Malver Lopez. Traffic was dense and slow as work came to a close and thousands of county employees fled the downtown office buildings. An ancient Pontiac screeched to a honking halt as she hurried across the street to the underground parking. There, in furious disbelief, she noted that a car door had been flung open into her car, creating an uneven rectangle where the paint had been chipped. She carefully touched the exposed area. A fragment of white peeled away and fell to the ground. She cursed out loud in the emptying structure.

The library was located on an intersection with international mom and pop *tiendas* selling Central American and oriental products, fast foods, and foreign newspapers. An improbably wealthy steel magnate had put up the money for the library and commissioned an architect who built it in the style of the Italian Renaissance. Across town, in Sandy's neighborhood, the same conceptual dreamers had built vaulted archways, pink palaces, and flooded the streets to make canals. From where she parked half a block away, the library was simply an incongruous work of masonry faded by the perpetual southern California

149

sun and eroded by the smog until it was the same dull color as a used nail file. Sandy thought she understood how Malver Lopez had selected this particular meeting place. White Russians, Armenian refugees from Turkey, blacks, orientals, Mexicans, and then others from Latin America moved in. The whites moved out. East Hollywood, former center of the motion picture dream industry, had become the place where many immigrants found their first home.

Malver Lopez was seated at a long table near the front door with a book about astronomy propped in front of her. It was a serious work. Malver apparently had considered its size and weight, the proportion and symmetry of its edges, the number of lengthy and unfamiliar words in the introduction, the contrast of the black binding against the white pages. Watching from just inside the door, Sandy smiled. It would be easy to believe a book that heavy must have all the answers written in it. Plus, it had a photograph of Venus on the cover. Malver Lopez had been waiting so long she'd stopped looking up at every person who came in through the door. Quietly, Sandy crossed the room and sat down beside the girl.

"What are you reading about?" Sandy whispered. She had already concluded from the telephone call the girl didn't want to speak Spanish with her. It would be too intimate.

"Black holes and the beginning of the universe." Malver Lopez pointed to a diagram.

Sandy examined it briefly with some surprise. "Are they teaching this in your school?"

"No, I just wanted to see these pictures."

Sandy nodded approvingly as she studied the concentric circles and arrows on the chart. The girl was obviously bright.

"How do you think the world began?" Malver asked in a tone at once inquisitive and slightly agitated.

Could it be the girl was having the same disturbed dreams that she was, wondered Sandy. The same dreams where the landscapes shifted and the wind blew?

The librarian, a short woman with wavy gray hair, peered impatiently from her desk, placing her finger across her lips in warning.

Hastily, Sandy stood and closed the book, pushing it back toward Malver Lopez; she didn't want the librarian to remember them. While Malver put the book away, she waited outside on the stairs. The Mayans daubed the steps to the temple with blue unguent, the special color of the vain gods. It was good that the girl wanted to study the sky. Most people had lost their memory of the night and forgotten what the stars were for. Malver skipped down the steps. Silently they began to walk toward Sandy's car.

"Did you eat today?" she thought to ask Malver.

"Sure. I had breakfast." Malver tried not to look too eager, but she did glance over at the small market across the street.

"Stay here." Sandy didn't want to take the chance of anyone seeing her with the girl. She went into the store and hurriedly picked up a large bag of potato chips. She chose an orange soda for Malver. Her hand lingered over the wide selection of Mexican beers, but she made herself take a diet cola.

They walked to the car, which Sandy unlocked. If Malver Lopez knew this was a classic machine with restored leather upholstery she didn't say anything; she was busy looking in the paper bag Sandy had handed her. Malver's long black hair, which had been pulled back into braids when she was at court, hung carelessly to her waist. The girl was much smaller and more delicate than Sandy remembered. Her wrists and throat were quite slender, which further accentuated the round moon shape of her face in which her dark eyes were wide set and overhung by unusually thick eyebrows. She was actually quite tiny.

151

Suddenly Sandy felt overwhelmed and ill prepared. "Keep your door locked."

"So how did you get here?" she asked after they opened the drinks and the girl slowed down from gobbling the potato chips offered to her.

Malver Lopez licked her lips, then wiped her hands daintily on the stiff new jeans she was wearing. "I told them at the foster home I was going to school. I had two dollars I'd been saving, so I went to a bus stop and learned how to ride the bus to Hollywood."

"Didn't you think about what might happen to you if you got off the bus in Hollywood and your mom or someone wouldn't come to get you?"

Malver shook her head. "No, I decided I was going home and if I had to go alone, I would."

"Why didn't you just call your social worker if there was a problem?" Sandy asked with some irritation, mostly at herself for having agreed to meet the girl. "Was there something wrong with the foster home you were in?"

"There wasn't anything wrong. They were nice people. See, they even bought me these new shoes." Malver held up one foot and displayed a shiny red patent pump with a tiny heel. "I just want to be home with my mother. She needs me. The social worker would say no." Malver pressed her eyes shut for a second to keep from crying before lifting her head with a sad smile. "*¿Me entiendes, no?*"

Sandy wondered about Malver's mother, who had seemed assertive enough at court. She reached for the potato chip bag Malver was holding and took a handful of chips. As she ate she studied Malver Lopez's face thoughtfully. "Did your mother tell you to run away and call me?"

"No," Malver exclaimed in surprise.

"Is that the truth?"

"Yes, I swear. I decided on my own. I don't want my mother to get into any more trouble."

Unable to detect any deceit in the girl's face, Sandy leaned forward and started the car. "Okay, I'll drive you. If your mom is there, I'll let you out of the car, you go in and figure out your own story. If she's not, you come back and I take you to the foster home. That's the deal, okay?"

Malver nodded her head. A real smile lit her face. "Thanks. This is a beautiful car."

Sure, Sandy thought. We're just out for a nice little spin. "Where are we going?"

"Fifth Street over by the freeway. You know, west of the freeway."

"In Varrio Loco Nuevo?" Sandy guessed.

"Yeah."

Sandy had seen the name spray-painted on walls when she drove from the courthouse to the Tango Room. It was a neighborhood of old two- and four-story buildings, many of them condemned, where apartments were rented to the poor and undocumented. She pointed the car around the block back toward downtown Los Angeles.

"Do you have any children?" asked Malver.

"No."

"I didn't think so," Malver said thoughtfully as she sat back in her seat smoothing the crinkled edges of the potato chip bag in her lap.

"Why did you think that?"

Malver shrugged. "You just seem alone."

Sandy got into the right lane to make the transition to Sunset where Santa Monica Boulevard dead-ended in Silver Lake and the last Thai restaurant divided its neighborhood from a string of gay bars and midnight coffee shops.

"Wouldn't you like to have any children?" Malver continued.

"I never thought about it," Sandy lied. "I'm not married."

153

Malver studied her with increased interest and some concern. "You don't have to be married to have a baby."

Sandy took her eyes off the car in front of her and looked at Malver.

"Hey, watch out!"

Glancing up, Sandy slammed on the brakes just in time to avoid hitting a red Mustang, which had come to a sudden stop at an intersection. "I guess you know more than I thought you did."

Malver nodded her head grimly but then brightened and added reassuringly, "You're not too old to have a baby."

"That's true," Sandy replied so noncommittally that Malver continued to scrutinize her until Sandy became uncomfortable under the girl's direct examination. "Just tell me where to turn, all right?"

They were on Sunset where it sloped uphill, making a broad curve through Echo Park. A few elderly and tenacious eucalyptus trees clung to the hillside that rose on the north side of the street behind the *panaderías*, auto body repair and tailor shops. Off to the left ran the road up to Elysian Park and the police academy. Sandy wondered what Francisco Gomez was doing now. Probably arresting people who broke the law.

"Don't you ever get afraid of being alone?" Malver persisted.

"Sure, but there's lots of times when it's nicer to be alone." Sandy regretted having this slip out.

"Yeah," Malver sighed. "When I had to be with my dad I used to pretend I was alone or invisible."

Sandy was getting a headache. She didn't want to talk anymore. She adjusted the air conditioner and turned it toward her.

"Did your father do something to you when you were a girl?" Malver asked.

Outside was a blur of chain-link fences. With her left

154

hand Sandy massaged her forehead, which felt tight. "Yes, Malver," she acknowledged reluctantly.

"Do you sometimes still feel bad about it?"

All the time. I can't love. Not even myself. I can't hate. I can't help anyone. Or even take care of myself. I don't know what I'm doing here. To Malver she said as calmly as she could, "It's something you always remember, but you learn ways to live your life that make it seem less important." Sandy forced a smile, which was supposed to convey encouragement. "Right now, the thing is to keep you safe."

Christ, Malver, how did you talk me into this?

The girl laid one small hand greasy from potato chips over Sandy's and told her to turn right on the next street.

"Are we close to the apartment now?"

Malver Lopez nodded and left her hand on Sandy's. Sandy could feel the girl's pulse jumping against her own skin.

She pulled to the curb. It was the usual four-story building, painted yellow, a torn white lampshade in a second-floor window, and a sycamore tree planted near the front door. Sandy scanned the building for some form of activity.

"How will you know if your mother is home or not?"

"I have to run upstairs real quiet, open the door a little, and peek in. If my mom's there, I'll wave to you," Malver pointed to a window on the third floor. "If she's not, I'll come right back."

"I'm waiting for you, so make it quick."

Nothing was moving on the street. The door of a nearby corner market was open and a stalk of bananas hung in the shade. Two small boys rested against the wall of a nearby apartment, their heads propped against the brick, a soccer ball between them. Malver jumped out of the car, slamming the door behind her.

With the engine still running, Sandy lit a cigarette as

155

she watched Malver Lopez run across the street and into the building. She looked at her watch and mentally reviewed the provisions of her malpractice insurance. Five minutes passed. Sandy had lit another cigarette and was tapping it nervously on the ashtray when the door to the apartment building swung open. She looked up anxiously. Three teenage boys came out smoothing back their hair, tucking in their shirts.

Switching off the motor, Sandy grabbed her purse, opened the door, and jumped out of the car. She took another drag on the cigarette and threw it into the middle of the street as she darted over to Malver Lopez's building.

The hall was gloomy and smelled of old orange peels and sweat. A rusted bicycle was shoved into a corner. Names were barely legible on the kicked-in metal mailboxes. Lopez. Number 11.

She ran up the stairs. It was very quiet except for the sound of her high heels and a Spanish news program coming from somewhere in the building. Number 11 was dark. Sandy knocked once, but no one answered. She put her hand on the doorknob. It was unlocked. I'm already in contempt of a court order, she thought, I might as well try breaking and entering.

The living room was sparsely furnished. There was a couch, a couple of chairs, and a low table.

"Malver," Sandy moved slowly through the room. A tiny hall with worn carpeting led into the interior of the apartment. "Malver," she called, measuring cautious steps toward the rear of the dwelling. "Malver!"

Malver Lopez and her father were in the small kitchen where the hall ended. The man's back was to a window overlooking Fifth Street. He held the girl in front of him like a weapon.

Sandy caught the sides of the door frame, her breathing loud and ragged. For an instant everything froze like a photograph where three objects draw the eye to a triangle shape. "I need to take Malver with me," she said simply to Mr. Lopez.

He grasped the child closer to him as he backed toward the window. Malver, her eyes enormous and frightened, watched Sandy; Sandy tried desperately to remember movies she had seen with similar situations to help her decide if it would be best to stand still or advance toward him. She knew she was more terrified than either Malver Lopez or the father.

Finally Sandy let go of the door and took one step forward.

"Mr. Lopez, the police are looking for you. It's not safe for you to stay here. Let me take Malver." She cast what she hoped was a quick subtle glance around the room to see if there were any knives lying out on the counter.

"She is my daughter. She stays with me." His features were shadowed as he gripped Malver's shoulder more tightly and inched toward the window.

"Mr. Lopez, believe me, the police are on their way here now."

"¡Hijos de putas!"

The light from behind the man and girl wavered as the wind blew the thin curtain slightly away from the window so that she saw Malver's father clearly for the first time. There were heavy creases in his forehead and he had the same enormous bushy eyebrows as his daughter.

"If they take you to jail, the other men there will kill you. They don't like child molesters."

"I didn't do it," he screamed, his face frenzied and contorted with fear.

"Malver, come here," said Sandy, taking a couple more steps. They were all close enough to touch now.

Malver suddenly, savagely, leaned forward and bit her father in the thick dark brown of his forearm. He yelled in surprise as he let go of her.

157

"Get in the car," Sandy shouted as Malver ran past her. "Lock the doors!" Sandy backed into the hall that separated the kitchen from the living room.

Across the space that now existed between them, Sandy and Mr. Lopez stared at each other. "She's my little girl," he said weakly, rubbing his arm. "My little princess."

Instead of feeling angry, Sandy wanted to cry, quickly she turned away into the living room. She tripped on the low table in front of the couch, knocking over a small plaster statue of the Blessed Virgin; it fell to the floor. The Blessed Virgin sprawled in an ungainly posture on her back and her head rolled under the couch.

Sandy nearly tumbled down the stairs to the ground floor. The heavy leather purse slapped against her hip. Varrio Loco Nuevo was still nearly deserted at this hot and smoggy hour except for the two young boys who were now listlessly kicking the soccer ball between themselves on the opposite sidewalk. Stumbling, she scraped her new navy-blue heels. Malver threw the car door open for her. Sandy got in, gunned the motor, and squealed away from the curb down Fifth Street.

At that same moment, across the street on the second floor of an almost identical building, Jesus Velaria was moving about in his kitchen preparing dinner for himself and his daughter. He stood by the stove stirring a can of vegetable soup he had opened and mixed with water. He heard a car start up, its tires squeal as it pulled away fast, but when he glanced out the window, all he saw was two small boys playing a listless game of soccer. It was his sixteenth day alone with his daughter; he was both worried and resigned to the fact that he was on his own. Now he would have to remind Señora Cruz to be especially careful when she took Soledad out to the street for walks. Sandy had to stop at a traffic light. She pushed the car

158

cigarette lighter in and inhaled deeply a few times to try to quiet her breathing.

"You ought to stop smoking," Malver said. "It's very bad for your health."

At Wilshire she slowed down into the right lane. There were many people waiting at bus stops, walking down the street between the tall illuminated buildings, and past the shimmering fountains of water erupting from the center of MacArthur Park Lake.

"I wonder where your mother is," she blurted out.

Malver Lopez looked sadly out the open window.

Looking for a new apartment, a new job, a new man, a new neighborhood, a new identity. Stop it, Sandy screamed to herself. Don't let her see you're scared.

"Maybe she had to work late or she's staying with a friend," Sandy suggested hopefully.

They continued in silence. Sandy debated with herself about congratulating Malver for her courage, or leaving the subject alone in case Malver hadn't realized how much danger they had all been in.

"How about some dinner now?" asked Sandy, to put an end to her own increasingly morose thoughts. She pulled into the lot of a large coffee shop located on the part of Wilshire Boulevard euphemistically referred to as "Miracle Mile."

"Go get us a table to sit at," she directed Malver, pushing her toward the dining area. At Chichén Itza she had seen two decapitated skulls together with pieces of jade. Sandy went into the women's bathroom and locked herself into the last stall with the sense of someone entering a confessional. Dropping her shoulder bag on the floor she knelt by it, feeling blindly until her hand hit the now nearly empty half pint of brandy. She took a drink and thought about the girl outside who was now her responsibility. This made her take another drink. The hot, sweet brandy carved its way into her stomach. It gave her strength. Like the microscopic star-shaped fossils that made up beaches along the Pacific coast, it was miraculous in its ability to reduce the universe to finite and comprehensible terms. Sandy realized Mr. Lopez didn't know who she was. Relieved, she screwed the top on the bottle and put it back in her purse.

Malver was halfheartedly studying the menu with its glossy pictures of fried foods and ice cream.

"You can have a sundae if you want," offered Sandy.

Dinner was quiet. Sandy already knew certain things about Malver Lopez. The social worker's report had said she was born in Guerrero. She was the oldest child of Mercedes and Hector Lopez. They had entered California in 1979. Mercedes Lopez worked in, and here Sandy's memory failed, in either a nursing home or a hospital cafeteria. She couldn't remember what Hector Lopez did and it didn't seem the time to ask. Sandy wanted to keep the conversation on Malver's school and neighborhood, so what was happening between them would be as simple as possible. Malver said she was in the choir at Our Lady of Grace but lately she had been having doubts.

Sandy, obsessed with more temporal problems, like what she should do with Malver Lopez, merely smiled politely, and said, "I don't know, Malver, you have to talk to the priest about that."

Malver made a scornful face. "They're all men. What do they know? They should have women instead."

"How do you know that?" Sandy asked despite herself. The girl was wise beyond her years.

"You know what I mean," Malver replied. Then, as if guessing that this hurt Sandy, she continued, hurriedly trying to erase the moment. "There's a woman where I live who has powers. My mother told me about her. Her name's Consuela and she's in a *botanica* near my house."

Sandy stopped tracing patterns in the damp trail made by her water glass. "What can she do?"

160

"Anything. Fly through walls. Predict the future. Change the past. Change into a wolf. That's what people say. I've never seen her." The girl stopped, laughed uncomfortably, and returned to her grilled cheese sandwich.

While they waited for the check, Malver, who had been quiet for some time, suddenly drew herself up with great formality and asked directly, "Are you going to take me home with you?"

Sandy imagined taking Malver to her apartment, spreading some sheets and blankets on the couch, giving her a towel to use, stopping to buy a toothbrush at some all-night market. There was a school a few blocks away. . . .

"No, Malver. I'm taking you back to the foster home. That's the law."

"I'd rather stay with you," Malver pouted.

"You can't. You don't belong to your mother or to your father now. You belong to the court. You have to stay where they tell you. Those are the rules. You don't have any choice."

Sandy studied her nail polish so she wouldn't have to look at Malver Lopez. She could feel the girl's pain. "Besides, I don't know how to take care of little girls."

Malver stopped stirring the soupy remains of her hot fudge sundae with the long sticky spoon, which dribbled chocolate down her hand. "I wouldn't be any trouble. I promise. I can take care of myself. I could help you around the house. I'm really very responsible. I take care of my little brothers all the time. It would be good for you to have somebody with you."

Hesitating in her explanation, Sandy said, "You're still a little girl." No matter what has happened. "You deserve time to grow up."

"I thought you liked me," Malver said, almost crying.

Trembling with fear of this little girl so like herself, Sandy made her voice firm, rough. "Malver, I barely

161

know you. You seem like a very smart girl. It's been nice meeting you." Sandy took the check and left some money on the table as she stood up. The girl looked sadly up at her. Impulsively, Sandy took a twenty-dollar bill and crumbled it in Malver's hand.

"Don't go on any more bus rides. Buy yourself a book about astronomy or something."

Malver was able to remember the address in Panorama City where the foster home was located. At least it wouldn't be necessary to drop her off in front of a police station in the middle of the night. Sandy got onto the Santa Monica freeway and then north onto the San Diego heading for the San Fernando Valley.

As they crested Mulholland Drive, above the millions of lights of the valley, Sandy remembered Malver's question in the library and the book about black holes and creation. Sandy thought of the story she had been told. In the beginning the world was supported on the back of a crocodile and the Milky Way was a woman's skeleton. Neither stones nor trees existed then. Time was a circling dance held fast in the blinding flame of the sun. The constellations changed constantly, erratically, like whores with a contagious form of hysteria, blackened wombs stabbed and torn by lightning. This had been told to her some years ago by a man with a humped back in the Lunamar Bar in Zihuatanejo.

Now Sandy would tell the girl it was like tumbling into a bowl of stars. She saw that Malver had fallen asleep with her head lolling against the door. Sandy put her arm around the girl's shoulders and pulled her closer so that Malver's head could rest on her shoulder.

8

The room smelled of gardenias. Sandy reached behind herself for a small black bottle and poured another capful of perfume into the bathwater. For a long time she lay in the tub watching the water nudging and moving her pubic hair like seaweed caught in a shallow current. *La noche triste, la noche triste.* Sandy tried to make herself remember the names of the last three Aztec emperors. Cuauhtémoc, Cuauhtémoc, but she could get no further because she kept thinking of Malver Lopez.

Finally she stood, wrapping a towel around her, strands of her long hair coiled around her shoulders and stuck to her breasts. Before Cuauhtémoc there was, yes, Cuitahua. Satisfied, she got into bed, propped her knees up and put two pillows behind her neck. After some deliberation, she selected a book about pottery of the Zapotecs from the stack piled on the table next to the bed. Within a minute, however, she put it back unopened, poured a shot of brandy and drank it before turning out the light.

But instead of sleeping, she was imagining for the fifteenth time what might have happened in Malver Lopez's kitchen if the man had decided to fight, if he had had a weapon, if Malver hadn't bitten him, if the planets at that moment had tilted slightly on axis. The possibilities that came to mind were all bloody and horrible.

The phone rang.

Francisco Gomez's voice was cool and sarcastic. "Was that one of your many boyfriends I saw you with today?"

Sandy searched her memory. It seemed centuries ago. Certainly longer ago than when Cuauhtémoc had been emperor.

"The fat guy, is that one of your boyfriends?" Francisco prodded.

She was too tired for the strange subtleties of romance. "What's it to you?"

"Are you making it with him?"

"What if I am? As it happens, he's just a friend of mine who's a criminal attorney." She wondered why she bothered to explain.

Francisco Gomez's laugh was unpleasantly triumphant. "And I thought we were the ones people called pigs."

"Why do you keep phoning me?"

"I want to keep the riffraff out of there."

"What are you talking about?"

"You heard me. Out of your pants. Out of your life."

To her surprise, she felt aroused, not angry. "I'm sure you've noticed I don't pry into your personal life."

"Maybe you're not the jealous type like I am. Maybe it's the latin blood," he bandied, sensing her ambivalence. "I could change you, Sandy."

"Oh, I get it, you want me to play jealous and ask what you've been doing lately, is that it? Okay. What have you been doing lately?" She moved her hand down between her legs in case it was a good story.

"Not much really," he paused for effect. "There is June."

"June?" Sandy cooed.

"June's a whore who works around here."

"Is this the one about the hooker with the heart of gold and the mother on the dialysis machine? I think I've heard it before." Sandy pulled her hand back and dropped it on top of the sheet. "I would have guessed you were waiting for the madonna."

Francisco Gomez ignored this. "I like June. She's an independent woman, like you. Maybe she's a whore but she has a proper respect for the establishment. Yeah," he ended smugly, "that's what I like about June—she's smart."

She wondered why he was telling her this, why it excited her, why she wanted to feel dirty. "You want to come over here and fuck me?"

"Don't try to be so tough."

Sandy dropped her voice suggestively and whispered, "You want to come over here and tell me a bedtime story, Daddy?"

"That's better."

Her voice dropped another half octave. "Well? What time?"

"I can't. I'm on a special assignment tonight."

"Busting prostitutes?" Her voice jumped back to its normal range.

"Come on, Sandy. I just wanted to call and see how you were. Don't you watch the news? There's a little girl missing down here and they have a bunch of us assigned to look for her."

Malver Lopez. "How old is she?"

"Nine."

Slowly Sandy exhaled. "I hope you find her."

"We will. That's our job." He said something in response to someone who was with him. "I got to go now. Don't do anything I wouldn't do."

She reached for the brandy and curled up in the dark, sucking on the bottle.

* * *

165

The clock radio went off like a bomb. In her dream she had been very close to a temple outlined in a wild jungle. The air was thick and sweet.

The only thing between her and the peace she sought had been a clearing and the twittering of birds. As she staggered from bed, it all dissolved to the too-bright morning light and the sound of the couple next door arguing about money.

She had a headache. It was getting harder to get up every day. She staggered into the bathroom and patted her face with cleansing cream. Her eyes were bloodshot, her face pale. She was probably the only woman in southern California without a suntan in the middle of August. Her hair and her skin were nearly the same color; it was almost as though she were disappearing. She thought about this as she stood in the closet trying to find something to wear. At last, shaking herself from this numb reverie, she put on a black silk suit with a straight skirt, a shell necklace, and a pair of ridiculously high pumps.

Traffic moved bumper to bumper on the Santa Monica freeway eastbound into downtown Los Angeles. Sandy smoked and twirled the dial of the radio, searching for a station that would tell her the temperature, but all there was was loud music and more war in Central America, so she snapped it off. She felt on the passenger seat for the morning newspaper, shook off the front section, and placed it on the steering wheel. After a quick glance at the headline, she flipped it over to look at the weather. There was the article.

BODY DISCOVERED MAY BE MISSING GIRL, 9

A body had been found behind a trash bin in a commercial area some fourteen miles from the home of the missing girl. The police had not yet positively identified the corpse as the missing girl nor did they know the cause

166

of death. She appeared to have been strangled and was fully clothed. No names, no suspects, no motives. Knocking the paper aside, Sandy forced herself to concentrate on driving.

It was hectic in the cafeteria where she went to try to pull herself together. Two busboys pushed an ill-balanced cart of dishes and glasses through the crowded aisles. A group of jurors in their third week of jury duty was having a raucous breakfast before reporting upstairs for another armed robbery trial. She was sitting alone at the usual table where the dependency court attorneys congregated rereading the article when Michael Fillipini wandered in.

He sat down clumsily, causing her coffee to spill. "What's new, pussycat?"

Sandy pointed to the article. He skimmed it quickly then tossed it aside. "That's the trouble with kids today. Can't take a joke. You know what I say? If they can't take a joke, fuck 'em. You got the sports page?"

She handed him the sports page as she searched in her purse with her other hand for aspirin.

"So what you got scheduled today?" he asked after checking the baseball scores.

"More of the same, I guess." Pulling her battered black calendar out of the shoulder bag, she ruffled through the pages.

The Jeanette Ray case. She had forgotten all about it.

"I have to get upstairs." Since she hadn't gone to her office yesterday, she didn't even have the police report with her. She would have to use one of the files from the day before so she'd have something to hold and doodle on. She had already told Jeanette Ray they were going to lose.

Sandy took one last look at the newspaper before stuffing it in her purse as she ran up the stairs to the courtroom on the third floor where she and Jeanette Ray would have to flounder through the morning together.

167

Her heart pumped a hard rhythm, repeating the last sentence of the gruesome article. "The place is a dumping ground." Dumping ground, dumping ground.

Jeanette Ray was prompt. Sandy cursed to herself when she saw the woman waiting for her. Jeanette Ray, her hair pinned into a cumbersome and lumpy bun, was dressed in an incongruously juvenile yellow dress with long puffy sleeves and a ribbon tied around her throat. This made Sandy's head ache even more.

"Mornin', Ms. Ray." Sandy felt herself slipping into a folksy and unnatural drawl. "Sure looks like it's going to be a nice day. You feel ready for the trial? We're going to have a different judge today." But they'll still know you did five days in SBI for contempt and they'll have doubled the number of bailiffs in the courtroom. "You know, it's not too late to enter a plea of no contest to some kind of amended petition. You could . . ."

"I know. I know," chirped Jeanette Ray with unreasonable cheerfulness. "You explained all that to me. I've been praying and asking the good Lord for guidance."

I hope to Christ he told you to go for a fast plea so we can get the hell out of here, thought Sandy, fixing an expression of innocence and concern on her face.

"No, I've decided that I must have a full trial, that right and might must surely prevail and . . ."

"Save it for the judge," said Sandy, her sudden burst of effervescence exhausted. "Let's you and me keep it simple. Here are the rules. You don't talk, you don't get out of your chair, you stay off your knees, and you keep your legs together this time. I'm advising you not to take the witness stand, but I can't stop you from doing it if that's what you want."

Jeanette Ray nodded enthusiastically. "I brought the tape recordings with me today."

It was all too much. The tape recorder. Her own father reading her diary. She thought about Malver Lopez, about the dead girl somewhere in downtown Los Angeles. Hidden lives, the endless succession of unlucky accidents and bizarre coincidence. "You don't care about your daughter, do you?"

"What do you mean?" Jeanette Ray tried to show Sandy a photograph she removed from the Bible she was carrying. "I've done everything."

"Ms. Ray, I couldn't help but notice when I read the file that all your children have different fathers. I don't care. The judge doesn't care. Even God doesn't care. Why don't you just enter a plea, get into some kind of counseling program, work out your own guilt or anger that you slept around and ended up with nothing to show for it except three kids whose fathers won't support them, and get the fuck off your daughter's back before you push her into doing something that you'll both have to regret the rest of your lives."

Jeanette Ray flushed furiously, sputtering, "You're fired. I'm getting another lawyer."

"No, you're not. Listen to me. What's going to happen is inevitable unless you tell your daughter you were wrong. I'm your only chance. Don't you understand, I make more money if you go to trial. I'm giving you the chance to make it right with your daughter. Tell her."

A slow eternity passed as the two women, oblivious to the ebb and flow around them, scrutinized each other. Sandy waited for some alteration of Jeanette Ray's countenance that would signal her acceptance. She was still waiting when the bailiff came out into the hall calling their names to find out if they were ready.

Within an hour they were concluding the trial. Jeanette Ray still had not seen her daughter. The girl was taken directly into the judge's chambers to give her testimony. When the county counsel rested his case, and the judge peered down over her horn-rimmed glasses, Sandy turned warily to Jeanette Ray. "This is your time to testify if you want."

Jeanette Ray bounded to her feet. The bailiff led her to the witness stand and pointed her in the direction of the clerk.

"Do you promise to tell the truth, the whole truth, and nothing but the truth, so help you God?"

"Amen."

Sandy buried her forehead in her hand so she could avoid having to see either Jeanette Ray or the judge while she asked a short series of questions. The county counsel coughed and closed his file. Having proved his case, he had lost interest. Sandy quickly ran out of simple leading questions and sat for so long staring at the table that the judge finally excused Jeanette Ray from the stand. After a brief argument, the judge sustained the petition.

"Ms. Walker, I'd like to see you in chambers," the judge said, getting up and exiting the bench.

She had heard this lecture before. Encourage the client to enter pleas. Don't waste judicial time with open-and-shut cases.

Constance Faith O'Leary, pro tem for eight years, was sitting behind her desk with her shoes kicked off, a cigarette dangling from her lips, winding a ball of blue yarn from the immense mountain of variegated wools that cluttered the desk's surface. Sandy was about to knock on the open door when the judge looked up.

"Come on in, Sandy. Shut the door behind you."

"I'm sorry, Your Honor. I wanted to get a plea but my client wouldn't budge." Sandy lifted her hands beseechingly and let them drop loosely to demonstrate her efforts.

"I understand that." The judge's long, graying, brown hair was pulled severely back from her face by tortoiseshell barrettes. Behind her back she was known as "The Grim Reaper" for her quick but virtually unappealable decisions. She put down the yarn and folded her hands tightly on the desk. "That's not what I wanted to see you about. I had a complaint this morning."

Sandy's mind raced. Coming into court late? Did she look hung over?

"It's about a dependent child named . . ." the judge discreetly referred to a telephone message wedged under a cut glass paperweight, ". . . Malver Lopez. I understand she disappeared from her foster home yesterday and somehow you drove her home."

Sandy held her breath.

"I'm not going to ask what you were doing. I will assume it was nothing inappropriate. I don't want to hear an explanation."

Sandy waited, looking out the large picture window down Broadway.

"That's all."

She turned to open the door to let herself out.

"I'm glad you decided to take her back to the foster home, Sandy, or I would have had you in jail this morning."

There were no explanations. There was only a little girl who had tried to go to a home that didn't exist in the invisible part of the city known as Varrio Loco Nuevo. There was only a dead girl beginning to rot in the horrible heat infecting the city. Cops who could only find bodies and invent sequences of events that mimicked logic. All that separated them from the horrible desert and killing winds was a few sheets of plate glass, a thin strand of palm trees, and the law. And the law was only a fragile permutation of the indelible history recorded in the primitive reptile part of the brain.

Sandy left the door open.

Jeanette Ray was waiting in the courtroom. "Nobody gave me a chance to explain," she screamed.

"There is nothing to explain," Sandy exploded, pushing past her into the hallway. "You see your daughter

171

living your life and you're horrified. You want to pull her back, shake her as though she were a dreamer. You want her to believe that you love her, but you are incapable of love. Incapable of real, sacrificing love. You could have stopped it all this morning, but you didn't."

Breathless, she made an effort to compose herself but she was shaking with rage at Jeanette Ray, at the system, quaking with the terrors that possessed her at night and were now spilling over into the daylight. Ambling toward them she saw Michael Fillipini and her opportunity to get away from Jeanette Ray. Sandy waved, hurrying over to where Michael had stopped rather gloomily to watch the comings and goings in the hall.

"What's happening?" she asked, refusing to look back in the direction of Jeanette Ray. She felt sick of it all but she managed a smile.

"I got a client with an eight-month-old baby with a fractured arm and she doesn't know how it happened."

"Time for the old 'the baby fell off the couch' routine, huh?" she said, hurrying past him and further down the hall away from Jeanette Ray.

She went into Department 27 where she had a couple more cases and to speak with the heavy oriental woman with bad skin who was Judge Lawler's clerk. The clerk squinted over her shoulder at Sandy.

"How nice you could join us today."

Sandy blushed. Late again. There were going to be problems soon, she knew, but she couldn't prevent them; she was as powerless as if she were trying to stop the buffeting forces of El Niño.

"I told the judge you checked in earlier this morning. You know the kinds of problems this creates for me when you don't show up on time?"

Gratefully, Sandy patted the woman on the arm.

"Don't do it anymore, Sandy. I'm not going to keep checking you in when you're not here."

172

The morning dragged on. Sandy was reading a paperback mystery in the last row of the courtroom when someone tapped her on the shoulder. It was Lacey Potter.

"You're not going to believe this," said Lacey. "Remember that nut I told you about the other day? Harvey Otis?"

Sandy nodded.

"Guess what he did last night." She looked expectantly at Sandy. "He kidnapped his daughter from Mac!"

"How? They have all kinds of security there."

"Yesterday we had to come to court for a change-of-placement order because the little girl's foster home wouldn't keep her. She was showing the other kids how to make the dolls fuck each other and she kept touching one of the little boys who lived there."

Sandy clapped her hand over her mouth.

"Otis was here and created a scene, saying he demanded she be released to him immediately. He must have lurked around the courthouse till the end of the day and then followed them back to Mac. He rammed his car into the back of the van, pulled a knife on the social workers, and took off with his daughter."

"Have you heard from him yet?"

"No. I don't think I will. Maybe the police will pick him up."

They sat for some time not saying anything as they watched a case being tried by two other lawyers.

"Goddamn," Lacey sighed finally. "Guy like that, I could have been going to court forever. Ex parte orders, change of orders. I could have made a little money."

When Sandy left the courthouse, the gray halls were quiet, lifeless. One lone janitor was pushing a mop. It was an abandoned stage where tragedies were recreated and morality tales enacted. An unpleasant chill ran through her as she hurried out to the street.

The sun had dropped to an obtuse angle. Los Angeles

was busy with movement and brilliant with color. The tall smoked-glass buildings along Olive were struck by the sun so that their massive windows turned gold, red, pink, and orange. Entire structures glowed like volcanoes. Sandy found herself driving again into Varrio Loco Nuevo past buildings smoldering with late afternoon heat, irradiated, flaming like the very fires of Mexico the Mayans described as the point of creation.

Abstractedly, she drove as though seeking connections, examining intersections, turning at every corner where traffic required her to stop, weaving her way deeper and deeper into the neighborhood. Although it was in the shadows of the center of the city, the buildings here were old, nameless, their windows gouged and blind. Malver Lopez and her father had stood in such a window.

A half a block from Malver Lopez's apartment she parked the car near the Grove Hotel, a dilapidated tenement frequented by winos. A wrinkled old man with a sparse beard stuck out his hand tiredly and let it dangle. Sandy looked away and drew closer to the edge of the sidewalk as she passed by him.

What good would a quarter do? Or even a dollar? What good could a court system and a handful of social workers do for Malver Lopez or the dead girl in central Los Angeles? Only at that one certain instant in the late afternoon when the walls of all the millions of houses and apartments in Los Angeles turned pink and glowed luminescent, did it seem possible that there were any miracles. There was some loose change in her pocket. She turned back to give it to the man but he had fallen asleep again, his mouth gaping open. These lives were fixed, inevitable. The exorcisms they would require were too painful and costly, with little chance of success. She repocketed the money.

Sandy walked toward Seventh Street, where she had noticed a store that sold frilly dresses for *fiestas rosadas* or

174

quinceañeras, the parties where fifteen-year-old girls were presented to the community as young women. Sandy Walker stared through her reflection in the store window at the white dresses. She remembered being fifteen, waking up hot and sweaty, naked, a white sheet wrapped around her like a shroud after she had been raped, and a crimson stain between her legs spreading into a pool of blood. The sense of loss, fear, anger, desperation, and inevitable catastrophe had saturated her, stained her, making her heavy with knowledge and awkward with grief. Malver Lopez knew these things also. Restless and unhappy, Sandy turned from the window.

From where she stood, she could see a small shop called *Botanica La Ayuda* on the corner. The name was spelled out in black across the top of the door in a sloping, though formal, Gothic lettering. In the window was a clumsily hand-painted sign announcing CONSEJOS ESPIRITUALES. Spiritual advice.

Of course there were *brujas,* shamans, herbalists, and *curanderas* in Los Angeles. The land itself was surreal, the air potent and charged. This must be the place Malver Lopez had been trying to tell her about.

She crossed the street. A heavy black metal gate was pushed back against the wall. The doorknob stuck. Bells jingled when Sandy pushed the door open.

The room was dark. A multitude of flickering candles in glass jars of various sizes were placed on counters, on shelves, on the floor. A battered black-and-white television screen with a Spanish soap opera cast an ominous gray light around the room. Two women leaning against each other, asleep on a sagging couch, started awake as Sandy pushed the door open.

A young woman with long black hair and a white blouse stood thoughtfully behind a counter of enclosed glass shelves containing rosaries, scapulars, tiny mirrors

175

laminated with pictures of the Virgin Mary, plastic bags of herbs and dried flowers.

"Bueñas tardes." The young woman's slender silver bracelets laden with medallions shimmered and danced in the light as she scrutinized Sandy.

"I'm just looking," Sandy stammered in Spanish.

The pantheon of saints and deities was large and varied. Sandy walked the length of the counter examining its contents, then crossed over to the wall by the couch where the two women were dividing their attention between the soap opera and her movements. A curtain of floral material partitioned the room in half. The same Gothic lettering, but smaller, painted on the wall demarcated the space. "Members only—Consultations."

The three women watched Sandy so intently as she read the sign, she made a point of not lingering beside the curtain. The radiant purity of the candles was soothing. She retraced her steps back to the counter where the young woman was waiting.

"I am looking for some special candles."

"For what purpose?"

Startled, Sandy hesitated. Yes, she had known about witchcraft from her studies of anthropology but she had been more interested in patterns of migration, in pottery. She had always considered the spiritual arcane and naive. Yet, obviously, she was here. Something had drawn her in. She remembered what Malver Lopez had told her about a Consuela, a mistress of magic who lived in the neighborhood dispensing cures and advice.

"Purpose? Does each candle have a different purpose?"

The woman placed one slender finger carefully beside a mole on her left cheek. "It is unusual that a blond woman comes here speaking our language. What is it you want?"

Sandy pondered this question, then addressed her with great formality. "Imagine that I am a woman like yourself. That we have a common history. That our lives have been darkened and we now seek light."

With great deliberation the woman studied Sandy. "You understand that there is no margin for error in what you are requesting. It is doubly difficult, or impossible, to undo what has already been done. The antidotes are potent and often overwhelming. Consider this carefully because we work neither with the immoral nor the irreverent," the woman warned in a deep throaty voice. "Perhaps you require a consultation," she suggested, pointing to the floral curtain.

Sandy shook her head sadly. "I have lost faith in those who predict the future. I have even lost faith in the future. I am interested in deciphering the past and curing its pain."

The young woman laid her hands palm down on the glass counter and studied them. Finally, she looked up. "I sense that there is some danger around you now. That you are torn between your desire to explode the past and create the future. That your balance is tenuous and your vision in question. So it is with the study of the past. It is as though pictures and symbols were drawn on both sides of very thin parchment and when one holds it to the light, both sides are visible and legible." She turned around and took a plain white candle in a glass jar from the shelf, then reached down and opened a drawer, taking out a small bottle of green oil that was labeled *"Tranquilo."*

"Put this in your bedroom. Anoint the candle. Burn it all night long. You must illuminate the past. You must let the man who is searching for you find you. You cannot hide from him forever. Come back again if you choose and we will talk." She inclined her head in the direction of the room on the other side of the curtain.

Sandy fumbled in her purse for her wallet and laid out some money, which the young woman counted carefully.

Neither of the two women on the couch looked up as Sandy walked out the door.

Feeling foolish, Sandy dropped the bottle of oil in her purse and unlocked her car. Something fluttering caught her eye, and as she looked up to the second floor of a nearby building she saw an open window out of which hung a peach-colored shirt gently rocking in the light breeze.

She decided to go to the Tango Room a dozen blocks away to have a few drinks. The Tango Room was across the street from MacArthur Park, a place where the surface of the earth had collapsed, exposing an extensive underground water hole, which was now ringed by cement walkways and grass areas. It was used as a recreational facility by the poor and recently arrived, as a political rallying point for the left, and an oasis for the desperate and diseased.

Sandy sat at a table near the front door under a large photo of a naked blond reclining in a jungle setting with vines plaited around her ankles. A weary bartender with a drawn face shuffled over.

"Brandy and water tall."

She slumped back into the chair. A row of alternating white and red lights in the black ceiling illuminated the beer and shot drinkers who were reflected in the thin panel of mirror above the bar. The only other woman was a dispirited hooker drinking a Coke. She heard a man asking the bartender about her.

"Yeah, she comes in here every once in a while, usually about this time of day."

Out the door she could see the traffic light at Seventh and Alvarado, crowds of people passing in both directions.

"No, let her be. She's not working now."

The bartender put the drink down in front of Sandy and looked at her knowingly.

178

Without taking her eyes off the street corner, Sandy drank the first drink. An old man carrying a plastic shopping bag full of his clothing and personal effects slouched in; gingerly he set the bag on the floor next to an empty bar stool and studied the careful display of bottles in the shape of boats, ducks, soldiers, and Greek urns. A fat, young Salvadorean in a green T-shirt with doubles lined up in front of him stood and walked over to the jukebox, which he examined for a long time before dropping in a quarter. There were heartache and get-drunk songs in both English and Spanish as well as Frank Sinatra singing, "Fly Me to the Moon."

She held up the empty glass for the bartender.

The sky changed from gold to copper. The sun began to fall into the ocean as she drank the second drink. Her thoughts kept returning to the details of Malver Lopez's apartment and the father silhouetted against the window.

This led Sandy to consider ordering a third drink. She was oblivious now to the men and women outside hurrying by to begin their evening activities in Varrio Loco Nuevo.

Jesus Velaria was swept away like a speck of dust in the crowd. He was returning from his job at the auto body repair shop on Sunset to pick up his daughter Soledad from the widow in the apartment building who baby-sat. He knew the little girl would be waiting for him with her hair brushed and a cotton T-shirt tucked into a blue pair of corduroy bib overalls.

Jesus Velaria knocked on the door. "Good evening, Señora Cruz," he announced cordially.

The old woman opened the door slightly and peered around it to verify his identity. She could not believe the little girl's mother had left for good and she kept expecting that the mother herself would appear one evening. How could a woman leave her child? Señora Cruz had concluded that Jesus Velaria must have done something terribly wrong to drive his wife away, so she regarded him with distaste.

He ran his hand uncomfortably across the nape of his neck; he needed a haircut. Although he sensed Señora Cruz's disapproval and didn't understand it, he made himself stand patiently and wait for his daughter to come to the door. He was not invited into the apartment. It was like this every night since his wife left.

"¡Papi, papi!"

The little girl ran and threw herself around Jesus Velaria's knees. He leaned down, picked her up, and kissed her on both cheeks. Bowing his head, he bid good night to the old woman, who only partially closed the door as she watched them go into their apartment. For some moments she stood in the doorway listening carefully.

Still carrying the little girl, who hugged him tightly, Jesus Velaria went into the kitchen. Talking to her, he took things from cabinets and out of the small rented refrigerator. He poured a fruit juice for Soledad and grabbed a bottle of beer for himself.

"¿Te gusta el jugo? Bueno, voy a cocinar."

Placing the child by the table so she could watch, he scrambled some eggs and sliced some tomatoes. He put beans in a pan to heat them and laid some tortillas over the flame of the stove. On the weekend when he had the time, he would boil a chicken. It would be easier to buy canned or baby products, but he thought she should have real food. Besides, once his initial panic subsided, he had decided he was a good cook.

The kitchen was painted yellow. A red-and-blue poster from Nicaragua hung over the sink. They had lived in the apartment for more than a year. Tearing a tortilla into strips and handing them to Soledad, he sat her in the high chair bought down on Broadway when she was four months old. She looked more like his wife, he realized, her face rounder than his, her forehead somewhat lower. This

180

unexpected memory of his wife caused him to stir the eggs more violently.

Jesus Velaria looked at the calendar with its color photograph of the floating gardens of Xochimilco. It had been more than two weeks and still no word from her. His cousin who lived over on Witmar Street claimed she was living with a man, a drug dealer from the state of Michoacán, and that she was occasionally seen at the market. Jesus Velaria avoided that area because he didn't want to have to look for her. She should come to him.

He scraped the eggs onto one plate. Sooner or later she would contact him about Soledad. He had told Señora Cruz not to let the girl go off with her mother, but he wasn't sure what Señora Cruz would do if the situation arose. He was afraid if his wife was able to take Soledad, he would never see the girl again. Pushing aside a stack of his history and poetry books, he made room for the plate. Jesus Velaria watched his daughter touch the food with her hands, chew it, and shriek with laughter. This had something to do with the meaning of life, he marveled, something so delicate and pure that not even the most brilliant or ancient of the writers he admired were able to capture it in their many pages. Gleefully, she grabbed a tiny handful of the eggs and threw them onto his chest. He brushed the eggs off but they had made a wet stain on his shirt.

It had grown completely dark. Sandy shifted her attention from the neon red, yellow, green, and black signs above the bus stop on the corner to her empty glass, the third, which she examined, shaking the ice. The bartender looked in her direction, but she laid some money on the table, then put another dollar on top of it. It was time to go.

Manuel had been at her apartment. A note on the door

181

said he was out getting something to eat or walking on the beach. He would come back later. Sandy crumpled the paper and threw it away. She was getting tired of wondering where he was at night and she had reached the point where she had no expectation that there were any further revelations he could make to her. The depth of his relationship to the past was of no value to him; it was a danger. His only desire was to be assimilated.

Further, she thought irritably, he was careless and obstinately unsophisticated. The fine cotton shirts she bought made no impression on him, he preferred the tight, garish, polyester ones he got on Hollywood Boulevard. He seemed to lack an innate sense of texture or elegance. He couldn't even remember to keep his napkin in his lap in restaurants. That left only their sex life. His ardor in bed was fueled, Sandy sometimes believed, by his desire to obtain a green card.

These were her thoughts as she stood gazing out the window with a glass of brandy in her hand. Manuel knocked, then let himself in when Sandy failed to open the door. She didn't even turn to acknowledge him. He came up behind her, took the glass and put his nose in it. "How can you drink this stuff?"

She shrugged her shoulders as she took the glass from him.

"Are you in a bad mood again?" he inquired warily, peering into her eyes to determine how drunk she was.

"Not particularly. The same as usual."

"I don't understand it," he sighed in true bewilderment. "You have everything. A nice apartment at the beach, a hot car, a job. You should be happy. You're not illegal. You don't have to hide all the time or worry like I do."

"Give me a break. You worry about *la migra* catching you. I worry about the past. Are they really any different? You used to say you wanted to go home to Mexico. You

182

don't say that anymore. And it's not just the money. You're afraid everything will have changed, that people won't remember you, that the streets won't look the same, that you won't know where you belong. It's the same with the past. You think the boundaries are fixed but the topography keeps changing. *Así es la vida*, so why don't you fix yourself a drink."

Manuel fished a half-smoked joint out of his shirt pocket and lit it. A trail of white smoke appeared briefly, then disappeared. The sorrow that she felt was so much larger than she was. Woefully, she put her arms around his neck, gently but firmly pulling him close. He was so young, with a face both exquisitely handsome and simple, almost childlike. He had a firm, strong body and slept with his back pressed against hers, which she found tender and comforting.

She unbuttoned the loud print shirt and dropped it on the couch. Manuel's chest was like a perfect bronze sculpture, the small dark nipples erect. He was hairless, flawless, molten metal. She ran her hand over the pectoral muscles and felt along the rib cage, which moved under her touch. Stepping back, she fumbled with the zipper of his pants. He took another long hit off the joint before throwing it on the end table. Manuel sat on the couch and pulled off his ankle-high boots so she could get his pants down. His cock was large, uncircumcised, dark purple, nearly black.

Night like heat expanded. In Varrio Loco Nuevo, Jesus Velaria finished washing and putting away the dishes and pans from dinner. He wiped off the kitchen table and laid out a box of paper diapers, a can of baby powder, and a little nightgown printed with pink flowers. In the sink he ran warm water, which he tested frequently as he sang a song called "La Adelita." He laid Soledad down on the

183

table and untied her white shoes, which were nearly new, unfastened the metal snaps that held her bib overalls at the shoulders, and tugged her T-shirt off.

Jesus Velaria felt the diaper between her legs. As he removed it and looked at her body, she wriggled happily. Again he noticed how much Soledad's eyes were like his wife's. He felt a certain sadness sweeping over him like the wind that blew in, rustling the towel hung over the sink. For an instant, he turned toward the window behind him, which faced *Botanica La Ayuda*. He felt so alone. Then he heard the drumming of her feet on the metal table and turned to her with a smile.

Sandy knelt between Manuel's legs. She grasped his cock with her hand and then closed her mouth around it. Manuel gripped her neck, kneading the tight muscles with one hand. He slipped his other hand down into the front of her bikini underpants, working two fingers into her vagina. "Wouldn't you like to have a baby? We could have a family, get married, settle down. You'd be happy then."

She stretched up so she could put her tongue in his mouth to stop him from talking. She rocked on her buttocks so his hand moved deeper inside her. Slowly, he pulled her blouse above her breasts and inched his hand under her bra. Wrapping her arms around his waist, Sandy silently motioned him to lay her on the floor.

The noise from the street subsided in Varrio Loco Nuevo. Someone changed the station and adjusted the volume of a radio playing *norteño* music; a green sedan was parked on the street; the sycamore tree leaned into the building. Jesus Velaria took a washcloth. Soledad splashed in the sink as he picked up her arms and washed them carefully.

Drops of water streamed down her light-brown skin as he dipped the cloth into the warm water and rinsed his daughter's chest.

He recalled the last time his wife had been in the apartment. It had been morning, an impossible Tuesday in late July, the city waking, the street already tasting dry and parched, the sky unremarkable, dishes stacked by the sink, a quick cup of coffee, all reminders of the impermanence of things. She had been putting on a pair of red high heels with ankle straps to go to work. She was meticulously made up. Her hair glistened. Her nails were vermilion. The scent of tropical flowers hovered about her. Her ass curved round and smooth beneath a silky white dress. She had not come home from work.

Jesus Velaria wrung out the washcloth and fit a corner of it around his finger. He spread his daughter's vagina with one hand to wash it and inserted the finger wrapped in pink terry cloth. He hoped he was doing this the right way. Sandy shuddered. She stroked the black hair on the nape of Manuel's neck and traced a design on his shoulder. They lay sprawled on the living room floor, listening to the waves breaking on the nearby beach. Manuel was curved around her with his face against her stomach. Sandy lit a cigarette and held the match in her hands.

"Did I tell you I had a case the other day with some parents who burned their son on the back to punish him? Can you believe that?"

"Were they Mexican?"

"How did you know?"

He shrugged, pressing closer against her. "The mother did it."

"Why do you say that?"

"Because women usually have responsibility for children." Manuel stopped playing with the ends of her hair, which were spread out on the floor. "You know what the Mayans did to their children? They hit them, pinched

185

them, rubbed chili peppers on them, even burned them if it was necessary."

At one time every house had an altar but they had been smashed and cast aside. It is all as brittle as bone, she brooded, scarcely hearing him. The abandonment and destruction of great cities, fatal circumstances, the internal disintegration of a rhythmic and sequential flow.

"But that was a long time ago," Manuel was saying with disgust. "Haven't they learned any better?"

An apocalypse is coming. Fear is the heart of civilization. We are making the only bargains of which we are capable to appease the gods and we are either unaware of the inadequacy of our actions or ignorant of the consequences.

"These are hidden aspects of our lives, governed by the part of the brain that understands only rituals and repetition," Sandy mumbled drunkenly.

He lifted his head and put his lips between her breasts. "People can change," he insisted.

"They don't." Sandy closed her eyes and turned her face to the window. "That's why the rituals are so important."

His lips moved downward. "Do you want me to do it again? Now?"

The telephone rang before she could reply. She pushed him aside and reached for the receiver.

"Hello, *rubia*. What are you doing?"

She muffled the mouthpiece with one hand, with the other she held out her empty glass to Manuel. A look of jealousy flashed across his face but he took the glass and got up. The light went on in the kitchen and there was the scrape of a bottle being taken off the top of the refrigerator.

"I saw in the newspaper that they found the little girl you were looking for."

186

"Yeah." Francisco Gomez sounded tired. "It's been a lousy day."

Manuel returned and sullenly set the glass beside her. Then he went into the bedroom, closing the door behind him. Sandy didn't care if he heard about the girl. Brutality was a fact of life.

"The newspaper said she'd been strangled. Was she raped, too?"

"I can't tell you things like that."

Sandy knew this meant yes but she bit her lip with annoyance. "Why not? Why can't you tell me? Do you think that if I went around and told people that it would make any difference, that they would even care?"

"Come on, Sandy, baby, don't be like that. I don't feel much like talking about work now."

"I want to know."

"No," he was adamant. "Why is it so important to you? We're doing the best we can."

"I'm sure you are. What do you care about this investigation unless it makes you look like a hero?"

"What?" he asked in surprise.

"You make me sick. It's just a job with long hours and bad coffee after all, isn't it?" Her voice rose unpleasantly, uncontrollably. "I'll bet you never wonder why people commit these crimes, do you?"

"No. Thank God."

This is no simple alignment of planets. It's a history of the senses based on deplorable legends and amnesia of the future. The Mayans understood that.

"Are you scared?" Francisco Gomez asked, his voice changing to a smooth, seductive tone. "Are you alone? You don't have anybody there with you tonight?"

Manuel must be lying on the bed. The door was still closed and the light was off.

"Good." Francisco Gomez answered the question for himself.

187

Sandy pulled the phone cord and looped it tight around her ankle like the photograph in the Tango Room of the big blond with the vines entangling her legs.

"I wish I could come over to take care of you, but I'm still working."

Draining the last half inch of brandy, Sandy hung up without waiting to hear if he had anything more to say. All of the unseemly mortifications of the flesh that she had attempted were useless, without redemptive power. She took her purse from the low table near the couch and removed the glass candle and the bottle of green oil.

The woman in the *botanica* had told her to rub the oil on the candle. She unscrewed the top and held the small bottle to her nose. It smelled of grass, palms, oranges, papayas, fertile seasons, half-remembered landscapes, the damp soft crook of a baby's arm, a man's hair on a pillow, the edge of the city. The oil glistened on her fingertips and she began to coat the candle with it.

Sandy thought about Malver Lopez, the dead girl in downtown Los Angeles, the reflection she had seen of herself in the window of white dresses.

She thought about her father as she lit the candle.

9

The man next to Tricia Spivey kept nervously clearing his throat. He was about twenty-five years old, thought Sandy. White. Neatly and appropriately dressed in a sports coat and tie. His son had been removed from his home because he dreamed there were bruises on the boy. The man's psychologist, honoring his legal duty to call the authorities if there appeared to be some danger of child abuse, had reported this unusual dream.

Now the psychologist was on the witness stand explaining the objective relation between conscious thought and dreams, but Sandy couldn't follow all of what he was saying. She kept thinking of a fifteenth-century Aztec poet.

"We have come only to sleep./We have come only to dream./It is not true, it is not true/We have come to live on the earth."

She was so engrossed in this combination of the psychologist's testimony and her thoughts, she didn't notice the clerk motioning until the bailiff came over and tapped her on the shoulder.

"You know a Nadra Taylor?" whispered the clerk.

Sandy leaned across the woman's desk. "I don't think so. Who is she?"

"A client of yours recently. She's asking for you."

Wrinkling her brow, Sandy thought about this. "I think I know who you mean. Does she sound black?"

"I don't know. I haven't talked to her. She wants you."

"Why doesn't she call my office?"

"Because she's on the roof of the Talmadge Building. Says she's going to jump. She wants to talk with you."

"I remember her! Black hooker with braided hair and a couple of little boys. Tell the judge I had to leave." Throwing her purse over her shoulder, Sandy raced out of the courtroom in the direction of the stairs and past Sonia Perez, who was waiting for the elevator.

"What's happening? *¿A donde vas?*"

Sandy flung open the door leading to the stairs. "The Talmadge," she called back.

"Lucky you. Fabulous pasta salad."

She drove as fast as she could down Broadway, cutting in and out of traffic, then made a sharp right at Olive, scattering a group of people in a crosswalk as she headed south toward Ninth Street. At the Talmadge, she abandoned her car to a red-jacketed valet for the swank restaurant perched on top of the building where it overlooked the entire city.

The head of security was waiting for her in the cloakroom of the restaurant. He was a huge man in his late forties wearing a light-blue cotton suit with sweat stains under the arms. A walkie-talkie he held sputtered sporadic, indistinguishable words as he quickly explained how Nadra Taylor had been spotted on the roof by a couple of accountants who were seated at a window table. He was indignant she had managed to penetrate the security system.

The roof was open and rimmed all around by a four-and-a-half-foot steel wall. The head of security escorted Sandy discreetly through the restaurant to a door that led outside and pointed for her to turn right. The restaurant was set in the corner of the roof and surrounded by an elegantly manicured Japanese garden with tiny bridges and stone lanterns. The insurance company that had built this massive tower probably threw fancy cocktail parties out here on summer evenings, imagined Sandy as she stood staring across the empty roof toward the lonely figure of Nadra Taylor. That would be nice. Set a bar up, people serving trays of hors d'oeuvres. Maybe some kind of string quartet.

Nadra Taylor had hoisted herself on top of the wall and was seated straddling it, peering down into Ninth Street. She's gonna do it, marveled Sandy, jamming her sweaty, shaking hands into the pockets of her gray silk dress. A magnification of perception took place. It was forty stories to Ninth Street. Molecules of air became visible.

"Ms. Taylor. Hi. It's me, Sandy Walker. I heard you were looking for me."

Sandy stood awkwardly, waiting for the woman to respond.

"Did you want to talk to me? I came right over as soon as I heard you were looking for me."

Despite the heat, which usually trapped a layer of smog above the city, it was surprisingly clear. A warm wind had blown the sky wide open. The San Bernardino Mountains were an opaque blue. To the north the Hollywood Hills were radiant in the noon sun and the observatory high in Griffith Park was nothing more than a shiny, useless plaster sculpture on a shelf. These winds can alter the chemistry of common environmental gases and create elemental madness.

Sandy tried to assume some casual stance between concerned friendship and professional authority. She didn't want to see Nadra Taylor go over the edge and leave a permanent stain on Ninth Street.

Nadra Taylor turned her face to Sandy and gave her a goofy smile. "Mrs. Walker. I been hoping you'd come. We had such a nice talk the other day."

191

Vainly, Sandy struggled to recall what she had said that might be serviceable now. She couldn't think of anything, either pleasant or helpful, she had said to the woman. "Well, I been wondering how you were."

A lie. Sandy hadn't even been able to remember who she was. She hoped that this was the type of lie that was considered only venial. Perhaps she should have paid more attention to Sister Adrian when she had the opportunity. She hoped that this lie would be examined under its particular circumstances and that the wind would be taken into account.

"They took my two little boys away from me."

"Who was that?"

"They did. The law. People I don't know. People who don't understand what my life is all about."

Sandy nodded sympathetically. The head of security had told her he would be behind her with a couple of policemen in the stairwell that led to the roof. It was odd how quiet it was so far above the traffic.

"You been having some bad luck lately, I'd say," agreed Sandy.

"I heard that. My boyfriend, Mr. Larry Samson, got put in jail. I been kidnapped. My babies got taken from me. There ain't nothin' going right." Nadra Taylor let go of her viselike grip on the wall. She tottered, her anguished hands puncturing the air and railing against the heavens.

I think I'm going to get sick, Sandy thought. She wanted to look away but couldn't.

"Your little boys miss you. I won't know how to explain this to them if anything happens to you." Sandy tried to swallow a large sore lump in her throat.

"Oh, they're smart little boys all right," Nadra Taylor laughed delightedly. Her teeth gleamed and the braids shook about her head. She rocked back and forth on the wall.

192

"Your little boys need you. If you die and I tell them you went to heaven, they won't understand. They'll think it's a street somewhere in Los Angeles. They'll keep waiting for you to come back. That's not fair, is it?"

Nadra Taylor slumped disconsolately.

Sandy took a step closer. "Don't you think we should go downstairs and try to visit them? You'd like that, wouldn't you?" She said this a little too eagerly for it to be completely believable. Besides being nervous, she was starting to feel angry. Why should she have to help this woman think of reasons to stay alive?

Nadra Taylor looked over the edge into the street again. Sandy could barely hear her because she was talking into the wind. "They don't let me see my boys. They don't even tell me where they are. They think I'm crazy." She whirled to face Sandy. Nadra Taylor was crying, her face pitifully contorted.

There are even some countries that permit a special legal defense for crimes committed during these freakish weather fronts.

"I don't think you're crazy." Sandy hung back, not knowing whether to get any closer to the woman. "I can find your boys. I can take you to see them."

"You know where they are?" Nadra Taylor shrilled suspiciously. "Then you must be one of them!" She started to put her other leg over the wall.

"No, no," cried Sandy. "I don't know where your boys are now. Nobody tells me these things. But I can find out if I want. If you want me to, I will."

There was nothing to do but wait. The sun had stopped dead in its path to the Pacific. Sandy felt sweat trickling down her neck.

"I want to see them." Nadra Taylor extended a hand toward Sandy, then waved one finger. "You find them."

"You have to get off the wall and come over here to me. If I'm going to help you, you have to come here."

193

"For sure you're going to help me?" Nadra Taylor leaned away so that she swayed over Ninth Street with an uncertain look in her eyes.

"Yes. I said I would."

The wind picked up, whipping Sandy's hair around her head.

"Now come over here. Please."

Nadra Taylor swung both legs heavily over the wall to face Sandy. She leaned back again, then took one more long look over the edge. "I'm counting on you. You promised you'd help me get my boys."

Sandy held her breath as Nadra Taylor ambled slowly and unsteadily toward her. She didn't move until the woman was standing directly in front of her. Nadra Taylor's breathing was rapid and her eyes were watery. Tentatively, Sandy reached out and touched one of the woman's long braids, which was bound at the ends with red and green beads.

"Come on, let's get out of here." Nadra Taylor answered, squaring her shoulders and lifting her chin. "This place gives me the creeps."

They turned and walked toward the stairwell. Bleached by the sun and silhouetted against the vast flat plain of east Los Angeles with its thick streaming clouds from distant smokestacks, the two women huddled close together for an instant before disappearing into the shade of the building. One of the two policemen hidden behind the door jumped out, grabbing Nadra Taylor by the arm, twisting it up behind her. Sandy dropped back and away from the convulsive woman, who stumbled and fought as the two men sought to restrain her.

"You lied to me, you bitch! You lied to me," Nadra Taylor screamed. White foam flecked her mouth. "I'm gonna kill you. You bitch. You are one of them!"

Sandy walked over to the wall and stood there looking over the edge for whatever Nadra Taylor had seen.

194

"Bitch!"

Nadra Taylor's voice receded and the door slammed shut. Sandy wondered if she would have time to go to the Tango Room or if she'd have to make do with someplace closer.

Michael Fillipini looked relieved when he saw Sandy coming through the crowd in the hall of the third floor. Sidestepping an arguing couple he hurried toward her with his hands shoved into his pockets, an unfortunate posturing for a man his size, since it made him waddle. "Did she jump?"

Sandy shrugged her shoulders laconically. The crowds in the hall never seemed to get any smaller. It made her job seem impossible.

"What happened?" he demanded impatiently.

"I promised to take her to see her kids. Then the police snatched her."

"Good. She's probably on her way to Metro by now. My hero." Michael grinned, clapping his arm around her shoulder to pull her closer. "Jesus Christ," his grin vanished. "You smell like a distillery."

"I stopped for a drink. Big deal."

He fumbled in his breast pocket. "It was more than one drink. Don't you have any breath mints? Here, take a piece of gum. Jesus, Sandy."

She wanted to get away from Michael Fillipini. She didn't want to talk. Sullenly she twisted away, the mass of long blond hair hiding her face.

He turned her around, walked her to the end of the hall past a clump of 82nd Street Crips who were horsing around while they waited for their various possession and concealed-weapon cases, and told her to sit down.

"What the fuck's wrong with you? Showing up drunk for court. Are you out of your mind?"

Sandy put her face in her hands.

"You got the woman off the roof. You saved her fucking life. Everything turned out fine. So what's the problem?"

"I lied to her," Sandy whispered.

"Of course you did. That's what you're supposed to do. You can't deal with crazy people like they're normal. And if they end up down here they're crazy."

Sandy looked up, her hands shook slightly as she put a cigarette to her lips. "Is that what you really think? That they're animals? That they're not the same as us?"

"You got it. Let me tell you about this nut today." He plucked at the crease of his trousers, getting comfortable to tell his story.

"I pick this guy up in arraignment court about two months ago. Scumbag. Looks older than he is. Beard stubble. Yellow stains on his fingers. Dirty shirt. Worn-out blue plaid sports jacket. Got the picture?

"Guy's accused of fingering his daughter. He says it's all a big mistake that he can explain. This jerkoff insists on coming to my office. I got time to sit around and hold hands with these clowns, right? I tell him, 'Look, buddy, I've heard it all before. There's no criminal charges against you. Cop a plea and I'll take care of you at the dispo.' But no, he's got to come see me to explain it.

"Anyhow, he gets to my office to tell me his story. Seems he doesn't work, but his wife does. He takes care of the house. When the wife gets home from the office, she mixes herself up a few cocktails while he's fixing dinner. You following this? He's putting the finishing touches on raspberry Jell-O mold and she's in the living room getting bagged. Then the whole family sits down and eats dinner in the dining room and guess what's hanging there on the wall?"

Sandy shook her head blankly without any interest in what Michael Fillipini was getting at. The millions of dots in the floor swirled in front of her.

"A calendar so they can keep track of the daughter's

196

period!" Michael exclaimed. "Eating dinner and they're sitting there thinking about her period. So I ask him what's the calendar for? Reasonable question, don't you think?"

Sandy stared at the floor. Michael continued without noticing.

"He says, real prissy, 'Our daughter's irregular.' I say, 'So?' The guy looks at me like I'm a nut. I ask him, 'Did you take her to a doctor? Is she banging the boys in the neighborhood?' He tells me no. I mean, I'm thinking up stories right and left for this guy and he keeps telling me no. Finally I ask him why he is keeping track of the daughter's period. Listen up, now it get's real screwy. . . ."

Sandy saw herself in the pine-paneled room of her parents' house. It was late afternoon in the spring—the gardenia buds trembling with the knowledge that they would soon bloom. Her mother was still at work. Sandy was reading a history book she had brought from school. Her father got up from the couch on the other side of the room and moved behind her. His shadow fell across the page.

". . . explains that while he does the dishes, his wife has a few more cocktails in front of the TV so she can relax. Adjusts her alpha rays. His wife finds this so relaxing she usually just goes to sleep watching TV. Then he has to go upstairs and tuck the baby in. Got it? Wife comes home, gets loaded, passes out cold in front of the tube and he's upstairs with the teenage daughter. I can barely control myself when he tells me. I'm busting up, so I have to excuse myself to go out and get a cup of coffee."

The shadow moved across the page of the book Sandy was reading. Her father placed his hands on the back of her chair. He leaned forward as though to look at the book, his breath rattling in her ear.

"Anyhow, I come back into my office and he's sitting

there talking to my desk. Never even noticed I got up and left. I'm about to piss my pants, but I say to him, 'Look, Mr. Ball,' no shit, that was his name, 'this story's not going to make it.' He tells me that since his wife is asleep, it's his job to take care of the girl. When she finally gets her period, she has terrible cramps. He has to give her massages to relieve the pain." Michael chuckled. "I guess he hasn't heard a good fuck is the best thing for cramps. . . ."

Sandy sat helplessly without speaking. She was waiting for her mother's car to pull into the driveway.

"I'm barely able to keep my composure and I tell him, 'Mr. Ball,' I love that name," said Michael, wiping his eyes. " 'You got a loser here. Your story is classic. Your wife's a drunk, the two of you don't have sex, you're alone with your teenage daughter, and you're telling me you gave her a massage?' So you know what this asshole does, Sandy?"

Sandy dragged her attention back to Michael Fillipini. "What?"

"We get into court and first thing he says to O'Leary, 'Give me another lawyer. This guy says I'm going to lose.' Of course, she tells him I'm a great lawyer." Michael chortled again. "The SOB has a heart attack."

"A real one?"

Michael nodded. "They had to call the paramedics and give him oxygen out here in the hall."

"You continue the case?"

"Are you kidding? Hell no. We went to trial and Ball lost."

Sandy unwrapped the piece of gum Michael had pressed upon her and pleated the silver paper into thin strips. "What are you trying to tell me?"

He chewed his lip. "That, uh, damn, what was it? I got so carried away with that story about Ball I forgot."

"Something about these people being different from us."

"Right. They come from a foreign world. They wouldn't know right from wrong if it bit them in the ass. You can't take it so serious, Sandy. You got the woman off the roof. The rest, that's her problem. Fuck her. We're not responsible."

He chuckled. "Can you imagine living in a screwy family like that? Good Lord, what happens to those people?"

What happens? Sandy thought. There are long nights, fear of the dark, your skin twitches.

She stood up. "Let's go back."

"Believe me, Sandy. They're from a different world."

They're people you never notice on the street. People whose lives are hidden. Whose lives are taboo words. Their pain is a veil. Or a checkpoint. A sentry post. We don't know what to do. We invent borders and we want to check their passports. We name the borders—court, the welfare and institutions code, psychotherapy.

"They're insane," Michael insisted.

We're afraid of these people. Of their horrifying nakedness. That's why we move like mediating animals in a passion play or we sit back and let the police try to take care of these problems for us. What can we do? It's better to imagine it's an alien world, isn't it?

Michael pushed himself to his feet. "How many people do you think we know like this?"

"At least one."

"Who?" he demanded.

"Me," she said over her shoulder as she walked back toward the juvenile courts.

Luther Bond's mother was said to have slapped her son. The doctors at Martin Luther King hospital said the boy

199

had trauma to the soft tissue of the head, bruises to the left eye, and swelling of the right eye. In the end, it turned out to be much simpler than that. There was a hand print visible on his face.

Wearily and with a headache that told her she needed another drink, Sandy closed the last file of the day; then went into Department 27 to pick up a copy of the disposition report for Jeanette Ray, who was scheduled to appear the following day. She was curious to know what Jeanette Ray had told the social worker, but more than that, she wondered how much of a problem she was going to have coercing Jeanette Ray into acceptance of the inevitable. Sandy kicked off her white high heels and curled her legs under her on an empty bench. Nibbling on a strand of her hair, she read the report. No surprises. Thirty-one-year-old woman from Brownsville, Texas, with a high school education. Whereabouts of fathers of children unknown. Unemployed, income from Aid for Dependent Children. Firm disciplinarian with little insight into emotional needs of daughter. The social worker concluded by recommending that the two younger children be returned but that Julie stay in a foster home.

The voice of Jeanette Ray was exuberant when Sandy called her from a pay phone in the hall. It changed dramatically and her detailed recitation of the prayer meetings she had been to in order to effect this turn of events broke off abruptly when she realized that Sandy was telling her that only two of the children were coming home.

"What the hell do you mean Julie's gonna stay where she is?" she roared.

"She doesn't want to be with you. Maybe she's still mad at you," Sandy mumbled as though courtesy demanded she think of some polite phrasing that would now convert Jeanette Ray's psychological failures into a minor social faux pas.

200

"She doesn't have the right to be mad at me," Jeanette Ray screamed. "I'm her mother. Do you mean to tell me they're letting children run this system?"

"The system is for the protection of minors, not the pleasure of parents."

Jeanette Ray was shrieking something about constitutional rights and Deuteronomy; Sandy leaned against the metal frame of the pay phone, trying to ease her aching back. How many times did you have to tell these people? Wasn't there a fundamental difference between right and wrong that demarcated all behavior like the broken white line running down the middle of a highway? Eventually the noise subsided.

"I'm trying to tell you what we have to do. You're going to have to work within the system. God doesn't have anything to do with this. I'll schedule you for a contested disposition."

"When do I get Julie back?"

"I don't know. That depends on you."

She had already decided to go to the Tango Room. More and more she found the meagerness of its ambiance and discretion of the bartender inviting. Of course, she realized she was drinking excessively. She had never appeared in court as loaded as that afternoon. Still, no one besides Michael had noticed anything. She should feel bad. She knew this, but she didn't. She had felt particularly alert and perceptive in court, though numb to what was happening around her. It was somewhere between dreaming and waking, if in fact there was a difference. At least this is what she decided as she headed the car west down Seventh Street to the Tango Room.

Suspended in a corner of the ceiling, the television was on but the five o'clock news was being universally ignored by the men and women at the bar. In the back of the room where Sandy sat it was dark. She held her glass up toward the white light emanating from the television and considered the way in which a drink could subtly alter the environment. Gray became pearl, then nacre. The red-and-black linoleum floor sloped slightly, almost imperceptibly, toward the rear of the bar. Voices came and went. It was the kind of bar where people got up suddenly from their bar stools, walked outside, came back in, and sat down. She found peace in the routine of the Tango Room. When the news was over, she got unsteadily to her feet and bowed her head in the direction of the bartender on her way out.

In the soft sheen of the summer's early evening, Los Angeles had relaxed into the languid rhythm of a sultry, heat-induced stupor and collective loss of memory. Variances of green beckoning from MacArthur Park attracted a slow but steady stream of people who trickled in and out of the public gardens. So refreshing and luxuriant were the possibilities promised by the shades of palms and giant hibiscus that Sandy forgot, as did the weary surging mass of humanity, that a man, a Salvadorean refugee, had drowned recently in the lake. Drunk, excited by the possibility of a five-dollar reward for retrieving a child's toy, misjudging the depth of the water, forgetting that he could not swim, the man plunged to his death. But he was not on Sandy's mind as she walked in the opposite direction to her car.

She was making a real effort to forget the shadow pattern of Malver Lopez and her father almost dancing above the street in the frame of an old window. She was trying to forget the harsh and desperate edge in Jeanette Ray's voice, she was trying to ignore the peculiar ominous infraction of light on the downtown roofs. She thought about buying herself a dress, getting a manicure, cutting recipes out of a magazine, planning a vacation, studying ballet, any of the myriad activities that require discipline and attention to detail. She should buy an expensive cut of meat, flowers, and a glass vase. She should line the interior of her dresser drawers with scented paper, buy new underwear, marry Manuel, learn to play backgammon, or at least one conventional card game. Lives, like the planets, she reasoned with drunken complacency, must be formed around solid cores. They must be held together by these small celebrative affirmations of the ordinary and unsullied.

The sun had not yet set when she tottered cheerfully up the wooden stairs to her front door. Long thin strips of white paper floated in the breeze. A small pile of green lay on the landing. Bewildered, she stopped for an instant, frightened as she sensed an intrusion. She approached the door deliberately and slowly.

A pile of broad, waxy green leaves pierced with stones and chicken bones was scattered in front of the door. Torn newspaper had been stuck to the red door, which appeared to be burning in the last hour of daylight. Had one of the angry women from court followed her home? Who knew her address? Was it Manuel? She ripped one of the strips of newspaper from the door. A word was printed crudely with black ink in the margin of the paper. *Puta.* Whore.

10

Three rows back someone was clipping his nails. Calendar call was nearly over when Jeanette Ray climbed clumsily into a seat indicated to her by the bailiff. A little boy howled as his mother pushed him aside to make room. Sandy's head felt like it was full of gravel; she looked over her shoulder and grimaced. Jeanette Ray was wearing a blinding pink sleeveless sundress with a full skirt. She had thrown a pale yellow cardigan over her shoulders and it was held around her throat by a simulated pearl sweater clip.

Tricia Spivey leaned toward Sandy to purr, "Fabulous. I haven't seen a sweater clip for at least twenty-five years. What a divine inspiration for an outfit."

"Why don't you lend me your Neiman-Marcus card so I can take my client shopping and get her something decent to wear?" Sandy snapped. "I'll bet you could get a charitable deduction."

"Touchy, aren't we, today? Sometimes I forget how much you love these little ragamuffins." Tricia Spivey patted Sandy's hand. "I love the ensemble. Truly. Real authentic nostalgia."

It was rumored Tricia Spivey had tried to write her Salvadorean housekeeper's salary off as a political contri-

205

bution. Sandy was just about to mention this, but the judge glared down at them.

Stiffly, Sandy got up and went back to Jeanette Ray. "We'll check in at second call. Read your report in the hall." Sandy lingered inside until she thought Jeanette Ray would have had enough time to digest the social worker's synthesis of her statements about her life, some sociological babble with several misspellings of polysyllabic words and the recommendation that Julie stay in a Mormon foster home in Huntington Park.

"This is all wrong," Jeanette Ray exploded as soon as Sandy came out the door. "My husband didn't leave me. I kicked him out. He'd come home drunk, lipstick on his shirt, smelling like he'd been with some cheap whore."

Exhaling wearily, Sandy rested her hand on her hip. "How about the rest of the report?"

"Wrong, all wrong. It says Julie doesn't want to come home. I know she does."

"She does?"

"Of course." Jeanette Ray replied with assurance. "What child doesn't want to be with her mother?"

Sandy looked around the hall. Plenty.

Jeanette Ray beamed. "The Lord will answer me."

Julie refused to see her mother in the courtroom.

"Don't worry. You'll be coming back soon," Sandy heard herself saying after she set the matter for a hearing in September.

"I tried so hard. I only wanted what was best for her. She hates me, doesn't she?" Jeanette Ray cried.

Sandy saw her father slumped on the living room couch, intently turning the radio dial from news station to news station as though searching for some new and global disaster that might bring them closer together. Something almost like pity ran through her. But for whom she didn't know. She started to put her arm around Jeanette Ray's

206

shoulder but at the last second dropped her arm and shoved her hand into her pocket.

"Come back on the twenty-seventh. Dress nice. We'll see what we can do in court."

After the elevator doors closed on Jeanette Ray, Sandy made her way through the sluggish crowd and down the stairs one floor to the clerk's office where juvenile records were kept. A woman looked up from her desk at the sound of the swinging door that separated the service counter from the stored files but, recognizing her as one of the attorneys who occasionally came in, she returned to her work without further interest. Sandy leafed through her calendar until she found the case number she had scribbled by Nadra Taylor's name. Miraculously, the file was exactly where it should have been. On top was the court's minute order, stamped, WHEREABOUTS OF MINORS TO REMAIN CONFIDENTIAL. Sandy glanced over at the woman at the desk. It should be fairly easy to find out where the boys were. She would come back into court on a motion and talk the judge into granting monitored visits. She copied the social worker's telephone number down. She could even drive Nadra Taylor out to the first visit.

Humming the refrain of a Mexican love song she had heard repeatedly on the radio the last several weeks, she gave the file an extra pat as she put it back on the shelf. It was so simple. She had promised to help Nadra Taylor and now she would make good on that promise. For the first time in weeks, she breathed easier. She swung her purse over her shoulder and left the building. Even the incredible heat seemed more manageable.

It was busy on Broadway, swarming with shoppers, street corner prophets, and pickpockets. Storekeepers in thin, brightly colored suits paced in front of their businesses trying to lure in customers. Sandy loved to walk on Broadway, losing herself in the crowd, studying the expanse of a certain cheekbone, a particular shade of skin, or the unequivocal movement of a hand sweeping hair off a stranger's forehead. Down past the *Los Angeles Daily*, past the driveways and stone ledges where workers in dark-blue overalls lounged as they ate their lunches and called out to the passing women. "Hey, baby, momma, I'm talking to you, *guapa.*"

Across Second Street a tall dirty white building with a seventy-foot-high blue mural of a bride and groom advertised a bridal shop and separated the staid government buildings from the carnival on Broadway. The wino with vacant eyes who sat on the sidewalk by this building every day, his hand laconically in front of him as though it were no longer connected to him, had been joined by an older man who lay with his head on the younger man's thigh as if he had fallen over. A thin, nearly invisible stream of saliva trickled from the older man's mouth onto the faded gray pant leg of the younger man. Sandy dropped some change into the man's hand while he stared dreamily ahead.

Clothing shops hung their flamboyantly tropical-colored shirts from awnings and baseball jackets flew out the open doors. Slick pants and pointed shoes were piled in the windows. There were jewelry stores with gold saints' medals and wedding rings. Salsa and ranchero music blared from numerous record stores. Sandy found herself lingering in front of one of the many bridal shops. Dresses of white organdy and tulle, blue velvet and rose trim, full bodices with ripples of lace and snowy net floated among plastic champagne glasses and pink paper streamers. Dark-skinned male mannequins with thick mustaches and delicate hands were dressed in blue and black tuxedoes with cummerbunds of light lavender satin. Examining the profile of one of these men, his face partially turned away, his gaze shallow, Sandy thought of Manuel and wondered where he had been recently. The female mannequins wore heavy black wigs that accentuated their pale skin and soaring, arched eyebrows. These statues were linked together by huge white beaded rosaries that the men and women held in their hands as if their common faith in this act were itself the link between them.

Sandy went into the store to look around. An elaborately coiffed and made-up woman in her late fifties wearing a tight yellow blouse and white knit pants observed her tactfully from the far end of the store by the dressing rooms. Wandering through the room, Sandy touched the dresses, pretending to examine the price tags. The glass counters were filled with special white prayer books, veils, gloves, and rosaries of clear crystal beads that shimmered when they caught the sunlight.

On the walls hung hundreds of photographs of couples dressed in ornate costumes and ritual colors, the man's arm around the woman's waist, faces turned three-quarters to the camera, eyes closed in permanent kisses. The photographs were all inscribed to a Margarita, presumably the owner of the store, thanking her for her help in the planning and arrangement of these ceremonies.

The room was covered with mirrors that reflected the dresses and mannequins in a disorganized and dizzying display of joy. Sandy walked over to the window that looked out on Broadway. A knee-high white wrought iron railing separated the showroom from the window and its theatrical display. Out on the street were drunks, the usual hustlers with imitation gold watches and necklaces that would turn green within forty-eight hours, and working people hurrying by too busy to stop to contemplate this small icon of faith in the middle of Broadway.

"I am Margarita. Is there something I can help you with?" the woman in the yellow top said in heavily accented English.

Sandy glanced back and found the woman directly behind her. "I'm just looking."

"For some particular occasion or event?" the woman inquired knowledgeably.

Sandy hesitated. "No, I was just looking because the things were all so . . ." She hesitated again, this time longer as a particularly garish spangled dress caught her attention, ". . . so lovely."

The woman nodded her head gracefully. "Yes, they are lovely. They are like the embodiment of dreams. They are fantasies upon which lives can be built."

"I see by the photographs that the people who come here are very pleased with what you offer them."

The woman pursed her lips and majestically gestured with one hand around the room. "It is an illusion we all seek. That there is some simplicity or order, that life can be dealt with if we approach it purposefully, directly, with respect, as a ritual. I, myself, have been married three times."

Sandy wondered if that was considered good or bad as together they examined the tableaux presented between the wrought iron railing and the glass window. "Well, thank you," Sandy murmured, somewhat uncomfortably. "I don't want to take up your time. I was just browsing."

"I understand you're not here to buy anything. You're just curious about this fantasy. The fantasy is," continued the woman, closing her eyes as though Sandy were no longer there, "that changes will take place in our lives. That we can direct and order these changes. The changes we seek are so elemental and so profound that God could not possibly trust us with them." Suddenly she opened her eyes. "There, look outside. Tell me what you see."

"A woman waiting at the corner to cross the street." Sandy squinted, wondering if she was looking at the right corner.

The woman laughed dryly. "A whore with three hungry children at home and no *palanca* or influence in the world except for what she keeps between her legs and the

210

hatred in her heart. See, there where she is standing have stood a million such women while I am here in this business of trying to assure the world that desire can deepen into something more useful, that there is hope and beauty, and the possibility of redemption through the conventionality of love."

Then the woman leaned into the display area and picked up a heart made of red velvet and trimmed around the edges with white feather boa. The word AMOR was written in silver glitter script and there were two hearts pierced with arrows also in silver glitter.

"Take this. It's a beautiful thing. The little girls carry the wedding rings on it into the chapel. One might also use it to dream of happiness. Examine it for yourself," she said, putting it in Sandy's reluctant hands.

Sandy held it awkwardly. Silver glitter stuck to her fingers. "Are you trying to tell me this is a magic pillow?"

The woman laughed again, this time arid as the wind that blew off the desert.

"There is no magic. There is merely history and fate, but if you feel there's some connection between fate and longing, between desire and destiny, then take it."

She retrieved the pillow from Sandy and carried it to the cash register.

"This is eighteen dollars, but for you, thirteen." She wrapped the pillow in a brown paper bag and looked expectantly at Sandy.

Fumbling in her purse, Sandy pushed the brandy bottle out of the way so she could get her wallet. She counted out the money. She was spared the necessity of having to express her covert pleasure in the pillow because at that moment a group of women came through the door chattering among themselves about yellow bridesmaid dresses. Margarita cast one last, brief, world-weary glance at Sandy as would the proprietor of any pornography store and turned, smiling, to her new customers.

211

Clouds of dust and paper swirled above the sidewalk. The sun, slightly past its midpoint, had driven many people indoors. The two men she had passed earlier had fallen asleep in the wind. Sandy turned again to the court building. Clutching the paper bag closer to her chest, she hurried to the pay phones on the third floor.

The phone in the office of Nadra Taylor's social worker rang many times. Sandy lit a cigarette and inspected her makeup in the scratched metal plate of the telephone. Maybe they could actually go have some pancakes with the little boys. Excitedly, she identified herself to the woman who finally answered the phone and told her Nadra Taylor's name and case number. She could hear papers being shuffled in the silence as she waited for the worker.

"I got the file now. Guess I'm not going to have the pleasure of meeting Ms. Taylor," said the social worker.

"What do you mean?"

"She committed suicide the other day. I got a note on top of the file from my supervisor."

Sandy pressed the phone against her breast for a moment before she could speak again.

"Isn't that the craziest thing," wondered the social worker more to herself than to Sandy. "She tried to commit suicide earlier the same day. She was up on the roof of some building but the police got her down. Well, I guess she finally did what she wanted."

"What happened?" Sandy demanded in a husky voice. "What happened?"

"Hard to tell. Looks like she managed to get out of the car that was transporting her. I guess she was trying to run away. They had her handcuffed but she smashed her hands through the car window. She broke out two windows and cut her wrists to ribbons before they could stop her. The cops said she was on PCP, she could have killed anyone who came near her."

212

Nadra Taylor hadn't been running away. Sandy knew that. She'd been trying to find her children. If she was dead now it was because of Sandy.

"What was it you wanted?" asked the social worker.

"Nothing, I guess."

"I'm going to close my file. You win some, you lose some. Oh well, I got a case load of seventy-eight families. That's enough to keep me busy."

Sandy dropped her cigarette to the ground and stepped on it. "Did anyone tell her children?"

"The police. They went out there."

She wondered how Francisco Gomez would have handled that. A tall stranger in a uniform, bending down, crouching in front of two tiny boys who looked at him blankly and with only a slight degree of interest. He wouldn't know if they understood him or not. He would explain it to them at least two and probably three times before he gave up. He would straighten uncomfortably and ruffle the tops of their heads before turning and striding more purposefully toward his patrol car.

"Are you sure about all this?" Sandy pleaded in a small voice.

The social worker had hung up and the halls were silent. Only a few women with children waited in the desultory quiet of the long afternoon. Sandy walked through the hall, seeing with an exceptional clarity those who were still waiting. They were like the woman she had seen on the street corner across from the bridal shop. They lounged on the yellow wooden benches, ankles crossed, smoking languorously, without hope or expectation, a slow rage simmering.

She felt the weight of her purse as it dug into her shoulder, reminding her that she had almost a full pint of brandy. Sandy went into the bathroom and locked herself in the last stall. It was covered with the melancholy graffiti

213

of La Payasa, Sad Eyes, and Mousie. She slumped heavily against the bolted door and drank.

The reason for all this suffering escaped her. There was no plausible explanation. That meant there was only destiny, inevitable as the waves, and history, which was the erosion of time. She wrapped her arms around herself, laid her face against the marble wall, and cried.

The connections between her life and the people she worked with were indelible, like tattoos. If she kept up with the drinking, she'd be out of a job soon. But she didn't want to stop. She needed it. She wanted to stop seeing her father, to stop hearing his breathing, insistent and infernal as the ceaseless wind in her ear. He was dead. Why didn't he stay that way? All of the cases she worked with just brought back the feeling that he was watching her and waiting for her to be alone in the dark.

As she leaned forward and flushed the toilet to cover the sound of her crying, something glass and silver on the floor caught her eye. She knelt down and picked up the shiny object. It was a hypodermic needle. It must belong to one of the women sitting in the hall. Sandy examined it. She turned the sharp steel point in her fingers; it was weightless in her hand. She wondered if drugs would help her sleep. Carefully, she wrapped it in toilet paper and hid it in her purse.

After washing her face and brushing her hair fifty strokes, Sandy retraced her steps out to the hall to call the office before going home. Jiggling coins in her dress pocket, she kept her back to the waiting women, some of whom looked up hopefully. A woman sighed loudly, feet shuffled past.

"Not much going on," reported the receptionist in the usual listless tone she assumed after lunch. "Just some girl named Malver. Said you'd remember who she is, she's at the same place you met her before, and she wants you to

214

come there. She'll wait until you get there. She called, let's see, about two hours ago."

There weren't any other messages.

Malver Lopez wasn't her responsibility. Fuck her. Let her get on a bus and go home or back to Panorama City, where she belonged. There was nothing Sandy could do. Everything she touched disintegrated. It was all as brittle as bone.

Sandy wanted to drive home but she was too confused; near Koreatown she simply felt she couldn't go any farther. Making a sharp turn, she pulled into the parking lot of a bar she had never been to. Any one of these places might be the sacred well. At this time in the afternoon it was nearly deserted. The place was empty except for a couple of Korean businessmen drinking Scotch and laughing with the fat bartender.

"Brandy," she called as she took a seat at a dark table near the back. "Make it a double."

Why had Malver Lopez called her? Why, out of all the people in Los Angeles, did the girl think that she could help her?

The bartender placed the drink in front of her. Grateful for its awful, searing distraction, she drank nearly half in one long swallow. "Let me have another."

The bartender padded away.

What was Malver Lopez to her? Why should she risk any more trouble to help this one little girl? What could she possibly do to help her? Sandy Walker knew she had been running from her father all her life, trying to evade him. There was no way to forgive what he had done.

Another drink silently appeared by the empty glass. Without noticing the bartender, she picked it up and brought it to her lips. Where was the someone, the guardian angel, who could have saved her when she was Malver's age? Her hand trembled; she was starting to feel drunk. Why hadn't anyone come forward for her? Tears began to well in her eyes. Wasn't she worth it? Was she just born bad? Had she deserved it? Were there some children created only to absorb the abuse of the world and the sins of its elders? She slammed the glass down on the table, grabbed her purse, and ran to her car.

Traffic was light on Beverly west toward Hollywood and the public library where Malver was waiting. The road climbed a small hill from the Civic Center to the oriental section of Beverly. Filipinos stood in front of whitewashed restaurants with pictures of palm trees painted on plate glass windows. Palm trees grew along the edge of the street. The air was heavy and sweet with the smell emanating from an ice-cream cone factory. Some women with their hair wrapped in white bandanas stood sleepily, smoking cigarettes and talking among themselves.

In the vicinity of the Rampart police station the road ascended another small hill at Vermont and the city became latin again. The local street gang had named it Paraíso but it looked like any other depressed subtropical neighborhood stretched out and laid flat under the blinding afternoon sun. Driving as fast as she could through Paraíso, she swung unhesitatingly around a bus that was blocking her from the right lane and headed north toward Santa Monica Boulevard. There, in the distance, the old library stood out from the surrounding cheaply constructed stucco apartments that dated from an unprecedented building boom in the thirties when the Silver Lake Reservoir had been completed. Cars were backed up for at least half a block. The red lights of a police car pulled over to the pavement flashed and a small crowd milled about, making it difficult to park.

Inside the library it was cool and partially dark. Many of the lights had been turned off to conserve energy. A large potted palm cast a broken shadow across the doorway as Sandy went into the reading room where she had met Malver. Only the hum of an air-conditioner greeted her. An old woman draped in scarves was seated at one of the tables with a large stack of magazines in front of her. The scarves fluttered about her head as she flipped through the pages mumbling to herself. At another table a middle-aged Oriental man dressed in black was reading a Filipino newspaper, clicking his tongue at important articles and making notes on a crumpled piece of note-book paper. Increasingly aware of the heavy sound her heels made on the floor, Sandy hurried among the stacks of books, looking for Malver. On the table closest to the door lay a large book open to a diagram of the solar system.

Malver was not in any of the reading rooms. Sandy went downstairs. She pushed open the door to the bath-room and called Malver's name. A startled young latin girl of about sixteen emerged from one of the stalls smell-ing of marijuana and smiled blissfully at her. Sandy let the door drop closed and rushed upstairs.

At the information desk she glanced around the room again, expecting Malver to come in any second. Sandy did not want to call any attention to herself but now she was worried. Impatiently she drummed her nails on the counter while the tall gray-haired librarian gave someone on the phone a lot of information about the origin of limestone caves.

"I'm looking for a little girl. About twelve years old. Mexican. I'm supposed to meet her here."

"Oh, thank God." The librarian's squeezed Sandy's hand. "We had no idea who she was. We didn't know what to tell the paramedics."

Sandy gripped the desk.

The lines around the librarian's eyes deepened and her amber necklace clattered against her breastbone as she leaned confidentially toward Sandy.

"She was here for a long time this morning. She kept

going out and coming back in. I thought she was going across the street to buy candy." The woman shook her head slightly as though this were the probable cause of all the trouble infesting the world. "I noticed she left about four-thirty but I thought she was coming back because she left her book open on the table." The librarian paused, patting the back of her hair, which was pinned up in a large, awkward roll. "We like to keep the tables clear and get the books back on the shelf so all the patrons can use them."

Sandy nodded a weak encouragement. She needed another drink.

"She went out and a few minutes later I heard brakes squealing, then people yelling. When I got outside to see what had happened, I saw the little girl in the street." The librarian looked slightly sick remembering this.

Feeling the breath knocked out of her, Sandy clutched the counter. "Was she hurt bad?"

"I think so." The woman cleared her throat uncomfortably and straightened some papers. "They took her to Queen of Angels Hospital."

Unsteadily, Sandy walked back to the table where she had seen the book with charts of the solar system. She flipped through it for a minute before closing it with a deep rattling sigh. The large color drawings of Venus on the cover stripped the planet of its opaque and permanent cloud cover, making it look fragile, vulnerable.

"Her name's Malver. She was looking for me." Sandy Walker handed her driver's license to the librarian. "I want to check this book out for her."

The cheerless yellow halls of the hospital were thronged with doctors, nurses' aides, and uncomfortable visitors who carried roses and carnations. Sandy elbowed her way through the corridors, searching for the emergency room. It seemed it took an endless amount of time to explain to the harried woman behind the counter of the pediatric section who she wanted to see but finally she was directed down the hall to the Intensive Care Unit. The nurse stopped her.

"Where are you going?"

"Malver Lopez. Little girl who got run over. She came in here about an hour and a half ago."

"It's relatives only."

"I'm her sister," Sandy announced definitively. She straightened her shoulders as the nurse studied her. The nurse hesitated as though trying to decide if it was possible that such a blond could be the sister of the little Mexican girl.

"Number three. Five minutes," the nurse said, stepping out of the way and pointing down the hall.

Hastening past her, Sandy found the room, which was separated from the nurses' station by a large glass window. Flashing lights from machines that beeped and droned pierced the dimly lit room. Malver Lopez, laid out in the bed, eyes closed, was wrapped in white like an angel.

Silently, Sandy moved to the bed, where she stood staring down at Malver, whose breathing was so shallow it appeared to have stopped. Dots and lines of electricity jumped across the screens of the machines but Sandy put her fingers gently across Malver's slightly opened mouth until she was satisfied that she felt some air move between the girl's lips.

"Hi, Malver. I'm sorry I'm late. I guess you thought I wasn't coming."

There was a naugahyde chair, which Sandy drew up and leaned against as she waited for Malver to respond. Sandy studied the recurrent specks of light pulsating across the machines with the same curiosity with which she had studied the lights of the boats that passed in front of the beach at her apartment at night; she was trying to find some recognizable or comprehensible pattern. The lights continued to flicker on and off. Finally she sat in the chair and coughed as though calling for Malver's attention.

"I got you the book from the library. The astronomy one you like. See." Sandy held the book up for Malver Lopez, who was hooked to three glass bottles dripping clear liquids into her.

"It has really lovely pictures, doesn't it?" She opened the book. "I was looking at the one you were looking at of the solar system." She ran her hand lightly over the surface of Venus for emphasis.

"Malver, don't die." You are my sister.

"They're looking for your mother. I'm sure she'll be here soon, so you just relax." Sandy winced at her clumsiness. It was all a matter of circumstance and rough edges arranged by some architect of adversity.

"Look, they have a nice explanation in here about the beginning of the universe. The big bang theory. It makes sense. That it was all swirling gases before time began and that these whirling shapeless forms met, collided, mingled to form an essence of life, a combination of elements that evolved to create the oceans, the jungles and mountains, even this space that is Los Angeles, even Santa Monica Boulevard and the guy that hit you. It was all an accident."

The police were still looking for the car that had hit Malver. Nobody had gotten the license number, although several people were able to identify the make and model of the car and something about the driver. He was young and latin, possibly illegal and uninsured because this fit the stereotype. He was also scared out of his mind. Sandy felt as sorry for him as she did for Malver and herself.

"I used to read astronomy books, too, when I was a girl. I even wanted to be an astronomer. Have you thought about that? That would be a nice job, wouldn't it?" To stay up all night and chart the rotations of the earth.

220

Instead of staying up all night worrying that he's going to come into your room again.

"To know there is some kind of certainty in movement, to understand the established patterns."

There was a shiny circular vaccination scar on Malver's plump bicep, Sandy noticed as she settled back in the chair.

"Malver. I've known these things for a long time. I understand a lot about your life because it's like mine. I had trouble with my father also. I know what it's like to be afraid and angry. We survive these things. Just like I know you're going to survive this accident. I know it."

The room was silent except for the hums and beeps of the machines. Sandy realized her voice had dropped to a whisper. Perhaps she was not speaking at all, perhaps she was just communicating these thoughts to Malver Lopez with her eyes.

"Malver, here's something I bet you didn't know. In all of Mexico, the Mayan empire, the wheel was unknown. All the great pyramids were built without it. Until around Remojados in Veracruz the Totonacs conceptualized the wheel and its use. You know what they used it for? Not palaces, temples, or wars. For toys! They mounted little animal figures on wheels for their children. Ha, I like that, don't you?"

Malver's face was sunken and flat against the backdrop of white. Planes and angles melted. Sandy had no idea what time it was or how long she had been there.

"As soon as you get better, I'll go to court with your mother. She won't take him back after what he did. We'll show the judge your father's gone. You'd like that, wouldn't you? You'll be able to go home, but you have to get better."

I'll even take you myself, Malver. I'll get a bigger house.

Yes, you have to get better because as terrible as things seem, we have a responsibility, Malver. We have the responsibility to speak out. Our lives are like the great cities of the world that have been destroyed in sequences of cyclical and episodic lunacy. New buildings are constructed, new heritages established, but their infrastructures are invisible and respond to subtle manipulations only.

"You're strong and brave, Malver." She grasped the girl's hand, which lay limply at her side. "I know. I saw you in the kitchen with your father."

That's the difference between belief and knowledge. If you believe something it's because someone told you or you read it in a book; but when you know, it's a direct connection like the link between dreaming and waking.

And you, Malver, you were the one who knew what to do that day. You took care of us both, you got us out of the apartment. You were wonderful. You fought back. Yes, you have the innate knowledge of tyranny, structures, governments, and forms.

"You know these things without me telling you, without me saying the words."

But the words give us strength.

The glass bottles continued dripping clear liquids into Malver Lopez's arm. Each drop seemed to echo in the room.

"I know you understand, Malver. I can feel it. You don't have to say anything. This is like one of those old movies. Have you ever seen them on television, Malver? They say 'Just lift up your hand' or 'Just tap your finger once and I'll know you understand.' But we don't need that, do we? We understand each other. I know you understand."

Sandy leaned forward, peering at Malver Lopez, whose eyelashes grazed the bone ridge of her upper cheek.

"But could you just, just once, tap your finger so I'll be sure?

"No? Well, it's not important."

I know you understand. There are so many people who don't. They don't see these acute connections between women, our innate comprehension of the details of politics and torture, our understanding of food chains and survival and the struggle to hope.

Sandy peeked at her watch. It was almost seven. It was still hot. "I don't know where your mother is. She must be on her way here by now. I'm going to go out in the hall and ask about her. Pardon me. I'll be right back."

Sweating, her hair damp around her face, Sandy stepped outside to the hall and smoked a cigarette. She tried to recall what Malver Lopez's mother looked like. It was easy to forget these things. There were a lot of women. Sandy looked around for someone to ask or whose eyes might meet hers in a flicker of recognition. There was no one. Malver was hers now. She went back into the room and pulled the chair closer to the bed.

"I feel like you're the only person who can understand what I'm saying. It's not a unique vision that we've both seen. Our recognition of it and each other is significant. We're survivors, given the ability to make these connections. Some people say they have extrasensory perception, but that's not so. Perhaps everyone has it, if they would only use it. It's effective sensory perception. It's all in the constant interplay of cause and effect, waking and dreaming. It's the ability to understand that our lives are random, mysterious, disordered yet preordained. We are all living in parallel times so that the drought in Ethiopia becomes an earthquake in Ecuador becomes a flood in El Salvador becomes a windstorm in the valley of the moon."

Outside the breeze was rising and the hospital was adrift like a ship in the night. Santa Monica Boulevard separated itself from the floor of the valley and rolled on the back of gentle waves.

Sandy examined her hands. The skin was dry and rough. She held her hand in front of Malver's face.

"Here is the secret of the universe. Malver, there is no good, no evil. It's all an accident. That's the only importance of the saints and rituals. They help us to refine our suffering and lend it some dignity. They're a code for our desires and a panacea for our persistent longings. It's all very simple.

"We're all at some indefinite distance from the sun. There's no more significance for the stars in the sky than there is for the telephone booth where you called me from today. We like to think the stars represent some kind of order, a plan we can use to assure ourselves our lives are systematic. But that's not true.

"It's like a photograph, Malver. Let's say you stand in front of your apartment building and take a photo of the door. You may have come to believe the door always appears as it does in the photograph, but that's not so. All you have is an image of the way the door appeared for one single instant in time. Our lives are a collection of these images, some of them horrible, all of them haphazard. But you know these things. Why am I telling you? You understand me perfectly."

The wind pounded the walls, making them tremble, and the flashing lights seemed to blink more rapidly.

"What about our fathers, Malver?"

Where do they fit into all of this? Men without vision, without the least comprehension of their actions, who have deformed the meaning of sacrifice, who ravish distant countries and terrains of flesh; they know nothing. They disrupt lives of established patterns. They fail to perceive our delicate, intrinsic symmetry. They destroy hearts like they destroy roads or telegraph systems in times of war, breaking lines of communication. They bump through our lives like atoms, bouncing off whatever is near to them. They leave stains, dark red and purple, like birthmarks, upon their children. One looks for all the possible explanations. My father was a weak man. He was crazy. He was under great stress due to his work. He was unemployed. He had a poor relationship with his own mother. He was ashamed because he let another boy blow him while they were in the Cub Scouts. He lacked appropriate and supportive peer group relationships. His father abandoned him. He owed the government money. A tumor was growing in his brain. "Malver, it's all an accident. Consider how beautiful that is and how liberating."

Sandy ran her fingers through her hair and shook her head so that her hair flared out and flashed around her head. In the shadows projected on the wall she saw her father. The heat in the room was the weight of his arm or the dry wind of memory. The flickering tips of her hair stood out like naked electricity.

"We did nothing wrong. We were in the wrong place at the wrong time. Our profiles caught the light in a certain way. The moon was a certain distance from the earth. Our mothers were asleep, or away, standing in the kitchen over the stove and streams of steam clouded their eyes. The floor slanted in a certain way, the door opened, darkness was a tangible texture, sound took a form we could hold in our hands, and in those moments we were opened up and made privy to the secrets and mutations of the universe."

She gripped Malver's hand tightly. "We have earned the right to communicate with the core of life. The Mayans drowned their children. They threw them into sacred wells to talk with the gods who lived underwater. Now we can say to the very axis of our earth, 'Here, take me, right here, stab me, wound me. I am already open. Pour in all the secrets, the horror, the kidnappings and assassinations, the incest, the murder of women and children, men shot in the back before dawn, shot in the back of the head and left for dead in rotting jungles without

225

names, give me all the specific details of this misery that traps us dreaming or waking. I can take it. I know it all. You don't have to tell me.' It is as clear as moonlight, as water, as transparent as an insect's wing. I know the sorrow of the world and now I understand the lack of penitence. What is there to be sorry for? It was all an accident."

Sandy stood and patted the bed, rearranging the sheets so they were folded neatly across the girl's chest.

"Hush, don't say anything, Malver. We understand."

She was still standing by the bed when a short, black, bearded doctor with a clipboard came in to check Malver. He looked at Sandy with such curiosity that she felt compelled to explain that she was a friend of the family and would wait outside to talk to him. She stumbled slightly when she leaned over and kissed the girl's forehead. It was moist and warm.

"Good-night, Malver. Be well." Sandy winked as she closed the door quietly behind herself.

Sandy was standing in the hall leaning against the wall in her rumpled black linen dress, smoking another cigarette when the doctor emerged from the room.

"I don't know why her mother hasn't arrived yet," Sandy apologized. "But you can tell me how she is. Will she be out of the hospital soon?"

The doctor rubbed his beard. "That's hard to say."

"Why? What's wrong?" Something about his tone of voice worried her.

"She's had a massive head trauma. An epidural hematoma."

Sandy lifted her hands in confusion. "What's that?" she stammered.

"There's been a severe blow to the brain. I'm sorry. I can't give you any more information. I can only discuss the prognosis with the family." As the doctor turned away Sandy understood what the doctor had said. She had not gone immediately to Malver. Instead she was drunk, useless. Malver Lopez had permanent brain damage.

Sprawled on the black couch in the darkness of her living room, Sandy managed to pull off her hose. The drive home from the hospital had been hideous. She had broken her own rule about drinking while driving. It was her fault Malver Lopez was in the hospital. Forget what she had told the girl about accidents and coincidences. If she had only been able to love her, to love her unconditionally, and from the very beginning, this never would have happened.

It was black. Like fever, a terrible tropical fever brought on by the insane wind. She didn't want to turn on the lights. The blinds were open. From the hidden position where she was lying on the couch, she could look over the top of the house next door directly into the apartment of the middle-aged man who kept odd hours and lived alone. He was home now, moving sporadically through his living room in his underwear, moving to an indeterminate rhythm that was silenced by his closed windows. Swaying to a silent beat, he appeared to be afflicted with some strange disorder that caused him to jump suddenly and skittishly through space like an exorcist.

She stretched out the hose, alternately wrapping them around her neck, her ankles, her wrists, tying knots, pulling the soft filmy material tight. The bottle of brandy stood on the table. Sandy wondered where Manuel was. She wanted a fuck. A warm hand laid on her breast. Spanish syllables in a voice pressed against her ear. The dark skin against white. She thought about getting back in her car to drive down to Western to look for his apartment. Although she'd never been there, she would rather walk around all night under the stark white lights and flashing yellow signs with the black hookers and junkie queens than stay in the apartment by herself.

She rolled off the couch and crawled across the floor,

227

groping for her bag and the car keys she'd dropped when she came in. Stumbling over the large leather purse, she fell to one elbow but still couldn't find the keys. Realizing she was too drunk to drive anywhere, she lay back on the floor, her legs open. She pushed her right hand down into the black bikini pants and moved the hand frantically for a quick, hard orgasm. The kind for headaches, menstrual cramps, and sleep.

Panting and dissatisfied, she felt impotent. No energy flowed from her fingers. She was dry and brittle, close to broken. Her impulses were shortened, faulty. The skin of her hand was parched; it scraped and pulled.

She tried to hold an image of Manuel in her mind. Black leather jacket, mahogany skin, impossibly white teeth, large, carefully shaped lips, tongue buried in between her legs moving like a rare and dangerous snake, but the image fled. She tried a picture of Francisco Gomez in the dark, kneeling behind her like a dog, hands clasped hard and tight around her breasts, a gold carved medal of Saint Anthony bumping against his chest. She was sore and her hand was tired. He, too, was an indistinct shadow, careless, fleeting. The sound of a car door slamming, metal hitting metal, voices and footsteps erased him.

Sandy moved her hand more slowly, listening for the sound of the sea, trying to synchronize her hand to the movement of the water. She strained but heard nothing. Night was impenetrable. She held her finger beneath her nose and smelled the ocean, then jammed the finger deep into her vagina, moving it with desperation. Tried to feel her cervix, to grab the process within herself that would suddenly illuminate her. Hold her for a single instant in eternity that would have one clear meaning. Her finger hit bone, cartilage, hard tissue. The flesh resisted. She wanted to tear out the secret inner part and hold it up to look at, but she was hollow to the core.

The lights went out in the apartment across the way. She pretended that the man had been watching from his window, that he had seen everything, the hose stripped off, the black bikinis pushed down around her ankles and kicked off. She arched her back and bent her leg to reveal more. Turning her face to the window, she tried to pull the man in with her. Tried to remember how tall he was, what his body was like, the color of his hair, the shape of his nose. She pulled him in and touched herself. She pulled him closer and closer so that his face was above her, sour breath, chin grizzled with hair, hair grayer than she remembered, his long fingernails pulling at her, tearing her, eyes cold and scared and gray. It was her father's face and she fought to push him away before she came.

11

Sandy winced with a painful headache and shielded her eyes against the day as she woke on the floor. The room smelled rank. Black underpants dangled from the couch. A glass had been knocked over and had soaked the green cover of a volume of poetry by Ruben Darío. She pushed herself to one elbow. It was stifling and she was sweating. The horrible yellow-and-orange painting over the couch made her sicker. She had to get out of the apartment, although it was much too early to go to work.

Driving down Pacific past the beach houses and small apartments of Venice, Sandy tried to distract herself from the killing throb between her eyes by studying the usual chaotic collage of people on the street. There were dog walkers, jive talkers, joggers, panhandlers, psychotics, rollerskaters, and a few secretaries on their way to work. She was watching a woman who walked like she had advanced syphilis, feet disjointed, heel hitting the ground first, then the toes plopping down without control, when she saw a dark young man with a strong profile like Manuel's come out of a stucco bungalow.

Sandy hit the brakes hard. A very young white woman with flowing brown hair followed the man out into a tiny whitewashed patio that was draped with bougainvilleas and potted plants. She wrapped her arms around his neck and whispered something in his ear. It was Manuel.

Angrily, Sandy drove the car around the end of the block, parked, and walked back toward the house. She had been betrayed, deceived. Pots of geraniums surrounded the door. The enormous silver-and-black-onyx bracelet she wore jangled noisily as she pushed the gate to the patio. The world was indeed wicked. Manuel and the woman were standing beneath the cascading plants. They didn't even notice her. He had one hand on the woman's shoulder and with the other hand he was caressing her cheek as he spoke to her in a tone so intimate nothing else around them existed. This was the general formula for the kind of news story that appeared every several weeks in the Metro section of the paper.

She forced open the gate.

Half turning, Manuel's face froze and he dropped back so he was standing beside the woman with his arm still around her shoulder. The woman blinked sleepily and nuzzled his neck before lifting her eyes to meet Sandy's.

Sandy glared at her. The last news story she remembered reading had taken place in the parking lot of La Gaviota, an overpriced Mexican restaurant in west Los Angeles with abysmal food and a busy bar. A cocktail waitress who had been having an affair with one of the cooks, a young kid from Matamoros, had suddenly decided to call it quits and return to her husband. These stories had always seemed so pathetic, but as she looked at Manuel and then at the woman, she felt all of the instincts telling her to fight and claw.

"You son of a bitch! What are you doing here?" she exploded. *"¿Quién es esa puta?"*

"Stop it! She understands what you're saying. She speaks Spanish, too." Manuel nodded toward the woman.

"I don't give a fuck if she does understand me," Sandy

232

snarled in rapid-fire Spanish, planting both hands on her hips. "I hope she does."

The woman, who was petite and slender as well as hazel-eyed, inched closer to Manuel.

Sandy's voice rose hysterically as she addressed the woman directly and in English so there could be no mistake as to whether she understood. "He's a liar, a thief. He's been in jail."

Manuel hooted derisively. "Crazy old witch." He pulled the woman closer to him. He was bare chested, his skin taut and unblemished. "That old broad got me to go to her house. She said she'd pay me money to go to bed with her. I was out of work. Then she wouldn't pay me. Can you believe that? Look at her." He spat on the ground. "Who'd go to bed with her for free?"

Sandy threw her head back, tossing her hair. "Are you kidding? You begged for it. You'd never eaten pussy before. You wanted to be an anglo, so I taught you. I paid money to help you stay here."

"Loca," Manuel tapped his head with his finger. *"Absolutamente loca."*

"Do you believe anything he's saying?" Sandy screamed at the woman. "I'm telling you, be careful of him." Plaintively, she put her hand on the woman's scrawny upper arm. "He'll do the same thing to you."

Manuel grabbed Sandy with one hand. Clutching the neckline of her black linen dress, he pulled her off balance, breaking her loose grasp on the woman, who turned quickly and ran into the house.

Sandy's jaw trembled and she extended her chin slightly as she fought back tears. Everything was falling apart. All that was left was unseemly begging. "You said you loved me."

For an instant Manuel appeared stunned by what he had done, but then he twisted the material more firmly and pushed her again toward the gate before he let go of

233

her. "Get out of here." His lilting English voice almost made her laugh.

"You said you needed me."

"I don't know what you're talking about. You're insane."

"You stole from me!" What did he want? Another shirt? A color television?

"You couldn't give it away. Look at yourself. You're ugly, sick. You think you can work witchcraft, like my people, but you're just a *gabacha*."

"She practices witchcraft," Manuel called after the woman who was hiding behind the screen door. "She believes she has some power to affect other people's lives. Insane." He turned abruptly and started to walk away.

"Manuel," Sandy dropped her voice entreatingly as she tried to smooth the bodice of the wrinkled dress. "I was good to you."

He shook his head, angrily, without looking at her. "Are you going to start with the money again? You think just because I'm some wetback you can treat me any way you want, that you can fuck around on me, that you can suck whatever you want out of me because you feel empty? Forget it. You can't buy love, and if you could, it would cost more than *chingado* fifteen hundred bucks." He said "bucks" hesitatingly. It was an expression he still wasn't used to.

"Why are you doing this?"

"You wanted to use me. Just like you want to use those fucking glass candles and little bottles of magic oil. You think I don't know what those are. They're supposed to keep away the darkness. There you are, lighting your candles with those cracked old hands that shake in the morning."

Sandy dropped her eyes to look at her hands, which were quivering.

"Sandy," he paused, his voice much softer, almost car-ing. "About the money, I haven't decided yet if I'll show up in court. If that's the worst thing that happens to you, you're lucky." She could hear the woman giggle as he closed the door.

Alone in the patio, the sun beating down, Sandy felt old, hung over, and frightened of being alone. At this point in the typical news story, someone would be dead or at least shot in the stomach. There would be some blood on the pavement. Sandy took one last look around the patio. She noticed how withered the potted plants were in the heat, that they were held upright by decaying strings lashed to plastic stakes. The geraniums were turning yellow and poisoning the air with a smell like crushed pepper. It was actually quite a squalid little place and devoid of charm. She straightened her back and walked with as much dignity as possible back to her car.

The steering wheel was hot, it burned her hands. The whole city was burning. Nauseous greens, dying trees, sick pink cloying flowers clinging to shabby sagging frame buildings, all impaled and irradiated by the awful sun. She wanted to find a cool spot. The car turned on Vermont seemingly of its own volition and headed through Koreatown's northern boundary toward Seventh Street and *Botanica La Ayuda*.

As she parked the car midway between the Grove Hotel and the *botanica*, Jesus Velaria was standing in his bedroom still half asleep in a pair of off-white boxer shorts that drooped slightly around his hips. He had lost weight since his wife had been gone, not more than four or five pounds, but since he was already thin, it was enough to make his stomach appear more chiseled and cast a hollow under his cheekbones. The sheets lay in a tangled pile at the foot of the bed where he had kicked them during the night. A reproduction of the Aztec calendar hung above the bed. The room was sparsely furnished. During the last several days, he had removed most of his wife's things. He put her cosmetics in a box, the professional but badly lit photograph of her parents in the bottom drawer of the dresser. Only her clothes in the closet remained, creating a jumble of red, green, yellow, and orange. He was peripherally aware of these colors; it was like a jungle growing in the corner of the room. For an instant he remembered a trip he'd made to Acapulco when he was twenty. The palm trees and tropical flowers danced constantly in the breeze, which was soft and humid and reeked of sex. He'd been there only three days and with his mother's older brother, Roberto. Jesus Velaria stared groggily at the alarm clock on the dresser and tried to remember what day it was. Buy some more tortillas, he thought, some more eggs, milk, oranges, and beans. It is not true time has stopped, he told himself. He laced his fingers and stretched his arms over his head before turning and going into the next room.

The black metal bars in front of the *botanica* were latched shut. A CLOSED sign hung on the door. Sandy reached through the gate and tapped loudly on the glass center pane of the door. She felt people in passing cars looking at her, a *güera* in a wrinkled black linen dress. They probably thought she was an investigator for the county or a tax collector. She turned her back and kept knocking until the young woman with long black hair answered.

The door opened slightly and the woman, who was wearing a scarlet-colored dressing gown, leaned into the door, filling the space so Sandy couldn't see in the *botanica*.

"We're not open yet. It's too early. You'll have to come back later."

"I need to see you now." Sandy tried to see the

woman's face more clearly, but it was hidden in shadows. "I have to talk with you."

"That's impossible. We have regular hours of business."

Sandy placed her hand on the door. "I can't wait that long."

A cat poked its head curiously around the woman's legs and looked at Sandy. It hissed, raising its back, and walked away. The woman laughed.

"Maybe you do have some special problem that merits consideration." She dropped the chain lock and jerked the door, which stuck, making the bells tinkle. Then she bent down and unlocked the grate between them, pushing it back against the wall. With one hand she indicated Sandy should enter the *botanica*.

A narrow path of light followed them through the door. The room was pitch black except for the flames of hundreds of candles flickering within glass jars. The walls receded in irregular shapes as the woman shut the door.

Sandy gestured at the candles surrounding them. "What's good for a broken heart?"

The woman didn't appear startled by this question, merely sleepy-eyed and perhaps a little bit bored.

"Carnation, a hot bath, a low-cut dress, a couple of drinks, a beckoning look in your eyes, a 'Say mister, have you got a light.' "

She waved dismissively so that her silver bracelets and medallions jingled. "But you already know these things. You don't have a broken heart."

"I do. Just this morning I saw . . ."

"So your lover has left you. Divorce and desertion are frequent." The young woman barely stifled a yawn. "Is that any reason for you to come banging on the door?"

Sandy nodded her head miserably. The woman with Manuel was at least ten years younger than she was.

The woman hadn't moved. She stood with her head

237

crooked slightly to one side and her lips pursed. "That is not the reason. You're looking for something else. You've been here before, haven't you?"

Sighing, Sandy walked over to the counter that held the bottles of oil such as the woman had sold her; apologetically she dusted her hand over the glass top. "I think you made a mistake and gave me the wrong thing the last time I was here. My life's getting worse instead of better."

Folding her arms loosely across her chest, the woman smiled. "You think I should give you some kind of refund or say that I've worked a faulty charm? That I have given you an incorrect accounting of your life?" She laughed again so loudly that the cat came back into the room to look at her. "No, I'm afraid it doesn't work that way."

"I came here for protection and guidance," Sandy pleaded hoarsely. "I expected that you would instruct me."

The woman sauntered over to the counter and took a pack of cigarettes from the pocket of her gown. She shook one out, put it between her lips, then offered one to Sandy. A match illuminated the space between them for a second before the woman lit her cigarette. Reaching under the counter, she pulled out a bottle of cheap Canadian whiskey and two small smudgy glasses.

"So you want me to instruct you. To share with you what I have learned from this *botanica*. I don't know if I have anything to teach anyone. I have a certain insight, an eye for color, and a steady hand. Perhaps that's the only thing I can tell you. But that wouldn't be enough, would it?"

She poured a neat shot into each glass, then pushed one glass toward Sandy. The woman picked up her glass, tilted it, muttered, *"Salud,"* and drank off half an inch of whiskey. She smacked her lips delicately as she set the glass down. "You imagine that I have some extraordinary gifts, that I work here with ghosts and dwarfs, and that at night, instead of falling asleep in front of the television, that I sail away on a raft of snakes, is that it?

"Still," she paused modestly, "I do have a certain success with a limited range of problems, the ordinary adversities of life in times beset by wars. There are still some things that are simple. For example, adultery, that is very simple."

From a cigar box that had been painted white the woman extracted a small mirror, some red stones, and a broken watch, which she arranged on the counter. "I know the intricacies of making love charms. Of casting wax images of adulterous spouses. The mixtures of ambergris, aloes wood, myrtle, and musk."

She withdrew a tube of fiery red lipstick from the other pocket of her dressing gown and picked up the mirror. Pouting slightly, then relaxing her lips, she drew an outline. "If you want him to love you, forget about clarity and truth. There is virtue in vanity and vice. Wear a necklace of polished teeth and say they are stars you have plucked from the sky. Wrap strings of bone objects around your hips. Paint your nails with red sandalwood, rose, and pigeon's blood. Bind a rope of hair and flowers around your ankle."

Satisfied, the woman blotted her lips and cleaned a trace of lipstick off her teeth. "Ignore the symbols of wind and water, the intricate scrolls of unknown meaning. It's very simple," she said, screwing the top back on the lipstick, "he loves the woman who goes down on him until her lips bleed."

The woman raised her eyebrows at Sandy, who was still clutching her drink in both hands. "You see the beauty of adultery? There are only two choices. The spouse can choose to kill or forget."

"That's elemental, but what about me?" Sandy snapped.

An enigmatic, though not impolite, half smile appeared

239

on the woman's face. The saints peered down from the shelves. Quivering light from the glass candles played across plaster statues of bleeding Christs and forlorn Marys.

"All I do is hand you the bottle of oil." The timbre of the woman's voice changed, as though she were speaking from far away. "It had been chosen for you. We simply play our parts in history."

Sandy saw her father's arm moving around the back of the chair in the darkened movie auditorium, his shadow falling across the page of the book she was reading, felt his breath against her cheek. "What is our responsibility to the past?"

"To recreate it so it becomes a guide to transform the future."

"That's why I came to you." Sandy spoke so excitedly her words tumbled over each other; she cleared her throat and emptied her glass. "That's why you're here, isn't it? To help in the selection of the proper saint, a candle of the correct color, the appropriate scent for attracting good luck or prosperity or a virile husband?"

"The saints are limited, defective. Why do you think there are so many of them?"

She had expected some better answers. It was, after all, a city settled by Mayan princes and the sons and daughters of wizards. Dejectedly, Sandy helped herself to the bottle and poured another drink. "Aren't there any new histories to be written?"

The woman scooped the stones and trinkets that lay on the counter back into the box and placed it neatly under the shelf. "We have barely learned rudimentary stone structure or the art of survival with grace. All movement is slow. However, we are a fortunate generation and there are unexpected wonders."

With the glass poised at her lips, Sandy waited for the wishes of the gods to become apparent either in omens or

240

epileptic spasms. Culture and faith were usually spread by force. But all she noticed was the unpleasant aftertaste of cheap booze and the overwhelming heat that was seeping into the room.

"Our lives are desperate," the woman continued without looking at Sandy; she had noticed a small stain on the glass counter and was rubbing at it with the sleeve of her robe. "Our families are separated, many of them dead. Our language mutated. We have lost the rhythm of the seasons. Only the insane among us feel the pull of the moon. We are all invisible in our own lives and living on borrowed time. Our heads are full of terrible thoughts and our hearts are empty. Here, take this statue and examine it."

She searched under the counter again and withdrew a small, painted, plaster statue. It was a man with brown hair and a beard who was wearing a green robe with silver stars so that it looked like he had been decorated for riding with a motorcycle gang. His right hand was clasped upon his breast and he had long thin fingers.

"Is this Joseph?"

"I've told you, it doesn't matter. They are all the same. Their names are unimportant. Inspect him. Tell me what you see."

Turning the statue several times, Sandy gently touched the slender hands and delicate feet. The green robe ended in molded folds around the ankles. The pale face was monotonously placid. His eyes were brown. Sandy spoke at last. "This must be the saint who represents stoicism, solidity. The patron of waiting. He is impassive and appears deaf to any appeal. He looks rather melancholy. It is ordinary in the execution. The stars are a nice touch, though."

"Anything else?"

Replacing the statue on the glass counter, Sandy shook her head in confusion. The woman picked up the statue, turned it upside down, and showed the bottom of the feet to Sandy. "You see, 'Made in the Philippines.' None of it is real. It is impossible to turn away from a preordained fate."

The unexpected scent of lemon and sage filled the room as Sandy paced back and forth, stopping to read invocations printed on some of the glass candles. Good luck. Health. Prosperity. Success. A red candle embossed with wedding rings and garlands of roses burned bright.

"It's all so terrible. Malver Lopez, the hospital, Nadra Taylor. If only Manuel hadn't left. . . ."

"He's not the problem. He is only a manifestation of the problem. Another mistake along the way. He was a gigolo. You got your money's worth, so what are you complaining about?"

"A gigolo?" His hot breath, his fingers laced around her neck. The long nights, torpid breezes. "You mean he planned the whole thing to get money from me?" Sandy buried her face in her hands.

"I don't know if it was all premeditated. Probably not. He was just learning. But what could he do? You have a frozen heart and an open wallet."

Sandy wheeled away from the counter in disgust, a deep, ugly wrinkle creasing her forehead. "That's the answer? I had it coming? Jesus, I don't believe this. I thought you were supposed to be able to help people with your charms." Infuriated, she hurried toward the door.

The woman's rich throaty laughter stopped her. "Okay, you want the whole routine? You think that would make you feel better?"

"Forget it. I'm . . ." When Sandy turned back to look at the woman, the scarlet robe had fallen away and she was dressed in the black skirt and white blouse Sandy had first seen her in. The room grew dark again. The woman's skin glowed, her outline radiant in the candlelight that came from behind her as she drew back the floral curtain

242

dividing the main room from the area marked "Consultations." Stepping aside, she motioned for Sandy.

It was a small space about the size of a clothes closet. Some of Sandy's clients had to use spaces like this for their children to sleep in. Occasionally a child suffocated to death during the night. But here there were two tiny black chairs and between them a card table draped with a shiny, lime-green piece of cloth with fringe around the edges. The two women sat in the chairs facing each other. Sandy pulled her hair back nervously and glanced at the bare walls.

The woman's features hardened into an impenetrable mask. She took Sandy's right hand, laid it up on the table, and studied it for a long time with great deliberation. Carefully, she touched several of the smaller lines.

"The planets do not shift positions relative to one another but remain fixed in place for generations. Sorrow is your north star. Venus is a junkie moaning on her knees in a night of falling asteroids and flailing comets. You must find your destiny leaping across galaxies, across centuries, across all the borders, heaven and hell, north and south, daughter of the wind, sister of blood, child of the broken heart." As the woman increased the pressure of her grip, prickling electricity seared Sandy's wrist.

Sandy nodded her head once as though some type of assent was called for on her part. Her hand was sweating. She didn't understand. The woman sensed this and continued speaking.

"Your past is a source of great pain and anger for you. You are surrounded by people and things that remind you of that past. You are powerless to help them. You will do one of two things, you will destroy that vision of the past or it will destroy you. I cannot tell you what will happen."

Startled, Sandy pulled back. The woman released her

243

grasp until only her fingertips curled around Sandy's wrist and rested gently over her pulse.

With her eyes closed, the woman chanted in an eerie, high, yet still sonorous, voice, *"All moons, all years, all days, all winds reach their completion and pass away. So does all blood reach its place of quiet."*

Wind and blood reverberated, the hot wind swept through the room, pulling on their dresses, blowing their hair. It was the beginning of the Mayan story of creation, which also foretold the end of the world.

Sandy jerked her hand off the table and out of the woman's loose fingers. The woman remained with her eyes closed, her breathing heavy and regular even when Sandy stood up, bumping the table with her knees. Sandy stumbled out of the claustrophobic confines of the woman's clutches and through the raging fires of the *botanica,* where glass candles seemed to howl and sing.

"Isn't that what you wanted? That's what you said you wanted." The woman was standing in the archway holding the curtain out of the way with one hand. The lights behind her had been extinguished and the cigarette she was smoking, a mere point of light, was the only remaining distinguishable feature in the darkness enveloping her.

"You had no reason to come here. You know the future as well as I do. You wanted me to deny it."

Tears ran down Sandy's face, then stained her breast as she hung her head. It was all as she had feared.

"You would never have believed me anyway," added the woman. She crossed the room to place her arm around Sandy's shoulders. She stroked Sandy's hair, which was gold and silver in the flickering light.

Comforted by this gesture, Sandy sniffed back the tears. She wondered if this was the same woman Malver Lopez had told her about. "How did you get here?"

"Los Angeles?" the woman exclaimed in amusement. "I was born here."

"No, here. *La Ayuda*. You're Consuela, aren't you?"

The muscles around the woman's mouth tensed, her eyes narrowed and turned orange for an instant before she smiled reassuringly. "Consuela? Who is she?" Dropping her arm from Sandy's shoulder, the woman laughed. "I studied psychology for two years at LA City College and then I decided to open this *botanica*."

Sandy tried to wipe at her face with the sleeve of her dress. "So here you are practicing without a license. That's funny."

The laughter faded from the woman's face. She looked stern. "No, I opened this *botanica* because I didn't want to fuck with people's heads. Psychotherapy is art for those with limited imagination. Here people come knowing what they want, what they believe in. They confirm it with the trinkets I sell."

"So this is all meaningless," Sandy sighed with great relief.

The woman frowned and shook her head. "Perhaps I was mistaken about you. You understand less than I believed. No, I am not a psychologist. I have no license. I don't need one. You have your license, your education. What are they worth? Law school, and you come here to ask me what to do with your life. I tell you and you run away. Perhaps that is best, for there is really only one thing I can tell you with any certainty, but I doubt you believe it."

The woman folded her arms across her chest and looked at Sandy for a long time as though debating with herself whether to say any more.

"The next one who comes to you, to love you, love him in return. It is the only thing that will save you. Your father loved you. He did the best he could."

Sandy turned away in disgust. The air was stale and unbearable. Breathing unevenly, she jerked the front door open and stepped out. The sun blinded her. It was then

245

she realized she had never told the woman she was a lawyer. Excitedly she turned back into the room but it was completely dark.

The sun continued moving in a methodical way across the sky above Varrio Loco Nuevo. Upstairs, across the street from the *botanica*, Jesus Velaria was heating some leftover coffee in a blue enamel pot on the stove. Soledad sat on the floor fidgeting and pulling at the hem of her overalls. The fidgeting was beginning to bother him.

He knelt on the floor to tie his daughter's shoes. She kicked so hard that he had to hold each foot between his knees. Rather wearily, he got to his feet and took the coffee off the back burner. He hadn't been sleeping well. The only thing he remembered about his dreams was that they were full of movement. He was also starting to spend a lot of time staring at patterns on walls and daydreaming. He thought about how different life was on this side of the border. The secrecy. His sheer amazement that buildings, entire blocks and streets of pulsating life could seemingly be lost in the middle of a city. He thought about politics, things he had done when he was a boy, about sex. He thought about the sudden and inexplicable disappearance of his wife. All over the world people were disappearing. Yes, all over the world people were disappearing only to resurface in another town, another country, another neighborhood, with a new driver's license, or social security number, a new husband or wife. It was amazing that everything lost could be found. Even *los desaparecidos* who disappeared in El Salvador or Chile or Guatemala resurfaced and lived again in the spirit of those who survived them. *Los muertos que nunca mueren*. The sun, which broke through the open window where a peach-colored shirt hung drying, played across his body. His chest glistened as he finished wiping off the counter. Perhaps it was as simple as finding another woman, one who understood him, who spoke the same language he did—not necessarily Spanish but that language of the soul. He slipped the shirt from the hanger and put it on, feeling less like an abandoned husband than a man who was being given a second chance.

Whistling, Jesus Velaria scooped his daughter up in his arms and carried her down the hall to the apartment of Señora Cruz. Anxiously, the baby-sitter opened the door, her heavy face set in a scowl, and took Soledad from him so quickly that he barely had time to glimpse the dark, old-fashioned furniture with its careful lace doilies. Soledad began to cry. The old woman barely glanced at Jesus Velaria. She locked the door behind her and shuffled into the living room with the girl.

Yes, he was late again, thought Señora Cruz, peeking out the window to watch him run to the corner where his friends picked him up each morning.

"Look, see. *Papi, papi,*" she said absentmindedly to the girl as she scrutinized Jesus Velaria climbing into the back seat of a freshly painted red car occupied by three boisterous men. Crazy *cholos*. Sniffing disapprovingly, she turned to the kitchen to fix the little girl's breakfast. Men did not know how to cook.

Señora Cruz was round-shouldered with massive breasts that hung nearly to her waist and jiggled as she beat an egg in a bowl. Her attention was on Soledad, who was propped in front of the television in the living room. The girl seemed distant, distracted. She wasn't watching the cartoons. Señora Cruz pursed her lips slightly in dissatisfaction. Soledad knew what the cartoon characters were saying. She had a vocabulary of a hundred words. Señora Cruz kept a list of new words on a piece of paper in the top drawer of a wood cabinet in the living room. At least a hundred words, maybe more. She had come to think of Soledad as her own granddaughter. Not that she

247

would consider Soledad's parents as her children. No. They were not good people. What kind of mother would go off and leave her child? Señora Cruz didn't for a minute believe the story that the woman had gone to visit her mother, who was ill. No daughter would go to visit her sick mother without a suitcase or dressed in a low-cut dress and a pair of flashy red high heels.

No, she was certain Jesus Velaria had done something so terrible that his wife had to leave him. True, she hadn't heard the sound of any fights coming from behind their door, but there are many ways that men and women can fight—with a look, with a shoulder turned away in bed, with a dish carelessly placed on the table. She was certain it was Jesus Velaria's fault. A woman knew instinctively no man that good-looking could be trusted. He was probably sleeping with women all over the *Varrio* and his wife had found out. Maybe he'd brought some social disease home with him. Señora Cruz grimaced and looked distastefully at the runny egg that she scraped onto a plate.

She chopped the egg briskly with a fork, her gray head bowed. It was very strange the mother had not come back even once to see the girl. Señora Cruz had been expecting that she would knock quietly on the door and slip into the apartment just to hold the baby in her arms. Yes, Jesus Velaria had done something so terrible and Soledad's mother was so frightened that she didn't dare to come to the apartment building.

What act could he have committed that was so brutal or crazy or immoral that it had driven his wife away? Certainly, it could have been another woman, but for that there are dishes thrown, weeks without sex, a stay of a night or two with a girlfriend. Maybe he took drugs. A heroin addict. Señora Cruz rejected that idea reluctantly after some further consideration. He did manage to get to work every day. She had only known one time when he hadn't returned home at the usual hour but that was months ago. Maybe like Lupe, her first husband, he wasn't bringing all his money home from work; he was spending it on booze or on the horses or card games. Señora Cruz frowned as she examined her fat wrinkled hands for a moment, remembering her first husband, Lupe, and the way he would study a racing form for names that had seven letters or referred to astrological symbols, then she wiped her hands on the white apron and untied it from her thick middle. Lupe was a bum, a thief. Her second husband, good riddance, had been no better. All men were dogs who wanted only one thing. She took the plate into the living room. She had to admit she had frequently seen Jesus Velaria carrying bags of groceries and toys up the stairs. He did seem to love the baby. For each reason Señora Cruz reluctantly found an answer.

Soledad pushed the fork away and began to cry. As Señora Cruz picked up the baby, she lost count of the reasons the mother could have had for abandoning the child. Automatically, she felt the baby's bottom, which appeared dry and solid. The baby continued crying, so she laid her down on the couch to see if a change was necessary. She pulled open the row of snaps that ran up each side of the baby's soft, fat, inner leg and into the crotch. Unpinning the diaper, she peered into it. It was dry. She patted on some powder and that caused the baby to wail with renewed shrillness. Señora Cruz laid her hand on the child's abdomen and then on her forehead. It seemed warmer than usual.

"Quiet, quiet little princess," she cooed as she started to fasten the diapers. The crying continued. Señora Cruz felt a nudge of trepidation like the tremor of leaves before a storm. "Now, now little rabbit, everything is all right." Her heart is breaking because her mother left her. Her father is feeding her terrible food that has made her sick.

Señora Cruz clicked her tongue with annoyance; she would have to speak to him about that.

She picked the baby up and held her. She had held many babies. Usually it was easy to determine why they were crying. The little girl's voice weakened and she stopped crying.

"That's better. You're all right now, aren't you, princess?" Señora Cruz gurgled. Gently, she laid Soledad back on the couch. The child howled again. Frustrated, the woman shook out more powder, which sprinkled across the bosom and skirt of her black dress.

"What's wrong, *mi corazón?* Does it hurt you?" Señora Cruz scowled again; gingerly she placed her fingers on the little girl's vagina, which she spread open. It was red and agitated. The baby cried louder than before. Señora Cruz had a sudden thought so disgusting it caused her to shudder. She examined the snaps on the overalls. Maybe they had pressed into the girl's delicate skin. Señora Cruz's heart began to palpitate erratically. Perhaps it was diaper rash she hadn't noticed. Impossible. She gave her better care than her mother ever had. Señora Cruz knew what it had to be. *"¿Papi, papi?"*

The baby screamed.

¡Madre de díos! It was as clear as the day outside. Señora Cruz crossed herself. Didn't the mother know what he had been doing? Had he threatened her? Bastard. Pervert. The mother should have killed him.

Señora Cruz had never called the police. In the small town where she was born there were uncles and cousins, respected heads of family, the priest who recognized each person's voice when he heard it in the dark confessional, but here there was no one she could go to. This building, this corner, the entire *Varrio* were all in flux. They came from everywhere, from Morelia in Mexico, Usulután in El Salvador, the mountains of Guatemala, the plains of Honduras. There was no one in the neighborhood who held a sufficient position of authority to confront Jesus Velaria. It was questionable, she brooded, whether there were any standards at all which could be relied upon. Here, they had all arrived as refugees. They came and went. She massaged her fat hands. We are all desperate in our own lives; between children, between jobs, between countries, cut off from all usual points of reference and adrift in the squalid wreckage called Los Angeles.

Would they have someone to speak to her in Spanish? Her throat was dry. She knew no words in English that could convey the horror and revulsion she felt overwhelming her. Pushing herself up from the couch, she moved quickly to the telephone and dialed. Would they ask her if she was legal? But the operator answered before she had time to give it any more thought. Señora Beatriz Cruz Garcia took a deep breath and looked across the street at *Botanica La Ayuda*. She would have to buy a candle in the afternoon.

12

Confused women. Endless cigarettes. Bad coffee in paper cups. Sudden trips to the bathroom for nips of brandy. Sandy had arrived perspiring and late to court, the incense from the *botanica* still clinging to her hair. There were women who locked their children in tiny apartments without food while they went to job interviews for which they were found unskilled, overweight, or simply too old. Women who drank away the afternoons and nights in bad bars while they waited for their luck to change. Women whose listless occasional lovers fondled the private parts of minors well below the age of consent. Women who couldn't decide whether to let the lover or the children go.

Women blind with drugs and grief, mad with indecision. Women with cheap perfume and blue eyeshadow. Women who painted their nails and then tore off the polish. There were young women who were almost used up. Women of indeterminate age and bad habits. Women with rigid lines around the eyes and a certain slackness about the mouth. Women with worthless wedding rings and no money. Women who carried immense purses and scraps of paper recording their personal histories.

Children. Their children were here. Stabbed, mutilated, born with drug withdrawal, scarred from beatings, elaborate tattoos of red raised lines wrapped around their backs and shoulders. Children laid face down, buttocks forced apart repeatedly, carelessly ripped open by their fathers, stepfathers, grandfathers, brothers, uncles, cousins, school janitors, playground directors, ministers, traveling salesmen, and passing strangers. Children who stared into space, who spoke to no one, banging their heads against walls and tables, inventing strange languages to express themselves with alphabets of pain.

But Sandy had stopped listening to all of this. Raw, open, receptive, she was tuned into a larger voice from somewhere in the air. Like the bandit Mexican radio stations a hundred and fifty thousand watts south of the border. It said this is Los Angeles. The mountains are floating. The light will be a rain of mirrors. What is happening to you is more than a vitamin deficiency or an unnatural fever. It is more than blood, phlegm, or yellow bile. It is beyond Jupiter, past the nightside of Mercury, caught in the vortex of stellar explosions. It is true that the symbols of wind and water mean nothing. Bleeding, laxatives, a purifying diet are of no use. You are wearing a mask of human skin.

Sandy turned, pale and sweating, from a woman who was describing a complicated chain of events involving a Saturday night, a bottle of bourbon, two men, the police, possibly a knife, and her missing children. Sandy thought she was going to be sick. Pushing roughly past the woman, she ran into the bathroom.

Locking herself in the last stall, she fell to her knees on the tile floor and leaned retching into the toilet. Gasping and coughing, she laid her cheek against the cool plastic and tried to control her breathing. The walls, vivid with thick black writing, proclaimed Mousie, La Payasa, and Sad Eyes. Struck across the names of the Happy Valley girls a newer, bolder hand erased them, declaring "NO MÁS PUTAS." As she swayed weakly on her knees, she observed low on the wall, in extremely tiny but neat letters, a piece

254

of graffiti she had never noticed before. *"If only I could be turned to stone or wood rather than suffer the future. But what can I do except await that which has been predicted."* The words of Montezuma before the conquest.

Wiping off her face, Sandy went out to the woman who had been talking to her. The woman started to say something more, some further amplification on the nature of her personal devastation, but Sandy stopped her. "Tell the judge anything, any goddamn thing you can think of. I'm going home."

Slumped on the shiny black couch, her jacket tossed over the edge, Sandy had pulled up her black linen dress and was concentrating on balancing a glass of Greek brandy on her knee. A well-worn book of photographs of the pyramids of Uxmal lay open beside her. She had lost track of time. The historians were immoral, obscene. And probably drunk, too, she thought. They wasted their time chronicling exquisite burials. It was simpler than that. The ancient men and women and anthropomorphic gods knew the world was in danger of annihilation so they sacrificed themselves to keep the universe from final destruction. They leaped, lucid and unfettered, from the tops of stone structures of incredibly intricate geometric designs. They spread themselves open and waiting across monumental slabs cut from the earth. At Uxmal, women lived the last year of their lives in a brothel adjoining the altars in the ultimate connection of sex and blood, of falling from great heights, inverted among the stars and random planets, limbs rolling, splayed, naked across the panorama of the vast forgiving night.

A knock on the door interrupted. Sandy got to her feet automatically, fluffing her hair and adjusting her skirt. Francisco Gomez stood against the crimson evening with his sports coat slung over his shoulder.

She was relieved to see him, anybody. She wanted to be impaled. Hard sex like a bloodletting. She wanted to say

255

file your teeth. Paint them black. Bite through my throat. Peel back this thin layer of white skin.

Instead, she moved away and leaned against the wall, watching while he prowled around the room as though checking to see that everything was in its usual place. Apparently satisfied, Francisco Gomez stopped next to her and pinched her cheek. "So how have you been? You look fine."

"*Sí, muy bien.* Just great." Her laugh was loud, shrill.

He stepped back, folding his jacket and laying it carefully across the old chair she had upholstered the year before with canvas. He wore a pale beige shirt with short sleeves. She had forgotten his arms were so large and well muscled.

Sandy sank down on the couch again, resting her head against the wall as she watched him. Her knees parted so that the thin linen pulled against her thighs. "Fuck me."

Francisco Gomez gave her a reproachful look, then shook his head as if he hadn't heard correctly. He paced around the living room again, stopping to touch a picture on a bookshelf. "What's this weird picture?"

It was a serenely blue archangel surrounded by clouds of silver. With gold rays emanating from her hands, she guided two small children across a bridge above a rushing stream. Sandy had bought it a few months ago in the basement of the Grand Central Market on Broadway and Second. At the time it amused her.

"It's nothing," she mumbled. "Just something that reminded me of work." She patted the couch for him to come sit beside her.

"What do you want to be reminded of your work for?" He sounded annoyed but he sat down next to her and put his arm along the back of the couch. "It's dirty business. Forget it."

"Is that what you do?" Sandy sat up sharply. The women with black eyes, eyes red from weeping and angel

dust, exhausted from childbirth, from being born poor
and female, from running from men with quick tempers
and qualms about imperfection. These horrible, pitiful
men hunched over small scarred tables in dimly lit rooms,
faces buried in their hands, weeping as they confessed,
hunched over a girl's body in a dark . . .

"Sure I do," he joked. "I have a clear conscience."

"How?" she exploded. "You were supposed to find a
missing little girl and what happens? By the time you get
there somebody's raped her and she's stone-cold dead."

Francisco Gomez started to stand up. "I think I should
leave."

I'm scared.

God. I want another drink. "I'm sorry. I'm just so
. . ." She put her hand on his chest and grabbed the open
collar of his shirt. Her fingernails grazed his throat as she
cuddled up to him. "I don't want to be alone anymore.

"Tell me about your family, your past," she pleaded.
You must have one. Solid. Unfragmented. Roots. Connections. Or have we all been cut loose, adrift in this
terrifying desert and tossed about by the maddening
wind?

He lifted his hand laconically, it fell heavily back on the
couch. She wondered if he'd noticed the bottle on the
table. She should have hidden it. "There's not much to
tell," he said. "They live out in Pico Rivera. The old man
had a heart attack last year. My mother just stays at home.
My brothers are married and work. I'm the youngest."
Having laid out these salient details, he stopped abruptly.

"I want to know where your family came from," she
prodded.

"Here." His lips tightened in a thin line. He'd probably
been asked questions like this at the Police Academy.

"Before that," Sandy persisted. Patterns and contours
were important. The topography of the soul.

"Somewhere in Sinaloa, I think."

He acted like these questions were insulting. As though they implied he was being looked down on. "Culiacán?"

"I don't know. I don't remember the name of the place."

"Don't you have any relatives there?"

Francisco Gomez shrugged impatiently. "I don't know. I doubt it."

"Aren't you curious?" Three thousand years of history. The development of dance. The invention of ceramics. The mastery of mathematics. And he acted as if he were ashamed of it. "Don't you want to go there someday?"

"What for?" he snapped. "I'd rather go to Puerto Vallarta, lie on the beach, soak up some rays."

The beginning of agriculture. The establishment of religion. The inception of government. He thought it meant they let him on the police force because he was a minority. "Is your family part Indio?"

"Spanish," he answered tersely.

The magnificent photographs of Uxmal that were between them fell to the floor.

The slaughter of the Aztec people. A time of violence and confusion. The destruction of astronomy. The erasure of language. Hundreds of thousands killed for the crimes of blasphemy, sodomy, the use of peyote and the practice of astrology. They died suddenly of smallpox introduced by the Spanish. Of venereal diseases. In the fires of their burning cities. Hundreds of thousands died uttering blood testaments and phenomenal curses.

"That's impossible," she argued. Manipulation of the past was dangerous. Aphasia of one's own history, deadly. "You must feel some connection to your past."

"The only connection I feel is to my badge."

"Why do you hate your people?" Sandy whispered, shaking her head.

He caught her by the chin, his fingers pressing hard into her cheeks, her mouth open and distorted. "You like

258

to fuck Mexicans; is that your trip? Does it make you feel superior?" With his other hand he tore at her underpants, ripping the purple silk, exposing the triangle of light-brown hair. "You want me to fuck you?" He jerked her face roughly, making her nod.

"*Puta,*" he swore.

Francisco Gomez leaned back, pulling Sandy toward him until her face was above his. She reeked of alcohol. "Don't you ever think you can tell me who or what I am." He slammed her face against the back of the couch. "I've never been with a whore and I'm not going to start now. I've never been drunk. There aren't any drunks in my family. And I'm not an Indian. Do we understand each other now?"

He released his grip. Her long blond hair fell across her mute face. Unsteadily, she got to her feet and went into the bathroom.

Leaning against the sink, she peered into the mirror, studying the red marks on her face where his fingers had been. Her mascara made dark circles under her eyes. With a trembling hand, she lifted her skirt and saw reflected in the mirror the purple panties with the hip band ripped apart on one side so that the material dangled uselessly from the other hip. Tentatively, she touched herself.

Her fingers traced the ridge of pink flesh that opened like ripe tropical fruit. The Mayans had executed women for drunkenness, but they had died with rouged nipples and cheeks. There had been festivals with dancers, musicians, and skilled contortionists honoring these slatterns deformed by magical powers. Sandy removed her torn underwear and stuffed it in the drawer with her makeup. She cleaned the mascara from her face. With fuchsia lipstick she painted a vivid mouth. Those women had been respected. Their brazenness was purity itself. She smudged kohl around her eyes and highlighted the color

259

of her cheekbones with copper powder. Their fears, arbitrary and sporadic as the heaving steam within fissures of the earth, had been recorded and studied as omens. They had been murdered in the throes of drunken ecstasy but only after they had been ripped apart by revelation. She flung her hair back from her face, which was pale and drained beneath the unnatural colors. As a final touch, she used an azure pencil on the inner rim of her eye so the whites would appear clearer and more brilliant.

Francisco Gomez had neatly placed the book of photographs on the table next to the couch. There was a strained, unhappy look on his face when Sandy returned to the room. Without looking at him, she poured a shot of brandy and drank it. She poured another and sat down across from him on the chair where he had placed his jacket.

"Sandy, I'm sorry." He put out his hand in her direction. "I don't know what happened. I just wanted you to listen."

The first conquistadores came without their own women. The religious men accompanying the army performed quick, mass marriages to save their men from the sin of carnality. These men probably moaned and screamed, "I love you, I'm coming, hold me tight, treat me good, I'm your only chance," in a language as strange and unfamiliar as the one Francisco was speaking to her. Sandy glanced up briefly, impatient with the distracting drone of his voice.

Why was he here? True, the world was arbitrary. But the accidental arrangement of substances and forces implied connections, convulsions, constructions. It implied random encounters, unexpected introductions. It implied rounding a corner and suddenly stepping into a street that had appeared in a dream. It implied catching a glimpse of a pair of eyes that glanced out a window at exactly 5:46 on a hot August afternoon when a moment of silence had occurred and for a millionth part of a second, the rotation of the earth stopped and a person's life was in flux.

Sandy's arm brushed against his sports jacket. Her elbow hit something hard as she sank back into the chair. She picked the jacket up and started to throw it at him.

"Be careful with that. It's got my gun in it."

She patted the jacket; from an inside pocket she removed the gun. It was black, smooth, cool. Obsidian. Deceptively light in her hand.

Francisco Gomez crossed the room swiftly and snatched the gun from her. "It's not a toy."

"I was only looking at it," she complained, rubbing her wrist. "I was just curious. Please."

He looked at her closely, then snapped open the cylinder and removed the bullets from the chamber. He checked it a second time and put the bullets in his pants pocket. Clicking the gun shut, he dropped it in her lap.

A surge of excitement and awe ran through her. There was something magnificent, yet intimate, in its proportion and symmetry.

A breeze seemed to issue from the barrel of the gun. It was whispering, Sandy, it has all been a mistake, a joke, a test, a tragedy, a preview of coming attractions. Look around you, it is written on the walls. You are blameless. It could have happened at any time. Time is mortal, an invention that invites despair. It could have happened anywhere. You are white, brown, black, yellow, mestizo, a Zambo Indian. You are father, daughter, mother, sister, whore, saint, and part-time bookkeeper. Remember, God is an accountant. You could have been clubbed to death by pagan villagers, slain by your own father, lost at sea, or crushed in the last embrace of dying gods in a nameless creation erected in artificial space and bounded by palm and lime trees. Only the weak among us associate terror with sacrifice.

Sandy, I am the Virgin Mother upon whose ruined

temples slums have been erected. I am the Madonna and I am hitchhiking. I could cause roses to bloom in the dust. I could turn the clouds into a rain of orchids. I could give you three million pesos in silver and cash. But everything you need is right here. Yes, you are going to die. Your form will be unrecognizable, your speech strange and slurred. You will see the fantastic costume of the quetzal. You will imagine you are a woman nursing a dog at her nipple. Your breath will become the night breeze. Your tears will smell like sweat and oranges. Your hand will grow steady and you will know that all of time is spent passing from one dream to the next.

Sandy stood and walked to the middle of the room. She pressed the trigger and made clicking noises to herself. She pointed the gun at the picture of the archangel and watched it disintegrate. She pointed the gun at the door and the windows, which melted. So this is it, she thought, as she examined the gun again; the handle was ridged with hieroglyphics. Demurely, she sat on the chair and smoothed her skirt neatly before looking into the barrel of the gun. She closed her eyes and put it in her mouth.

"Jesus Christ. Give me that thing. Are you out of your mind?" Francisco Gomez jerked the gun away from her and wiped it across his pants leg.

"I was just playing."

"I never took you for a coward," he said angrily. Turning his back, he slipped the gun into the coat, which he pulled on. He wheeled around to face her. "I thought you might be strong enough to learn to love someone."

Sandy pitched furiously to her feet. "How inspirational, Officer. You tell that to people you're arresting? You must have the happiest goddamn jail in the world over there at Rampart." She sneered and poked one finger at him. "I bet you got all kinds of arrests over there who hear this shit and say, 'Officer, you're right. I'm gonna go home and kiss my momma and look for a job. That's right. I'm gonna go love some pussy now and put down burglary.' "

Francisco stalked over to the window. He shoved his hands in his pockets and played with one of the bullets. On her way out Sandy slammed the door loudly so that the gold-framed picture of the archangel tottered on the bookshelf and fell.

The alley behind the apartment was deserted. An archipelago of isolated white islands created by streetlights stretched to the south. No one was in sight. The beach was black except for the luminous outline of the Venice Pier.

At the foot of the pier was the Playa del Sol bar. Sandy stood just inside the swinging doors watching the crowd. Boozers, users, losers with knives in hand-tooled leather sheaths, women missing their front teeth. She moved to the end of the bar. A stocky chicano came up and put his arms around her.

"Hello, beautiful," he slurred. "Let me buy you a drink."

The man was weaving slightly on the balls of his feet in an effort to appear taller. His nose had been broken at least twice. He lurched toward her and took her by the hand. "Come on, baby, don't be shy."

He was all the reasons why she avoided the Playa del Sol, home of the sixty-nine-cent wine margarita and hangout of half the SSI recipients of Venice. She started to say something, to protest, to walk back out the door, but she didn't want to go home. She let the man lead her to a stool at the end of the bar. The man smiled approvingly as she helped herself to a cigarette from a discarded pack in front of her.

"You're the prettiest girl I seen since I got out of prison," he whispered sloppily into her ear. "You married?"

A cheap tape player hooked up to a couple of stereo

263

speakers behind the bar grunted and ground up some tinny R and B. She shook her head slightly.

"What's your name?"

She brushed her hair back off her forehead and surveyed the rest of the room wearily. "Sandy."

He considered this for possible implications, then smacked his full lips and nodded several times in agreement.

"I'll have a brandy."

"A brandy for Sandy," he called down to the bartender.

As he leaned across the bar to pay for the drink, Sandy studied his profile. He had two tiny tears for hard time painted under the outside corner of his right eye. There was a V13 tattooed on his neck.

"Do you come here often?"

"No. I'm a Leo." The brandy burned its way down her throat.

He glowered at her suspiciously for a minute then laughed. "That's a joke, isn't it? That's pretty good." He turned down the length of the bar as though he were going to repeat the story but there was no one there; so he turned back to her. "I ain't been here for a long time." He laughed again loudly. "A long time. I'm waiting on my dad. He's going to come by here."

"That's nice," she mumbled politely. The brandy was harsh, cheap. The bottle at her place was sweet and smooth. Nectar. She wondered if it was safe to go home yet.

"Yeah. He's out on the pier fishing," the man was saying. "He'll be here in a while but if I don't see him tonight, that's okay. You know what I mean?" The man smirked and arched his neck, making the V13 elongate.

She took a large swallow of the terrible brandy, which seared her stomach. Probably an ulcer, she decided philosophically. The heat seemed to spread into her intestines.

264

Have to start drinking it in milk. She was already drunk, so it was hard to explain to herself why she continued to drink the cheap brandy except that it seemed to interfere with her thought process in a random but not unpleasant way. And it was a convenient substitute for prayer.

"Does he live around here?" she managed to ask.

"In Mar Vista. You know where that's at?"

"Of course. Why not?" she shrugged.

"I thought maybe you were just slumming tonight." His voice had changed.

Apparently she hadn't been paying attention. He sounded as mean as he looked. Sandy felt impelled to make some gentler, more solicitous inquiry. "Do you see him often?" She blinked, forcing herself to look into his dark, hard eyes.

"I try to. Whenever I can. I been gone from the area for a while, you understand?"

"Sure." Sandy hoped he wouldn't launch into a long involved explanation of where he'd been or what he'd been doing or why. She already had dreams about places where the walls were endless and the sky an illusion.

The man took a long drink from the glass that had been standing at his elbow. "It's hard to come back, expecting to find things the way you left them, knowing they won't be." He sucked his bushy mustache dry. "My kid brother, man, he's almost as tall as me now. My sister got married to a dude I don't even know and moved away. My old man, yeah, he's the only one that's solid."

"Good." She hoped the conversation would turn to another topic or that he would just stop talking to her. Her glass was full and she didn't want to have to leave it.

He nodded his head with enthusiasm. "You know what's so great about my old man? He said to me, 'When you get out of prison, you come back here. We'll still have a place for you.' He'd write me these letters, which was hard for him 'cause he don't write so good, and he'd call me *'hijo.'* And down at the bottom, he'd put PV. *Por Vida.* Forever. Get it?"

Sandy drank and looked away.

"My old man, he's the only one who ever really believed I was innocent. Not my partners, not my old lady. Just my old man."

There was a scar near his hairline and several more on the hand that held the glass.

"What were you in prison for?" Sandy interrupted.

The man refocused his attention on Sandy. He smiled. "Burglary, rape, assault with a deadly weapon."

Sandy reached for her drink again casually, pretending this was just another piece of information like the score of a Dodger game in the sixth inning or McDonnell-Douglas getting another aerospace contract. She wondered how she could get away from him. She could have told him she was an attorney, but then she'd have to listen to all the grisly details as well as the complaints about what a fuckup his public defender had been. Sandy wiped her damp hands across her skirt. All of this was, in some way, related to the weather. The bizarre sweltering heat that gripped the city. It was all related to the weather, to wind and unnatural seasonal fluctuations, to currents that were changing, temperatures rising, the flow of the ocean, which had reversed itself. She took another drink. "So did you do it?"

"Yeah."

"And your father stood by you? Did he know?"

"I told him but he didn't believe it. He thought I was taking the rap for someone else. He's always believed I was innocent." He shook his head again in wonderment. "That's what fathers are for, to love you no matter what, uh . . ." He faltered, trying to remember her name.

"Sandy."

Sandy. Her father spoke to her. You know I would never hurt you. I only wanted to protect you. Believe me,

266

the world is dangerous. Worse, it is stupid. Everything I have done was for your own good.

"Sandy, yeah." The man looked at her appreciatively. "My name's Sleepy. What do you say we go get high?"

The sudden warm breeze rocked the swinging doors of the Playa del Sol as Sandy thought about this. She looked out toward the ocean. The lights from the pier scorched the tips of the waves, turning them fluid silver and crystal.

Crystal. The needle in the bottom of her purse. To be burned open, naked, exposed, simple, pure as ash, without shame, without regret, all of it, without turning back. She turned to Sleepy. "Can you get drugs?"

"Shhh. Keep your voice down. We can talk about that outside."

"Well, can you?" insisted Sandy, about to get up off the bar stool.

"Yeah, baby. I'm the weatherman. I can shoot you full of stars. Brown Mexican like a hot breeze blowing up your skirt, a Santa Ana wind under your skin. But you got to pay for it."

Sleepy put his arm around Sandy and kissed her so that his tongue worked its way into her mouth.

"I got money." Sandy started to reach for her purse but realized she had left it in her apartment.

"Cash, *plata, dinero*. I don't take no credit cards. But what I want is some flesh. You know, flesh on flesh. You gotta make me think you love me."

"Is it true it makes you see pyramids, fires in the sky. . . ." Sandy pulled back to look him in the face.

"Sure, sure. Whatever you want. This ain't no hit-and-run accident. It's true love, so give me another kiss and we'll get out of here."

It was late. The band at the corner bar had taken a break and the night was strangely silent. She finished the brandy and put the glass down on the bar. As she wrapped her arms around Sleepy's neck to kiss him she looked up and saw Francisco Gomez in the entrance. Francisco Gomez turned away quickly and let the swinging door rock shut in the breeze.

The wind was rising in *Varrio Loco Nuevo* so that curtains fluttered in windows and the music from many radios playing *cumbias,* sambas, and inexplicably sad tangos blew through the air, meeting and merging in a dense and polyrhythmic serenade. Jesus Velaria was unaware of this. He was sitting at the kitchen table with his head propped in his hands. He had just gotten out of jail and he was still in shock.

His first reaction when the police who arrived at the body shop asked for him was anger, but he had carefully controlled himself as he felt the apprehensive eyes of his friends Jorge, Luis, and Raul on him. They were all worried. They were all illegal. Worse than maintaining his dignity in front of the men he worked with, Señor Aguilar, his boss, had been there. He was thankful that one of the cops, Peralta—the same name as a cousin of his from Zacatecas—could speak Spanish so that it had not been necessary to have Señor Aguilar translate their questions.

He couldn't believe it. They thought he had sexually molested his daughter! The questions they asked him! Did they think because he was a Mexican he was a dog who would rut with anything? A baby? His own daughter, for Christ's sake? If it had been just the chicano cop he would have explained that he liked women. With breasts. With hair between their legs. With tongues that sometimes tasted of cigarettes or chili or tequila.

But the white cop had done most of the talking in fractured Spanish. He had said, "I know you're illegal, you're scared, you're overworked and underpaid—and by one of your own people. You must be tired and angry when you get home. I can understand how it happened.

268

Maybe you had a few *cervezas.*" And here the white cop pantomimed, holding up a clenched fist with the thumb and little finger extended and tilted it toward his mouth. "You weren't aware of what you were doing. Why don't you just tell us how it happened and it will all be much easier." The white cop had said this several times while Jesus Velaria stared at him in disbelief. Finally the white cop turned back around in his seat and looked out the window while Peralta drove. Jesus Velaria knew enough English to understand that they were talking about what to have for lunch.

He believed it wasn't unusual for people to disappear on the way to jail, so he made an effort to sit tall and look alert when Peralta glanced at him in the rearview mirror. The only time he had spoken after they placed him in the car was to ask, "Where's my daughter?" The *pocho* cop explained in his faltering Spanish that she had been taken to a hospital for an examination and then to a foster home, where she was being cared for.

Madrededios. Jesus Velaria, who did not normally rely upon the Catholic saints, found himself praying. Would they know what to feed her? That she loved oranges and avocados? And a mashed banana. Peralta had then quickly read to him from a small printed card, running all the words together like he was offering mass. His rights as an arrestee.

They took him to a police station that was only fifteen or so blocks from his apartment. It occurred to him after the flurry of activity of booking, fingerprints, and photographs and he was put in a cell, that this must be the area where his cousin had seen his wife shopping in the market.

He wondered if his wife had reported him to the police. Maybe this was her way of trying to get Soledad from him. But why? All she had to do was come talk to him. They would come to some arrangement. Surely, she must

269

know that much about him after the three years they'd been together. He knew he was a rather formal man in many respects. He would insist they see a lawyer to arrange for a divorce. This he had decided after she'd been gone for five days, but he had done nothing to try to communicate with her. She should display some dignity and responsibility. She should come to him with some statement of her own desires in the matter. If she had ever looked at any of the books he brought home on women and their role in the revolutionary state, she would know that. He didn't expect apologies or explanations, just a plan for their daughter's care. They were adults and together accountable for Soledad's life. He couldn't believe she had done this to him. He was angry. And he was scared.

Still, he'd always known that there was an intrinsic weakness about his wife. It wasn't because she was a woman. It was because she failed to sense the inseparable connection between time and place. Once he had merely assumed that her traditional upbringing prevented her from fully exercising her choices. Later he realized her desires were more convenient than conventional. She thought that freedom was wearing short tight dresses and staying up late dancing at parties. It was true the only reason she'd married him was because she got pregnant and it was the easiest thing to do.

Sometimes at night, while they sat at the kitchen table, he would tell her about an article he'd read in the newspaper or heard on the radio. She would look at him blankly, then noisily stack the plates from dinner and carry them to the sink. If he tried to help her with the washing, she would turn away from the soapy water, walk into the living room, and turn on the television. He had frequently spoken to her about the wars in Central America, the power of the collective visions of revolutionaries, about equality. This bored her. When they lay in bed at night, he would sometimes recount the ancient myths of the Mayan and Aztec peoples, the fantastic *leyendas* of creation, death and rebirth. He could name the archaic emperors. He knew the stories of the conquest and the subsequent independence of Mexico. Relatives who had fought with the great armies of the people were real to him. He wanted to share his interest and pride in them. His great aunt had been a camp follower of Pancho Villa but even this meant nothing to her and before he reached the end of a story he would hear the soft, even breathing of his wife.

The police had let him use the telephone. He called Raul at the body shop and explained in a straightforward manner why he was in jail. It would cost five hundred dollars for bail. Raul sounded hesitant. He was probably overwhelmed by the amount of money. He would see what he could do. The policeman waiting for him to finish the call coughed impatiently and led him back to the cell, where he was left alone with his thoughts.

Certainly, there was a long list of grievances his wife could have presented against him. This, he acknowledged. He didn't tell her very often how beautiful she was. He assumed she knew this because of the long periods of time she spent in front of the mirror brushing her luxuriant black hair, playing with a rainbow of makeups in clear plastic boxes and little jars, or applying various sweet-smelling lotions and thick white creams to her face. He hadn't told her how pleased he had been that she found another job after Soledad's birth. He wondered if she was still working, or if she had quit when she ran away with the other man. Actually, Jesus Velaria had not devoted much time to thinking about the other man after the first several nights his wife had failed to return home. At first, he had been so jealous he assumed that his wife was in bed making love in every conceivable position, and he had scarcely been able to sleep himself. But this, he realized,

271

was not the reason his wife had left. She had been self-centered in her pleasures and yet so strangely modest in their expression that he had long ago concluded that she lacked the imagination necessary to find any satisfaction.

Suddenly he wondered if the police had asked her any questions about their sex life. Before they were married, they had both burned with a fever that made her rub against him when they danced to slow songs in darkened clubs; his hands would slowly move down her back until they cupped her buttocks and he would gently pull her toward him as he leaned down to kiss her on the mouth. They had stood at night in the shadow of the apartment building where she lived with her aunt, pressed against walls and doors, seeking each other's mouths and tongues. The city lights of the enormous office buildings and hotels to the east became their stars and planets. He would put his arm around her at the movies and sometimes she would allow her arm to be slowly nudged away from her side so that his fingers could slip lightly onto her breast.

Several times he took her to his cousin's apartment on Sunday afternoons when his cousin and roommates went to play soccer in the park. The first time he had laid a towel across his cousin's bed so her blood wouldn't stain the sheets, but there had been no blood. Jesus Velaria was not displeased about this, but she would not answer his questions or speak to him about how she lost her virginity. This reluctance seemed peculiar to him since he had already told her he loved her. In any event, she had not learned much from the experience. She was completely passive. Whether he was sucking her nipple, or rubbing her clitoris with his finger, or fucking her, she lay with her legs spread, her face turned to the side, and her eyes closed. He fantasized that one day she would squat above him with one hand rubbing her own nipple and the other hand stroking his cock, which she would perch above, so that the lips of her vagina opened and he could see the

272

rosy brown flesh grow wet as the tip of his cock grazed the opening. This did not happen; yet there was something beautiful in the angles and curves as her long hair spread across the pillow and curled around her breasts and her slightly rounded stomach rose and fell with her breathing. It was in this way that Soledad was created.

After she was pregnant and they were married, he tried to encourage her. What they did was called the missionary position, he knew this but he also remembered naked contorted statues of the Huaxtecs and Aztecs coupled in frenzy. There had always been variations. Trying to express himself in this regard, whether by speaking to her or turning her on her side, she had been resistant. After the fifth month of pregnancy when the doctor said she should no longer attempt the face-to-face position, she had simply made herself unavailable to him. One night he had knelt above her, placing her finger on her clitoris, stroking his cock until he came and the white come had erupted, shooting across her face and hair. She had said nothing to him but waited until he lay beside her, then she had gone into the bathroom, where the sound of running water continued for a long time and she returned to bed with her face glistening and smelling of rose petals.

She had complained constantly while pregnant about her weight, her ungainliness, the heaviness of her breasts, but her skin was radiant, slightly flushed, and her eyes sparkled. She said she didn't want to get pregnant again, so he playfully suggested that she could suck his cock if she remembered not to swallow the discharge. She hadn't done this either. For the last year, they had had sex two or three times a week but in the one position.

No, there was nothing unusual. Unless it was the time in the middle of February when he had come home drunk from drinking tequila after work with Jorge, Raul, and Luis, and he had gotten his wife to kneel on their bed. He had touched her until she was very wet and then, mixing

273

it with his own saliva, had lubricated the head of his cock and placed it against her asshole. She had turned wide-eyed to look at him, but he shook his head silently at her and then slowly worked his cock into her. This time the water had run in the bathroom for a much longer time and she had not spoken to him until the following evening. Had she told the police about this?

It was then he remembered the police had said the informant knew his wife was gone. He punched the wall. It had to be Señora Cruz! She was the only one who knew! Why would she make up such a story? The old bitch! Did she hate him? He had always been respectful and well mannered toward her. Bitch! She was jealous. She had no family of her own. She was old. Senile.

No, admitted Jesus Velaria, sighing and rubbing his hand, which throbbed with pain, he had never disliked Señora Cruz. She had done a good job taking care of Soledad; she loved the girl. Although he couldn't understand why she would do such a thing, she must have thought it was the right thing.

Jesus Velaria had observed that Señora Cruz was a great believer in the right thing. She adhered to a regular schedule of washing on Monday, marketing on Tuesday and Thursday, and ten o'clock mass on Sunday. She still dressed completely in black although it had been many years since the death of her husband. This unshakable belief in the right thing provided a solid base for her life and a consistency of action Jesus Velaria was forced to admire. In one way she was like his wife. She had seen the various options life offered and selected the one that was easiest. If he had any complaints about her, it was that she had turned her back on the challenging aspects of the world. He could understand her fear and the limited range of responses of which she believed she was capable. In the political terms Jesus Velaria often found himself using lately, she, like his wife, was a reactionary.

274

Jesus Velaria had a profound respect for law and order. In their uncorrupted forms. He would say that he believed in the laws of nature and the order of the universe. He believed that, although there were definite cycles in the passage of time, the subtle manipulation of fate was still possible. Not in the way Señora Cruz and the other women who went to *Botanica La Ayuda* across the street from his apartment believed, but through intense personal commitment. He had created his own life. He had been taught to read, he had learned as much as he could from his high school in the rather miserable neighborhood of *20 de noviembre* in Mexico City, he had a certain knowledge he picked up from the streets, he had come to Los Angeles, he had fathered a child, he had married, he had worked hard—first in a sweatshop on the second floor of an old building on Broadway where he carried immense bolts of cloth for women's clothing, then as a busboy in a luxurious downtown hotel, and now in a body shop. He had tried to win the love of his wife, he had participated in demonstrations against intervention in foreign countries, and he was studying English. He knew he was innocent.

The one failure had been with his wife. Jesus Velaria sighed as he tucked his shirt into his jeans and leaned back against the wall. He had known when he had first seen her at a dance hosted by the Matamoros Social and Sports Club to which he had been invited by Raul that it was a mistake to fall in love with her. Their conversation was simple and halting, as though they spoke two different languages. She had never heard of the people and places he spoke of. He would forget this when her hair brushed his face. He had gone the first time to visit her carrying a small volume of poetry; she had been puzzled and suggested they go for a movie. This was the reason his wife had left him. He read books.

The next woman would be different, he promised. She

would be bold and articulate. With visions. With a sense of the future, but a commitment to the past. Idealistic, but pragmatic. And a good pair of legs.

When he had been in Los Angeles for three months, he had found a job in one of the big hotels. That is how he became aware of a certain kind of prostitute. Of course he had seen, both in Mexico and Los Angeles, the whores who stood on street corners. These women were prostitutes and different. They dressed expensively in black high heels and simple cocktail dresses, which would reveal one eye-catching detail such as a plunging neckline, which displayed magnificent breasts or a draped back which fell in soft folds near the waist so the woman's entire back was exposed, or a straight skirt slit to the exact point slightly above mid-thigh that made it impossible to do anything but think of the upper part of the leg.

Jesus Cristo! How could they think he would have sex with a child?

After he discovered these women, he would dress carefully on the day he was paid and take the bus west along Wilshire to another large hotel. There he would sit for a while in the lobby until he saw the prostitutes enter. He would follow them into the bar and have two drinks where he could watch the women moving through the room, talking and dancing. He stopped doing this when he met his wife. He had never even spoken with one of the prostitutes, much less been with one of them, but he felt a strong and erotic bond with them. They, too, appeared to have carefully considered their options and constructed lives around the supposedly illicit choice they had made. That was what he had in common with them. They were all border crossers of one type or another.

The one time he had been with a whore, it had been in his second month in Los Angeles. It had cost him thirty-five dollars with a white woman. She had said, "Do you want to have a date?" At the time he hadn't understood, but he had let her open his wallet, take out some money, and lead him to a nearby motel. Jesus Velaria was starting to get hard thinking about this when a cop came in and announced Señor Aguilar had come to bail him out.

Tomorrow he would go to court and find out where Soledad was. The policeman who discharged him from jail explained that the county would appoint a lawyer for him if he couldn't afford to hire one. Jesus Velaria noticed that the wind had risen and was stirring the pages of books on the table. He got up and crossed the room. As he leaned out the window and felt the hot air against his face, he could see the downtown buildings lit by thousands of lights he pretended were stars.

13

"They got my baby. What do you think of that?" shouted a woman.

"They never even told me where mine was," answered another.

"I told those girls, I told them. . . ."

"Listen, baby, you know I'd . . ." A man in a white shirt, a tattoo of a pierced heart peeking out from beneath his sleeve, was whispering in a hoarse voice to a woman who gazed at him hopefully. He was explaining to her again that he had never touched her three-year-old daughter. The woman turned her jaw away from him but clutched her hands in front of her like a supplicant.

The crowded hall rolled as if it had been topographically altered to fit the land beneath it. Sandy was queasy. Hung over. Sleepy had lied to her. After she followed him into the alley behind the bar, let him kiss her and feel her breasts, he had finally produced a tiny worn piece of tin foil from which he grudgingly extracted two reds. Perfunctorily, she rubbed his cock, then told him she had to go use the bathroom.

Red.

Once inside the bar she dashed for the front door and ran out. Red. The color of the sun. The father of the sky. Red. Bloodstains on the sheets. Her father was dead and

279

each night the sun became a skeleton who needed to be fed.

Red. The traffic light on First and Broadway turned red. Jesus Velaria stood impatiently on the curb. In front of him, up the hill, was the criminal courts building. The great ceremonial centers had been misnamed by the anthropologists and called cities. The altars had been covered with slums and the sacred wells were poisoned by industry. He hadn't been able to sleep.

Sandy had thrown the reds away and stayed up all night drinking. The women and men and children who huddled around the courtroom doors looked up expectantly as she paced back and forth as if they thought she could help them. Sandy glared at them. They believed that hearts healed on schedule and through her skill she could make the legal process and the healing coincide. In the spring the rains had nearly flooded the city and now everything was on fire.

Jeanette Ray still expected to get her daughter back. Everyone waiting in the noisy, stifling hall was suffering from the same senseless and delusional fever, the belief that love in one of its awkward and strange permutations would somehow intervene in their behalf. Sandy was looking for Jeanette Ray to tell her it was hopeless. It was like trying to decipher the clouds through the use of physics or pinpoint the origin of El Niño.

"Son of a bitch!" A black woman was complaining loudly about her common-law husband. He was a drunk; he was never at home. She had given up trying to find out where he went. He only came home to sleep sometimes. "Son of a bitch." His two children were impossible. She barely knew them, she was too old to become their mother, and she'd already raised five of her own. She didn't want any more. This is why two days ago she told them to leave her house, took their clothing, put it outside. Locked the door. "Son of a bitch."

280

A man who was sitting nearby nodded his head in agreement, although the woman did not see him. He had called the police and demanded they come to take his children away. The man hit the children and kicked them because they had stolen money from his dresser.

This is the truth. Men are frightened of their bones.

"Oyé mujer." A couple from El Salvador sat by the courtroom door. The man was talking, the woman listening. They were discussing their fourteen-year-old daughter who came from San Salvador last year to live with them. She had arrived with breasts and menses, a bad vocabulary, and screaming nightmares. They wanted the judge to send her back to El Salvador.

In between everything a man and woman can do is death. And the moment of birth is the moment of surrender. This is why the ancient Mayans prayed squatting on their haunches in the same ungainly posture their women used for delivering children.

Sandy lit a cigarette. Tobacco had been a form of prayer. It protected people from being killed by lightning. She walked further down the hall but it also was full of those hidden lives that had been upturned for their histories and patterns to be examined under the fluorescent light like a diseased body. The sacrificial knife was called the hand of god.

"Corazón sagrado." A latina anxiously watched the comings and goings in the hall. The woman was getting a headache. Her head throbbed. Yesterday she had been fired from the restaurant where she worked. She never realized so much could happen as the result of a simple accident. Seven weeks ago, yes, it had been a Tuesday, she had gone to see her cousin who was going back to Mexico. They made a party in the small apartment her cousin lived in. The woman drank five beers to celebrate the happy event. Walking down Hollywood Boulevard to the bus stop, she stumbled, falling down on top of her

three-month-old baby. She was too drunk and too heavy from her last pregnancy to stand up. Passersby had to roll her off the child. *"Corazón sagrado,"* the woman kept repeating under her breath. She would have liked to say a rosary but she had so many things on her mind and it was so noisy in the hall that she kept forgetting the words.

"Corazón sagrado."

Oh heart of heaven who caused mountains to appear from the water and a heavy resin to fall from the sky, who caused it to rain so hard that all human beings were changed into fish.

"Get over here before I spank your butt." A child ran across the hall. "I'm not going to tell you again. One. Two . . ."

"Keeping busy, Counselor?" Lacey Potter suddenly stood beside Sandy with several neat white folders in her hand. "It just goes on and on, doesn't it? Look here, I got a case on a woman I represented two years ago. Same kind of case, but a new baby." Lacey Potter laughed and shook her head. "That's when you know you've been here too long, when you hear the same story from the same people. I can't stand it anymore. I'm quitting the panel. I'm gonna get into PI, some good clean auto accidents with permanent disabilities."

"Yeah," Sandy agreed absently as she watched a woman awkwardly clutching a little girl in a blue dress. "You can't get rich doing this."

"Rich? Shit. I think I'm losing my mind here. I'm ready to pay them to let me leave."

"Are you serious?" The little girl was trying to twist out of the woman's arms.

"I want you to take over my cases. You know what to say to these people, how to work with them. I don't know how you do it."

"But, Lacey . . ." The woman tightened her grip on the girl.

282

"I made up my mind. They don't ever change. These people are sick."

Only the land changed. Only the weather changed. There was a time when the sacrifice of children had been acknowledged. When the gods were perceived as living on the four corners of the earth and the regenerative power of the seasons was in doubt.

"I'm going to tell the presiding judge this afternoon," Lacey Potter was saying, her voice barely audible above the vibrating din of the hallway.

Sandy nodded without listening. She was watching a woman who sat nearby in a neat dress with the collar turned up. The woman had been discovered in the early evening walking down the center divider of one of the major boulevards of the San Fernando Valley with a dazed look upon her face, her baby in her arms, and a purse full of lithium. The woman was worried about the future and earthquakes.

Clapping her hand on Sandy's shoulder, Lacey Potter turned away. "I'll give you my files. We'll have lunch tomorrow."

An old woman with a bad back and two children sat in front of Sandy. The woman was wondering how long she'd have to sit there. She had been to court many times. These were her daughter's children. It had been almost two years since she'd seen her daughter. She had probably gone off with some other man. That was the pattern. One after another. It was hard to understand since none of them were any good. The man who was the father of the youngest child was a fine example. One night while he was loaded he tried to submerge the little girl in scalding water. The old woman had long since stopped wondering why he did this. Like an eclipse or a tidal wave, the explanations were scientific and incomprehensible. The old woman remembered it had been at the end of summer. It had been hot, the time of year when the winds began to blow from the desert. The old woman sensed the connection between the man's action and weather madness.

Sandy forced herself to turn away from the old woman whose thoughts were humming palpably and to look instead down the length of the hall. The unnatural white light from the neon panels in the ceiling bathed everything in an intolerable glow. The women's bright blouses and dresses were florid. Greens were harsh, yellows jaundiced, faces distorted. The noise was becoming deafening and Sandy was about to make a trip to the sanctuary of the bathroom when a silence fell.

It was Jeanette Ray. She was dressed in a pale pink taffeta ball gown. The hem was ragged and slightly stained. On top of her head, secured by a handful of bobby pins that she had carefully selected so they almost matched her hair color, Jeanette Ray wore a rhinestone tiara.

Unaware that all conversation around her ceased, that small children had taken their mothers' hands, Jeanette Ray smiled as she saw Sandy and approached with her arms outstretched.

"It is all over," Jeanette Ray announced jubilantly before Sandy could say anything. "I have sinned. As we all have. This is the time to put away the past. To give sorrow words. I have forgiven my daughter and now she will forgive me." Then, with the rustling of net and voile like the shattering sound of the angels themselves, Jeanette Ray had pirouetted and entered the courtroom.

At Broadway, just outside the criminal courts building, stood Jesus Velaria. It was almost nine. He glanced again at the paper in his hand to check the number of the courtroom he was going to. Department 28. He was nervous. He had put on a pair of black pants and a white shirt. There was something in the air, raw and fertile like the pollen from trees, although the season had passed. It put him on edge. He took a few deep breaths. The police told him they were looking for his wife. Would she be there? It was hot; sweat trickled down his brow. He was sweating inside his pants and it tickled his balls in a not unpleasant way, making him think of a woman's tongue. . . . *Hombre,* this is no time to be dreaming. He had come to get Soledad. Jesus Velaria glanced over his shoulder at the clock on top of the newspaper building and hurried up the stairs into the court building.

Sandy was still standing in the hall staring at the door Jeanette Ray had disappeared through when Michael rushed up behind her. "Wake up, Walker. Come down to Department Twenty-eight. All hell's breaking loose. Perez called in sick today, so they need another lawyer."

"Find someone else. I still got a case." Sandy started toward the door after Jeanette Ray.

"It can wait. They need someone who can *habla* the language." He grabbed her by the hand and tugged her firmly along after him. "Don't worry, folks," Michael assured a young couple who looked up in surprise as he dragged her to the stairwell. "This is my mother. She's come to take me home."

"Can't you ever control yourself?" she complained irritably, following him down the stairs.

Humming an old Sinatra tune, Michael Fillipini paused on the landing between the second and third floors, swept Sandy into his arms and began to dance her around in a fast fox trot. "Whoever said there isn't any magic anymore?" he crooned in a flat voice. He twirled her a few more times.

"You know, Sandy, you're really a rotten dancer." He stopped, out of breath, and let go of her. He wiped a few beads of sweat off his forehead and straightened his jacket. "My ex-wife was a rotten dancer, too. I ever tell you that before?"

285

Sandy combed her fingers through her hair. "Which one?"

"The first one."

"The one who's coming to visit you?"

Michael Fillipini started down the stairs again. "I called her and told her not to come."

"But you were so excited about it," Sandy said, hurrying after him.

"It was a fantasy. I haven't seen the woman in years. What is there to say to explain the past?" Michael Fillipini shrugged as he pulled open the door to the second floor.

The hall outside Department 28 was thronged with agitated men and women. Children were crying. Michael Fillipini disappeared inside and returned briefly to shove several files into Sandy's hand. People were smoking, arguing, weeping. The walls were glistening with sweat. An enormous woman was standing in the middle of the hall with her arms wrapped around herself. She was weaving back and forth in a great silence that would become a deafening roar when the full and explicit realization came to her that her son was dying in a hospital over at 53rd and Orange Grove because her boyfriend had hit him one time too many, one time too hard.

In the hall, Jesus Velaria had turned his back on the milling crowd after a quick glance. He saw there were men who had grown up hard on the streets, without as much love as a dog. Men who had been beaten when they were small by women who believed harsh discipline was the only alternative to jail, insanity, or an early grave. The women themselves were spread out around the hall like wilted blossoms after a fiesta. He gazed out the immense plate glass windows. The overwhelming intersection of torpid weather, of concrete and barren riverbeds, of linguistic maps, had conspired to draw him to this point where he stood overlooking Broadway and the endless migration of the spiritually disenfranchised. He lit a ciga-

286

rette, remembering that there had been a time when tobacco was a cure for black magic and that when rubbed inside the elbow and knee joints protected one from being seized by the dead. The sun was rising above the neighboring buildings so that their colors became intense, their edges sharp and shadows black. On the other side of the court buildings, on the other side of the freeway which was to the west, *Varrio Loco Nuevo* would begin another day. Each sunrise was a new exercise in the violent struggle between piety and history. Yes, he realized with a clarity beyond that produced by heat and the lack of sleep, it was all an accident. All the usual offerings, incense, resin, and rubber, the bones of jaguars, coral, and pumice had been rejected. The ancient rain gods had a predilection for children.

A noise rumbled through the hall like the center of the earth speaking, sorrowful and primordial. It was a woman wailing inconsolably.

Sandy felt the sound cut into her. Out of the rumble, like a thunderburst, came a voice saying, "The heart is a cruel climate. Extravagant rituals are necessary."

The veins in Jesus Velaria's arms began to twitch as the sound pierced his skin. It was the same as the sound that hung in the still night in the darkness around the sacred wells of Chichén Itzá, it was *el grito de dolores*, it was in the back rooms of Mexico City *cantinas*, in the border check points north of San Diego and in the sudden warm breezes that blew through *Varrio Loco Nuevo*. It was the true and universal language of the soul.

Sandy pushed her way through the silent crowd toward the window and the city stretched beneath them. Her father was dead, Nadra Taylor was dead, Malver Lopez for all intents and purposes was dead, Manolete was dead. Only the sound was alive, sighing, "Wear me around your neck like a Saint Jude medal. Keep me by you in the dark.

287

Light candles. Pray in Spanish. Love me like I was the last breath of air on a poison planet."

The sound washed over and cracked around Jesus Velaria like a wave. *"All moons, all years, all days, all winds reach their completion and pass away. So does all blood reach its place of quiet."*

The sound died away as the wailing woman sank to the floor.

Sandy Walker took another step closer to the window and looked out over Broadway. The traffic lights changed and crowds of people moved back and forth in a carefully measured moment. She looked down at the papers she held and took the one on top.

"Velaria, Jesus Velaria," she called.

The fronds of the palm trees around the building shuddered one last time. For an instant the wind, which is the breathing of the gods, stopped.